The Six-Week Solution

Other Books by Paula Darnell

DIY Diva Mystery Series

Death by Association

Death by Design

Death by Proxy

The Six-Week Solution

Paula Darnell

CR

Campbell and Rogers Press

Las Vegas

CR

Campbell and Rogers Press

Publisher's Cataloging-in-Publication Data
provided by Five Rainbows Cataloging Services

Names: Darnell, Paula, author.
Title: The six-week solution / Paula Darnell.
Description: Las Vegas : Campbell and Rogers Press, 2020.
Identifiers: LCCN 2019915974 (print) | ISBN 978-1-887402-01-9 (paperback) | ISBN 978-1-887402-02-6 (hardcover : large print) | ISBN 978-1-887402-00-2 (ebook)
Subjects: LCSH: Police—Fiction. | Murder—Fiction. | Divorce—Fiction. | Conspiracies—Fiction. | Nineteen fifties—Fiction. | Reno (Nev.)—Fiction. | Detective and mystery stories. | BISAC: FICTION / Mystery & Detective / Police Procedural. | FICTION / Mystery & Detective / Historical. | GSAFD: Mystery fiction. | Historical fiction.
Classification: LCC PS3604.A7478 S59 2020 (print) | LCC PS3604.A7478 (ebook) | DDC 813/.6—dc23.

First Edition

Published by:
Campbell and Rogers Press
P.O. Box 751111
Las Vegas, NV 89136

Printed in the United States of America

For my wonderful husband Gary with love and special thanks for his encouragement and excellent suggestions for my books

Chapter 1

"I can't see a wreck down there," Deputy Sheriff Ben Cameron said, swinging the beam of his flashlight from left to right. He stared at the dark mountainside below, before pointing his flashlight at the tire tracks in an earthen embankment. "But the car went off right here."

The lanky deputy stood at the side of Highway 27, the narrow road that wound its way up Mount Rose from Reno to Lake Tahoe. Two other deputies, the undersheriff, and the sheriff himself stood beside Ben, peering into the abyss below.

"Let's get a spotlight on it," Washoe County Sheriff Mark Rogers directed, his gravelly voice crackling. "Jeff, pull your car on over here and angle the front tires over that embankment."

Deputy Jeff Jergens, a twenty-year veteran of the department, broke into a sweat as he slowly inched his cruiser up and over the embankment.

"A little farther now," Undersheriff Al Mansfield guided him. "Whoa!" he shouted as the car's front tires approached the edge of the drop-off.

Jergens gripped the car's spotlight, sweeping it back and forth until they spotted the crumpled black Cadillac about fifty yards down the side of the mountain.

"Don't think anybody could've survived that," the sheriff said.

"Poor bastard," he added. "OK, boys, Al, you and Jeff set out the flares and block off this lane. Ben, you think you can climb down there without a rope?"

"Yes, sir, looks like it."

"Virgil, you go with him. I'll keep the spotlight ahead of you, so you can see where you're going."

Ben and Virgil inched their way down the rocky hillside. The steep terrain, covered with manzanita shrubs and tobacco brush, made the descent tricky, and the deputies, dislodging loose rocks along their way, struggled to stay on their feet. As they approached the long black Cadillac, now a mangled wreck, they could see that it had crashed into a huge Ponderosa pine tree directly in front of the passenger's side of the car. Rookie Virgil, who'd joined the sheriff's department just a month earlier, hung back as Ben shone his flashlight into the car.

"Empty. The driver went through the windshield," Ben told Virgil as he picked his way through shards of glass and circled to the front of the Caddy.

"There she is. Oh, God!"

"Is she . . . ?

"Dead. Smashed up pretty bad."

Retching, Virgil turned away from the bloody body.

"First accident scene?" Ben asked.

"First bad one."

Ben's walkie-talkie sizzled.

"Ben?"

"Sheriff, the driver's dead."

"Anyone else?"

"No, she was alone."

"A woman?" the sheriff's surprise registered in his question.

"Yes, sir. Looks like she was coming from a casino at Lake Tahoe.

She's all dolled up in a shiny silver evening gown."

"Damn shame. Coroner's standing by. Stay put till he gets here. He's going to need help getting the body back up here."

"Roger that," Ben said, reverting to the familiar military lingo that he hadn't quite shed, even though he'd been out of the army for a couple of years.

Ben climbed into the car and looked through the glove compartment, locating a few road maps, the owner's manual for the Cadillac, and a small white beaded evening bag. Inside the owner's manual, Ben found the car's registration card, which listed Adrian Beaumont of Pasadena, California, as the owner. The little purse contained a tube of red lipstick, a silver compact, a twenty-dollar bill, and a driver's license belonging to Phyllis Beaumont, also of Pasadena, California. The address on the vehicle registration matched the one on the driver's license. Ben stuffed the items into his jacket pocket and buttoned it before getting out of the car.

The walkie-talkie sputtered to life again.

"Coroner and his assistant coming down now."

"OK. I see their flashlights. Sheriff. The lady's name is Phyllis Beaumont, born 1930."

"Only twenty-five years old." The sheriff mused. "Damn shame."

"The Caddy's registered to Adrian Beaumont of Pasadena, same address as hers. Probably her husband or maybe her father," Ben speculated.

Ben and Virgil waited at the back of the Cadillac until the coroner and his assistant reached the accident scene. There was nothing they could do for the lady in the silver evening dress now—nothing except remove her body.

"Coroner's on scene now," Ben reported.

"Sending down the litter," the sheriff's voice crackled from Ben's walkie-talkie, and then he and his deputies up top played out the ropes, which were attached to the litter, and lowered it. Ben and the coroner's assistant secured the litter, and, with the help of the coroner, positioned it next to the woman's body.

"Virgil, check the back seat and the trunk of the Caddy for any other personal effects," Ben directed. "I have the contents of the glove compartment, but that's all."

"Sure thing," the relieved deputy responded.

Working quickly and mostly silently, the other three men hoisted the body onto the litter, where they covered it, and secured it with straps. While they guided and pushed the litter from below, the sheriff and his men hoisted the ropes from above. Gingerly holding the only other item he'd found in the car—a fur stole—Virgil trailed slowly behind, pausing long enough that he didn't have to watch the woman's body being loaded into the black coroner's wagon, which pulled away just as the rookie deputy reached the top of the hill.

"What'd you find, Virgil?" Ben asked the deputy whom he'd all but forgotten in the struggle to bring the body up the side of the mountain.

"Fur stole." Virgil turned it over and illuminated the silver fur's cream-colored silk lining with his flashlight. "Look here—a monogram."

The sheriff and Ben looked at the initials "PB" embroidered in elaborate script letters on the lining.

"PB for Phyllis Beaumont," the sheriff murmured. "Set that on the front seat of my car, Virgil."

Ben unbuttoned his jacket pocket and removed the items he'd found in the Caddy's glove compartment. "I got these, too, sheriff."

"OK, put 'em in my car with the fur." He turned to Deputy Jergens. "You boys can clear those flares now and take off. Tow truck can wait till morning."

Ben helped the other deputies clear the road and watched as they climbed into their vehicles—Jergens and Virgil in one and Al alone in the other—and departed. The sheriff leaned against the front of his car and pulled out a pack of Lucky Strikes. He tapped the pack and shook a couple of cigarettes out, offering one to Ben. Luckies happened to be Ben's brand, too. Ben struck a match and lit the sheriff's cigarette, then his own, before dropping the burning match on the gravel and grinding it out with his heel. The two men smoked in silence for a few minutes.

"Bad business," the sheriff said.

"Yes—awful."

"Ben, I'm turning over this investigation to you. It's a fatal accident, so we'll need a full work-up. With Carmine out, we're short a detective right now." Carmine Minelli, the sheriff's chief investigator, was in the hospital after suffering a heart attack a few days earlier. "You don't have any experience on the investigation side, but you're a bright guy, and you'll do fine."

"You want me to take care of notifying the family?"

"Yup, and make sure you confirm the victim's identity. Talk to the witnesses. Here." The sheriff handed Ben a scrap of paper. "Man and his wife driving down from Tahoe saw the car go off. They called in the accident from the Buckboard Stables, down below. They were real shook up, especially the lady, but in a hurry, too. Daughter's having a baby, and they were on their way to St. Mary's in Reno. Got their names and such there." He nodded toward the paper Ben now held in his hand. "Better stop by your place and change your pants before you do anything, though. You got blood all over 'em."

Ben, driving his own red 1953 Chevy pickup—he'd been off-duty when the sheriff had roused him with an after-midnight phone call to come to the accident scene—intended to follow the sheriff back into town, but he drove much faster than Ben wanted to, especially considering the accident scene he'd just attended, and the taillights of the sheriff's car soon disappeared.

The sky was beginning to lighten by the time Ben arrived at his apartment, a furnished room on the second floor above the Truckee Treasures Antiques Emporium, where he stopped long enough to take a quick shower and put on a fresh uniform. He stuffed his bloody pants into a paper grocery bag and brought them along when he left. He wasn't sure the uniform pants were salvageable, but he intended to find out. He'd drop them off at the Truckee Meadows Cleaners as soon as he had a chance. He didn't want to have to buy another pair of pants right now, not after all the money he'd just laid out for a new set of tires for his truck.

From his apartment on Virginia Street, Reno's main thoroughfare, he drove north to the Washoe County Courthouse and turned left onto Court Street, where the sheriff's office and county jail were located. There was only one sleepy civilian night clerk on duty in the administrative offices. She nodded to Ben and he nodded back as he made his way to Carmine's desk and sat down. As he rummaged through the top drawer, looking for a pencil and paper, the clerk eyed him, no doubt wondering what he was doing, but not curious enough to ask. With a shrug, she turned back to her paperwork. Ben picked up the receiver of the black rotary telephone, dialed 0, and asked to be connected with the long-distance operator. As he waited for the operator to come on the line, he lit a Lucky Strike before noticing that there was no ashtray on Carmine's desk. Rummaging through the desk, he found a large ceramic ashtray in the bottom drawer and snagged it just in time to tap off the ash from his cigarette.. As soon as the long-distance operator answered, Ben asked to be connected to the residence of Adrian Beaumont in Pasadena.

Ben smoked his cigarette while he waited several minutes until, finally, the telephone connection was made. Unfortunately, it proved a bad one, and Ben had difficulty hearing anything. That wasn't the only problem.

The woman who answered the phone at the Beaumont residence spoke with such a thick accent—maybe Eastern European, maybe Russian—that Ben couldn't understand her. He doubted that she could understand much of what he was saying, either. He hadn't told her about the dead woman, only asked for Adrian Beaumont. At last, she gave him a phone number, shouting something about "Mr. Adrian" and "studio." He wrote down the number, hung up, and dialed the operator again, this time providing her with the number he'd been given.

"No answer, sir," the operator told Ben.

"Thanks, I'll try again later," he said, realizing that if the number he'd given the operator was Mr. Beaumont's business phone, it was too early in the morning for anybody to be at work. But if Beaumont wasn't home or at work, where was he? Ben speculated that Beaumont could be in Reno, waiting for his wife to return from her excursion to Lake Tahoe, but somehow he doubted it. It didn't seem likely that Mrs. Beaumont would be driving down the mountain from Lake Tahoe alone in the middle of the night if she were visiting Reno with her husband. Ben reckoned that if he wasn't able to contact Beaumont, he could call the Pasadena Police Department and have someone go by the house. Maybe they'd have more luck talking to the woman there, in person, than he'd had trying to communicate over a phone line crackling with static.

Ben decided that he should wait at least a couple of hours before trying his call again. In the meantime, he could talk to the witnesses. He pulled out the scrap of paper the sheriff had given him and peered at it, trying to make out the sheriff's scribbled handwriting. He couldn't quite tell whether their last name was Conklin or Connors, but it shouldn't be too difficult to find them if they were still waiting at the hospital for the birth of their grandchild. Ben worried that they might not be too happy if he showed up there, but he reasoned that he had to talk to them sometime.

Outside, the cloudless June sky and pleasantly cool temperature inspired Ben to walk, rather than to drive, the seven blocks to St. Mary's Hospital. He couldn't make his next phone call for quite a while, anyway, and if the interview didn't take too long, he could stop for the breakfast special at the Riverside Hotel's coffee shop on his way back to the sheriff's office. He'd been up most of the night, and he was hungry. Besides, he could use some coffee to jumpstart his morning, especially now that the rush he'd felt from dealing with the accident was dwindling.

As Ben entered the lobby of St. Mary's Hospital on Sixth Street, he spotted an elderly nun making her way across the lobby. He approached her and asked for directions to the waiting room for the maternity ward. There he found two men, one who looked to be in his sixties and another man about Ben's age.

"Mr. Connors?" Ben guessed, directing his inquiry to the older man.

"That's me. You must be here about the accident."

"Yes, I'm Deputy Ben Cameron from the Sheriff's Department." The two men stood up and Connors shook hands with Ben.

"This is my son-in-law, Fred Jenkins," Connors said.

"Nice to meetcha," Jenkins said, shaking hands with Ben. "I'm a new daddy." He grinned. "My wife and I have a healthy baby boy."

"First grandchild for us," Connors added, beaming.

"Well, congratulations!"

"My wife's in with my daughter right now. Will you need to talk to her, too?"

"No need to interrupt her right now. I'll get her statement after she's done visiting."

"Say, Con, I'm going to run down to the cafeteria and get a cup of coffee while you talk to the deputy. Do you want me to bring back anything for you?"

"No, thanks. After the deputy's finished talking to Marge and me, maybe we'll grab some breakfast." Jenkins departed, and Connors and Ben sat down.

"It was a long night, in more ways than one," the older man said.

"Let me make sure I have all your contact information before you tell me what you saw."

Connors obliged, giving Ben his address and phone number in Reno as well as that of his daughter and son-in-law.

"My wife and I were at our cottage in Incline Village yesterday to make a few repairs. It was getting late when we finished, so we decided to stay the night. We usually stay up there ourselves all summer, but we decided to rent the cottage out this year, because of the baby coming and all. I knew I'd never get my wife to leave her first grandbaby for very long.

"Well, along about midnight last night, we got a phone call. Baby's on the way, so we drove back down the mountain. A couple of minutes after we passed the Christmas Tree—you know it?"

Ben nodded. He'd enjoyed a few steak dinners at the Christmas Tree since he'd moved to Reno to take the job of deputy sheriff. The restaurant was decorated with twinkling Christmas lights all year, not just during the holiday season. Perched on the side of Mount Rose, the Christmas Tree boasted a panoramic view of the valley below.

"I saw lights coming up behind me fast," Connors continued. "Then this big black car whipped around us—just missed hitting our car. It was weaving back and forth, and then it disappeared—ran right off the side of the mountain. I hightailed it down the hill to the Buckboard Stables and called for the sheriff from there. My wife was plenty shaken up, let me tell you."

"Did the driver ever slow down at all?"

"Never saw a brake light come on. Did anybody get out alive?"

"I'm afraid not. There was one fatality."

"A tourist?"

"I can't really say anything more at this point. We haven't been able to reach the next of kin yet."

"I understand. Here comes my wife now." Connors stood and rushed to his wife's side.

Mrs. Connors' account confirmed her husband's. It didn't shed any new light on the circumstances of the accident, so Ben thanked the couple, wished them and their family well, and told them to get in touch with him if they remembered anything else about the accident.

Glancing at his wristwatch, Ben saw that he had enough time to stop at the Riverside for breakfast. The Riverside Hotel and Casino provided a hub for much of the activity in downtown Reno, and both locals and tourists frequented it. Waitresses in the coffee shop were buzzing between their customers and the kitchen when Ben arrived, and neither they nor the hostess greeted him, but he spotted the undersheriff and Hank Sorenson, a deputy, sitting at a small round table near the back and joined them. Soon he'd ordered the breakfast special—two eggs, ham, toast, and fried potatoes, all for four bits—and settled down with a cup of steaming coffee. He added a dollop of cream and practically inhaled his first cup of the day.

"I hear you're investigating that accident up on Mount Rose," Al said. "Mark told me he was going to ask you to do it." Al and the sheriff were the two oldest men in the department, and they went way back, so Ben wasn't surprised that Al already knew about his new assignment. Ben suspected that the sheriff sometimes deliberately leaked news to Al when he didn't necessarily want to deliver it himself. "Better you than me, for sure. I only have four months to go before I retire."

"What're you going to do with all that time on your hands?" Hank, who was also known in the department as the "Big Swede," asked. "I'd go nuts if I didn't work."

"You're young yet. Just you wait and see. By the time you're my age, you'll change your tune. Anyway, I have plenty to keep me busy. The first project is remodeling our kitchen. After that, I'm going to turn our carport into a real garage, and then I'm going to paint the house."

"I take it back, Al." Hank said. "Sounds like you're going to be busier retired than you are on the job."

"I'm going to take my time with all my projects. No reporting for duty in the middle of the night and no alarm clock early in the morning, so it won't be as hectic."

"Sounds good, Al." Ben commented. "How long have you been with the department, anyway?"

"It'll be thirty years on the day I retire and leave all the sheriffing to you younger guys. By the way, Ben, you're in a good position now to take over for Carmine."

"I thought he was going to come back to work when he got out of the hospital," Hank said.

"Doesn't sound like it. I went over to visit him yesterday, and they wouldn't even let me peek into his room. No visitors except for family, but I saw his wife out in the hallway, and she said he wasn't doing too well."

Ben had just come from St. Mary's, and he hadn't even thought about checking on Carmine after he'd interviewed the two witnesses. Although he didn't know Carmine well, Ben felt somewhat guilty that it hadn't occurred to him to see how the stricken detective was getting along. Ben had to admit that his excitement about being tapped for detective duty, even if it was temporary, had momentarily made him forget everything else.

After gobbling down his breakfast and drinking two more cups of coffee, Ben headed back to the office, leaving Al and Hank sitting at the table. When he returned to the sheriff's office, Ben hoped he'd be able to contact Adrian Beaumont at his workplace. He didn't want to have to involve the Pasadena Police Department if he could avoid it.

"Ben, someone's here to see you," Anita Ferris, the day clerk told him as he walked in the door. An attractive thirtyish widow with two small boys to support, Anita was grateful to have a full-time job. In the two years Ben had been a deputy sheriff, he'd never known the perky strawberry blond mother to miss a day of work. Although he'd thought about asking Anita out a time or two, he'd overheard a couple of the other deputies asking her for a date, and she'd turned them both down. Ben didn't want that to happen to him. Besides, dating cost money, and his savings account was far from fat.

"Over there," she said quietly, motioning to a gaunt man wearing a light summer suit who had taken a seat next to Carmine's desk.

"OK, thanks, Anita," Ben said, flashing her a smile.

Ben went over to Carmine's desk and sat in his chair. "I'm Deputy Ben Cameron. I hear you're looking for me. What can I do for you?"

"Oh, good, deputy, you're here." The man withdrew a business card from his pocket and handed it to Ben.

Ben stared at the card. He probably should have realized that the press would be inquiring about the accident, but he hadn't given it a thought. Now a reporter from the local newspapers—the *Reno Evening Gazette* and the morning-delivered *Nevada State Journal*—was sitting in front of him, no doubt wanting some kind of a statement. Although he'd never had to deal with the press before, Ben had read enough newspaper articles with official statements quoting the sheriff to know how to handle the situation. With a pencil poised over a small spiral-bound notebook, Cal Harris, the reporter, asked for information about the accident on Mount Rose Highway.

"Well, Mr. Harris, all I can tell you right now is that there was an accident involving one vehicle, and there was one fatality."

"Can you give me a name?"

"I'm afraid not. We're withholding the name of the deceased pending notification of next of kin."

"Anyone else injured?"

"No, only the driver. There were no passengers."

"Cause?"

"It's still under investigation, so I can't comment on that right now."

"Can you give me something? My deadline is one o'clock, and my editor's going to expect more than this."

Ben felt mildly irritated, but he wasn't totally unsympathetic with the reporter's plight. After all, he was a man just trying to do his job.

"Tell you what, Mr. Harris, I'll call you at the newspaper as soon as we're able to locate the next of kin."

"Any idea how long it's going to take?" Harris pressed.

"I'm hoping we'll know this morning, but I can't guarantee anything."

"OK, deputy, I'd really appreciate anything you can come up with. I'll wait for your call."

After Harris left the building, Ben asked Anita to give the same statement to any other reporters who inquired about the accident. He figured that the radio stations and KZTV, the only TV station in Reno, might be calling to check on the accident, too, and he didn't especially want to deal with them, at least not until he had more information.

Back at Carmine's desk, he picked up the phone to try his call again. This time, a switchboard operator answered, "Excelsior Studio, home of Hollywood's finest motion pictures."

Ben asked for Adrian Beaumont, and the call was transferred, but Beaumont didn't answer it. Instead, his secretary came on the line. Ben asked to speak to Beaumont, saying that the matter was urgent.

"Mr. Beaumont's out of the country right now. He's in Africa, directing a picture."

"I'm afraid I have some very bad news." Ben told Beaumont's secretary about the accident and asked if Adrian Beaumont's wife's name was Phyllis.

"Yes," the secretary replied in a tremulous voice. There was a long silence, and Ben was starting to wonder whether the call had been disconnected when the woman continued. "What a tragedy! I didn't realize she was out of town. I'll send a telegram to his hotel in Nairobi immediately, but if he's out in the field filming, it could be days before he gets it."

"Is there another relative I could contact?"

"Yes, there's a sister. She lives in San Francisco. Just a minute while I find the Christmas card list, and I'll give you her address." How about that? The Beaumonts didn't even write their own Christmas cards. Mr. Beaumont's secretary did it for them. "Here it is."

Ben wrote down the address—that and the name would be all the long-distance operator would need to make the connection—and thanked the secretary for her help. He gave her his own name again, along with the address and phone number of the sheriff's department so that Mr. Beaumont could contact them when he received the tragic news of his wife's untimely death.

Although Ben had little doubt that the woman driving the Cadillac was Phyllis Beaumont, he needed to confirm her identity. He knew he was going to have to not only deliver the bad news about the accident to her sister, but also ask the lady to identify her sister's body. Dreading to make the phone call, especially because she was likely to start crying and Ben always felt helpless when a woman cried, Ben stalled for a few minutes while he went to the tiny area that served as a break room for the deputies and filled the brown ceramic mug he kept there with coffee. Back at Carmine's desk, he drank his coffee while he reviewed the notes he'd made about the accident.

He fiddled around for a few more minutes before he finally made the phone call to San Francisco and delivered the bad news to Phillis Beaumont's sister, Wanda Cartwright. Just as he'd feared, Mrs. Cartwright broke down sobbing. Luckily for Ben, who couldn't understand anything Mrs. Cartwright was saying while she cried, her husband came on the line. Evidently, he'd understood the gist of his wife's conversation, and he told Ben that the couple would drive to Reno right away. He estimated that they'd arrive by mid-afternoon. After giving Mr. Cartwright directions to the sheriff's department, Ben offered his condolences and rang off.

It wasn't nine o'clock yet, but already it seemed like a very long day to the deputy.

He was headed back to the break room for another cup of coffee when a tall woman wearing Western garb entered the office. She spoke briefly to Anita, and then Anita called him over to meet the gray-haired, blue-eyed woman who made an imposing impression in her tan Stetson hat, cowboy boots, and plaid Western shirt tucked into her jeans, cinched with a silver and turquoise concho belt.

"Ben, this is Mrs. Ellis from the Circle E Guest Ranch," Anita said. "This is Deputy Cameron," she told Mrs. Ellis.

"Ma'am," Ben nodded politely to the older woman. "How can I help you?"

"One of our guests has gone missing, and I'm worried that something may have happened to her. She left yesterday afternoon for Lake Tahoe—all dressed up in a silver evening gown and carrying her mink stole—to go to a show at the Cal Neva, and we haven't seen her since. The maid reported that her bed hadn't been slept in, and her Cadillac's still gone, too."

"Why don't we go back here," Ben said, motioning toward Carmine's desk, "and you can tell me about it." Ben pulled out the chair that the newspaper reporter had occupied and set it beside the desk for Mrs. Ellis before he sat down in Carmine's chair. Before Ben could prompt her, Mrs. Ellis began talking.

"It's not like guests haven't taken a powder before. They're adults, free to come and go as they please, but I warn the women who stay with us that I can't act as their witness if they aren't in Nevada every single day for six weeks. I won't lie for anyone. It'd mean a fourteen-year prison sentence, if I did, and I wouldn't risk that for the queen of England."

"Yes, ma'am," Ben said, slightly confused. He knew about the many dude ranches around the Reno area that catered to people, mainly women, who came to Nevada to establish residency so that they could get a divorce much more quickly and easily than they could in their home states, but he wasn't familiar with the way the process worked.

"The point is, deputy, that I've never seen a woman who was so absolutely determined to do whatever she had to do to get a quick divorce as Phyllis Beaumont."

Chapter 2

"All aboard," the porter sang out as Southern Pacific's sleek streamliner, the *City of San Francisco*, slowly pulled away from the station in Sparks and gradually picked up speed. Reno, its next stop, was only a few miles away.

Mary Garrison, a petite young woman with blue eyes and dark brown hair cut in a stylish bob, glanced around to make sure that the other passengers couldn't see her. Satisfied that their view was blocked by a pile of her belongings on the aisle seat next to her, she furtively pulled up her silk stockings, straightening the seams, before she attached them to the garters of her girdle.

Luckily, the passenger who had been sitting next to her for much of the trip had debarked in Elko, leaving an empty seat next to Mary, one she'd quickly filled with her make-up case, handbag, and jacket so that the cigar-smoking gent who'd eyed her since the train left Chicago wouldn't appropriate the seat. After spending the last forty-five hours on the train, including a day of unrelenting nausea, caused by the train's constant swaying motion, and two sleepless nights cramped in a coach seat, the last thing she wanted was unwelcome company.

Mary set her jaunty new navy felt hat on her head and secured it with a long hat pin before pulling on her white cotton gloves, tucking her white blouse into her navy pencil skirt and putting on her matching suit jacket. She wore navy and white spectator pumps with two-inch heels and carried a matching navy and white handbag. She looked clean and fresh in her smart ensemble, but the truth was that, since the train's facilities didn't include showers or bathtubs, it had been two days since she'd bathed, and she felt grubby from traveling. Taking her compact and a tube of lipstick out of her handbag, she gazed at the reflection of her lips in the compact's small mirror while she applied bright red lipstick. Then Mary gathered her things and lurched toward the end of the coach. Standing between two coach cars where they were coupled together, the porter waited with her three large suitcases, a matched set of light blue Samsonite luggage that she'd received as a gift from her grandparents when she'd graduated from high school four years earlier.

She'd had occasion to use the heavy, hard-cased luggage only one other time—on her honeymoon. Her travels with those suitcases marked both a beginning and an end, she thought somewhat morosely. Mary was headed to Reno for the six-week solution for a bad marriage recommended by her New York attorney—a divorce from her husband John Garrison.

The porter opened the door to the coach and beckoned to Mary.

"Coming into Reno, ma'am."

Mary gingerly stepped into the area between the two coach cars. All during the trip she'd hated to walk between the cars, but she'd had no choice if she wanted to go to the club car or the dining car. The swaying movement of the train jostling her back and forth felt more pronounced in the coupling areas than in the cars themselves. When she walked through them, she saw the ground rushing by under her feet, and she imagined that the cars would part and the earth would rise up to swallow her.

Bracing herself against the side of the car, Mary jerked as the train pulled into the station and stopped with a jolt, great clouds of steam belching from its underside. The porter swung down easily to the cement platform, setting Mary's heavy bags on the ground before he placed a small step stool directly under the last step of the train car.

"Watch your step, ma'am," he warned as he helped her down the steps. A couple with two small children waited a few feet away, and when she turned to thank the porter, he was already assisting them to board the train, which stopped only briefly in Reno.

Mary scanned the platform. Her hosts had promised to meet her when she arrived in Reno. Although the train was a few hours late, Mary hoped that her late arrival wouldn't be too great an inconvenience to the couple who owned the dude ranch where her husband's lawyer had arranged for her to stay during her six weeks in Reno.

Then she saw them—a strikingly tall older couple both dressed in Western clothing wearing matching red plaid shirts and holding a cardboard sign with Mary's maiden name, Marchetti, neatly printed on it. Mary didn't ever want to have to call herself Garrison again. She planned to take back her maiden name as soon as a Reno judge granted her a divorce. Her soon-to-be ex-husband had insisted that her train tickets and her stay at the guest ranch in Reno be booked under her maiden name. Mary knew that her husband didn't want any record of Mrs. John Garrison traveling to the divorce capital of America, just in case she should come to her senses, as he put it, and reconcile with him. Mary also knew that she would never go back to him, and, in the meantime, she was content to call herself Mary Marchetti once again, even though she didn't feel like the old Mary Marchetti.

Mary waved at the couple as they approached her.

"Mr. and Mrs. Ellis?"

"Glad to have you with us, Mrs. Marchetti," the old gent, whose hair and mustache were snowy white, said heartily. "I'm a-going to grab a luggage carrier from the station, and then I'll get your bags."

"Oh, thank you, and please call me Mary," she said, and the Ellises smiled and nodded.

"I'm Carol, and this is my husband Chuck," Mrs. Ellis said. "Mary, you must be exhausted after traveling all the way out here from New York."

"I am a little tired," she admitted.

"Let's get you back to the ranch where you can relax, maybe take a nap."

"That sounds heavenly. I didn't get much sleep on the train."

"We'll have you back there in two shakes of a lamb's tail. The Circle E's only a couple miles south of town," she said, as her husband placed the suitcases on the rolling luggage carrier.

"Here, Mary, let me take your make-up case, too," Chuck said, and Mary gratefully handed it over to him. "Shall we, ladies?"

Carol Ellis led Mary to a wood-paneled station wagon parked down the street from the railroad station. While Chuck stowed Mary's luggage in the back, Mary settled herself in the front seat, at Carol's insistence, and then, to Mary's surprise, Carol slid in next to her, leaving Mary sandwiched between the Ellises on the wide bench seat. As Chuck drove, the couple pointed out various landmarks in downtown Reno, including the famous arch that spanned Virginia Street, proclaiming Reno "The Biggest Little City in the World."

"It don't look like much during the day," Chuck said, "but it's real pretty at night, all lit up."

"I'd like to see it at night," Mary said politely.

"There'll be plenty of time for that, Mary," Carol said, patting Mary's hand, "after you've had a chance to get some rest."

"Here's the bridge where some of the gals throw their wedding rings away," Chuck said as he drove over the Truckee River Bridge.

"Oh, Chuck, you know they don't throw their real gold rings away. I guess some of them do throw dime-store rings in, though."

Chuck laughed. "Yeah, like the ring that little filly Joan got out of a Crackerjack box last week. She throwed it in right over there." Chuck pointed to the low cement railing on the bridge. Half a block later, he gestured toward an imposing Neoclassical building with tall Corinthian columns on the right. "That there's the courthouse where you'll be a-going in six weeks. Now this ain't no lie—some of the gals kiss them columns when they come out, free as birds."

"Oh, dear." Mary said in a low voice. She didn't understand how a woman could take getting a divorce so lightly, and Chuck's recitation of Reno's divorce lore made her feel sad.

Carol looked at Mary and patted her hand. "Don't worry, Mary. It'll be over with before you know it, and you'll be on your way back to New York." She leaned forward to speak to her husband, "Step on it, will you, Chuck?"

"Sure thing," Chuck said, as he accelerated and sped out of town on South Virginia Street. Soon he was turning onto the gravel road that led to the Circle E.

About a mile down the gravel road, Mary saw an open gate, framed by two long log pillars and a high wooden beam. The Circle E logo and name were carved deeply into the solid pine beam. The short road from the gate to the ranch house was paved, and Mary could see that it continued beyond the large house, which sat on the left, about half a mile farther to a stable and corral. A two-story log building, the ranch house had a wide front porch that ran the length of the building. A white wooden slat swing hung on sturdy chains from the porch's ceiling, and several white wicker chairs and a couple of small tables sat nearby. On the railing, a dozen boxes of red geraniums brightened the porch.

"You can't see them from here," Carol said, "but the swimming pool and tennis court are behind the house. We have five guest cottages back there, too. Let's get you settled in, and I'll show you around the place later."

Chuck pulled the woodie up to the front lawn where flagstones formed a path to the porch steps, and they all piled out.

"You ladies go ahead," Chuck said. "I'll bring them bags."

The front door opened directly into a large living room where a brown leather sofa, draped with a colorful, striped Mexican blanket, and several upholstered chairs were arranged around a red-and-tan Navajo rug. An old framed map of Lake Tahoe and several paintings, mostly Western landscapes with rustic wooden frames, decorated the pine-paneled walls. One painting—a handsome young cowboy standing proudly beside his horse—stood out among the landscapes, and Mary recognized its subject immediately, despite the fact that he was at least three decades older now.

"What a great picture of Chuck!" Mary exclaimed.

"Thank you, Mary. It's always been one of my favorites. I painted it about a month after Chuck and I were married."

"It's really wonderful. You're a talented artist."

"Oh, I dabble a bit—keeps me out of trouble." Carol laughed. "This way, Mary," Carol motioned to the staircase that led to the ranch house's second floor. "The guest rooms are all on the second floor, and here's your room, right at the top of the stairs."

Mary followed Carol into the cheerful, sunny room. Sheer white ruffled cottage curtains hung at the window with a roller shade beneath. The shade was all the way up, its little round pull dangling from a cord, permitting light to flood the room. A pink-and-white chenille cover topped the bed. The only other furniture was a long, low maple dresser with a large mirror attached to the back of it and a maple bed stand, on which sat a brass lamp with a white shade edged with pink fringe. The oak floor had been polished to a high gloss.

"Here's your own private bathroom with both a tub and a shower," Carol pointed out, as she slid open a pocket door that Mary hadn't even noticed. "And here's your closet right next to the bathroom."

"Thanks, Carol, everything looks great. I can't wait to soak in a nice hot bath and take a nap in a real bed. It's kind of hard to sleep on the train."

"I can imagine. You've had a long trip, and I'm sure you're exhausted, so just relax and holler if you need anything. Whenever you're ready, I'll give you the grand tour. Here comes Chuck with your bags."

Chuck came in with Mary's suitcases and set them neatly in a row at the foot of the bed.

"Here you are, Mary." Chuck looked as though he were about to say something else, but Carol caught his eye and, with an almost imperceptible toss of her head, motioned for them to go.

"Have a nice nap," she said and gently closed the door.

Mary went straight to the bathtub and turned on the faucet, running her fingers under the water until she'd adjusted it to just the right temperature. There were plenty of fluffy white towels hanging on a rack above the tub, and a fresh bar of Ivory soap sat in a tiny alcove next to the tub. She let the water fill the tub to very near the top before turning it off. She was just about ready to rummage through the smallest of her suitcases to find her blue satin summer robe when she remembered the letter she'd intended to mail as soon as she arrived in Reno.

Taking the letter from her handbag, she stepped out into the hallway. Perhaps it wasn't too late. If the ranch's mail hadn't gone out yet today, she could ask Carol to post the letter. In the letter, she'd written a cheerful account of her train travels and the scenery along the multi-state route so that her parents wouldn't be so worried about her. Native New Yorkers, their knowledge of the West was pretty much limited to the Western dramas they had seen on television, and they were afraid that the West was as uncivilized as it had been a century earlier. Mary knew that her divorce was causing her parents almost as much grief as it was causing her. She wanted to reassure them that she'd be all right, although she wasn't too confident on that score herself.

Mary walked the few steps to the top of the staircase, but paused when she heard Carol talking to her husband in a muted voice. Despite the fact that Carol was almost whispering, her voice carried up the stairs, and Mary could hear her quite clearly.

"I'm so upset, Chuck," Carol said. "We barely had a chance to talk before you met me at the train station, and I didn't want to say anything in front of Mary."

"I know, darlin'. The poor kid looked exhausted, and she has troubles enough of her own."

"Chuck, I should have warned Phyllis about that road. I knew she'd have to drive back from Lake Tahoe after dark, and all I said to her was to be careful."

"It ain't your fault, Carol. She was a grown woman. You were her hostess, not her babysitter. Accidents happen."

"First ever with one of our guests, though."

"True enough, and I feel real bad about it, too. Why'd she go up there all by her lonesome anyways?"

"Don't you remember, Chuck? She said one of her friends was in a show at the Cal Neva, and she wanted to see it."

"I'm surprised none of the other gals went with her."

"Most of them had already signed up for the twilight trail ride and barbeque. Thank the Lord that a whole carload of them didn't go up there with Phyllis."

Carol started crying, and Mary could hear Chuck murmuring to her, undoubtedly trying to comfort his distressed wife. Mary didn't want to disturb the couple, so she tip-toed back to her room, quietly closed the door, and laid the letter on the bed. Tomorrow would be soon enough to mail it. She doubted that Carol would appreciate being interrupted when she was crying.

Mary had been afraid that she might fall asleep in the bathtub, but after hearing such distressing news, she felt wide awake as she soaked. Obviously, one of the Circle E's guest's had died in an auto accident. How horrible! It was no wonder Carol was crying. Mary felt like crying, too—for the unknown dead woman, for her failed marriage, and for putting her parents through hell.

Mary's six weeks in Nevada hadn't gotten off to a very good start, but, unlike many of the women who came to Reno for a quickie divorce, Mary hadn't really thought of the six-week solution as a time to vacation, but more like a time in limbo, so she had no high expectations. As she lay down to nap, she crossed herself and said a silent prayer for the woman who had died.

Chapter 3

If Ben had had a shadow of a doubt as to the accident victim's identity, it was erased by his conversation with Carol Ellis. Evidently, Phyllis Beaumont had been a guest at the Circle E. From the little information he'd gleaned in his brief conversation with her sister Wanda, Ben had learned that she didn't know the reason Phyllis Beaumont was in Reno. Ben wondered whether or not Adrian Beaumont knew that his wife had come to Nevada to establish residency so that she could get a divorce. Neither the Beaumonts' housekeeper not Adrian Beaumont's secretary had known the whereabouts of Phyllis Beaumont. Ben surmised that the Beaumonts might have been trying to avoid unwanted publicity.

Picking up the business card that Cal Harris had left with him earlier, Ben found the newspaper's number and called Harris to give him an update. When the reporter learned that the accident victim was Adrian Beaumont's wife, he sounded excited.

"Adrian Beaumont, the Hollywood director?"

"Yes, that's the one. He lives in Pasadena, but he's in Africa right now shooting a movie."

"*African Safari?*"

"What?"

"The name of the movie—is it *African Safari?*"

"Oh, I don't know. You could check with his office at Excelsior Studio."

"Wow, thanks, deputy. This is big. The news wires will pick up my story for sure. Adrian Beaumont won this year's Academy Award for Best Director, and his next movie is supposed to be an even bigger blockbuster than his last one. I don't know much about his wife, but I think she had parts in some of his movies. Say, what was she doing in Reno, anyway?"

"She was staying at the Circle E."

"Holy cow! She was here to get a divorce, wasn't she?"

"Yes, it looks that way."

"Who's her lawyer; do you know?"

"No, I don't have that information."

"Never mind. I can find out from the owners of the Circle E. Thanks, deputy. I owe you one."

As he hung up, Ben had the sickening feeling that he'd made a mistake in contacting the reporter. Ben had never heard of Adrian Beaumont before today, and he didn't know that the sad story of a fatal, single-car accident on a steep, winding mountain road might become national news. In retrospect, Ben realized that he probably shouldn't have told the reporter about the reason for Phyllis Beaumont's stay in Reno. Harris had said he planned to contact the Ellises, and Ben feared that Carol Ellis would be angry when she found out that the reporter's information had come from Ben.

This new assignment that the sheriff had given him might just land him in hot water, but Ben refused to let himself dwell on that possibility. There was still plenty of work to do to wrap up the investigation. Ben knew who had died in the accident, but he still didn't know what caused it. Although he could have called the coroner, Ben didn't want to hang around the sheriff's office any longer, so he decided to see Dominik Petrowski, the coroner, in person. In his two years with the Washoe County Sheriff's Department, Ben had encountered the coroner a few times at accident scenes, but the only thing Ben knew about the wiry, little man, who always wore rimless glasses, a black suit, and a bow tie, was that when it came to his job, he brooked no nonsense.

Ben found the coroner sitting at his desk reading a report in his tiny cubbyhole of an office. Ben felt mildly claustrophobic on entering, but meeting the coroner in the autopsy room would have been worse. Although Ben had seen dead soldiers in both Europe and Korea, and as a deputy sheriff, he encountered death from time to time, he preferred to avoid any grim reminders of humanity's mortality when he could.

Petrowski looked up as Ben walked in.

"Deputy?" The coroner showed no sign that he recognized the man in the uniform.

"Dr. Petrowski, I'm one of the deputies who worked the accident this morning up on Mount Rose."

"Oh, yes. I'm sorry. I didn't recognize you." Petrowski apologized. "It was darker than hell up there," he added by way of explanation.

"Ben Cameron, sir," Ben said extending his hand to Petrowski. Petrowski rose from his chair and gave Ben a firm handshake.

"Sit down, deputy." The coroner gestured to a small wooden chair in front of his desk. He tapped a cigarette from the pack of Camels lying on his desk and lit it with a silver lighter that he pulled from his pocket. He nodded toward the pack of Camels. "Help yourself."

"Got my own right here," Ben said as he lit a Lucky Strike and took a few puffs.

"What can I do for you, deputy?"

"I'm investigating the accident, and I was wondering what you can tell me about the victim."

"Is Carmine still in the hospital?"

"Yes, sir."

"I'm sorry to hear that. He's a good man," Petrowski paused. "She wasn't drunk," he said abruptly.

"What?"

"The victim—Phyllis Beaumont—she wasn't drunk. Her blood alcohol level tested at zero. It's possible that she fell asleep at the wheel."

"From what the two witnesses told me, the driver was awake. They said she swerved around their car to pass them right before she drove off the side of the mountain."

"Hmm. Maybe she was driving too fast and lost control."

"That would be my guess, too. By the way, I couldn't reach her husband to notify him about the accident. He's out of the country right now. I was able to contact her sister—a Mrs. Wanda Cartwright—in San Francisco though, and her husband's driving her over. They should be here sometime this afternoon."

"Deputy, there's not a doubt in my mind that Mrs. Beaumont died as a result of injuries sustained in the accident although, as we've discussed, we don't really know why the accident happened. What I'm getting at is that I don't plan to do an autopsy. Do you have a problem with that?"

"No, sir. I suppose an autopsy would upset the family even more than they already are."

"Right. It's going to be traumatic enough for the lady to see her sister's face all smashed up. Her injuries are so bad I'm not sure her sister will be able to identify her."

Ben nodded.

"It's going to be awfully tough on her," he said as he stubbed his cigarette out in the glass ashtray that sat on the corner of Petrowski's desk. "I'll bring the Cartwrights over as soon as they arrive this afternoon."

Definitely not something to look forward to, Ben thought, as he left Petrowski's office. He flipped through his notebook to review what the Connors couple had told him. It had been their impression that the driver hadn't slowed down, but eyewitness accounts could be dicey, and he decided to drive back up to the scene of the accident to check the road for skid marks. He'd hadn't really looked at the road itself earlier. In any case, it would be much easier to see skid marks, if there were any, in the daytime than in the dark.

Traveling south on Virginia Street, Ben had left Reno a couple of miles behind when he noticed a small sign marking a gravel road on the right with the neatly lettered name of the Circle E on it. He'd passed this way many times in the past two years since he'd become a deputy, but he'd never noticed the sign before although he guessed that the ranch had probably been there for years. Until Carol Ellis reported her missing guest to him, Ben had had only a vague awareness of dude ranches in the Reno area, but he wasn't familiar with the ins and outs of the divorce ranch business.

Ben reached the turn-off for the Mount Rose Highway soon after passing the Circle E sign, and his trip up the mountain highway didn't take as long as it had in the early morning hours. Actually, it was a nice drive in the daylight, and Ben would have enjoyed it if he hadn't been returning to the accident scene. As he neared his destination, he passed a flatbed tow truck hauling the mangled remains of the black Cadillac, and he thought that he probably should have returned to the scene before the tow truck arrived. Parking at the turn-out, he crossed the road and examined the pavement for signs of skid marks, but there were none. Evidently, Phyllis Beaumont hadn't even applied the brakes before her car soared over the dirt embankment at the side of the highway and plunged down the hill.

As he headed back to town, it occurred to Ben that maybe the wreck hadn't been an accident at all. Maybe Phillis Beaumont, despondent over her impending divorce, had decided to take her own life. The lack of skid marks seemed to support that theory, especially since the coroner had determined that Mrs. Beaumont hadn't been drinking. Because the couple who had witnessed the accident said that the Cadillac had swerved around them, its driver couldn't have been asleep. Even if someone were driving recklessly, and Phyllis Beaumont certainly had been, he thought it likely that any driver not bent on suicide would brake, but the witnesses had reported that the Caddy's taillights hadn't flashed red.

Still, the suicide theory had its flaws. Ben doubted that a woman would choose to commit suicide by smashing herself up in a car crash. More likely, she'd take sleeping pills, as had happened in the two suicides Ben had responded to the previous year. Or she might leave her car running in a closed garage. Those methods would be more peaceful, less violent, and they wouldn't destroy a woman's looks.

Making a mental note to ask Petrowski about suicide statistics, Ben glanced at his watch and decided he didn't have time for a late lunch. He needed to get back to the sheriff's department before the Cartwrights arrived, and he should probably fill the sheriff in on what he'd learned about the accident. He felt a little twist in his gut at the thought of admitting to the sheriff that he'd most likely told the newspaper reporter more than he should have, but he also knew better than to try to hide anything from his boss. Things had a way of coming out, anyway—a newspaper story, especially—and he didn't want the sheriff to be blindsided because he'd failed to update him on the investigation.

Back at the department, he stopped at Anita's desk and learned that the sheriff was out of the building. In the tiny break room, he filled his mug with muddy coffee, added some cream, and had just sat down at Carmine's desk when a couple came in the door. He stood, sure that they were the Cartwrights. The short, beautiful, blond woman was dressed somberly in a black suit and hat. Her much-older husband stood only an inch or two taller than she did, and he also wore a black suit. Pudgy and bald, Cartwright certainly wasn't handsome, but from the way his wife looked at him, his looks didn't matter to her.

Anita greeted the couple as Ben approached them. He introduced himself and offered his condolences. When they accepted his offer to drive them to the coroner's office, he asked Anita to call Petrowski to alert him that they were on their way. The patrol car that Ben had exchanged for his pickup truck when he'd driven to the coroner's office earlier sat at the curb in front of the sheriff's department. Most of the people who sat in the back of the patrol car were prisoners, and Ben felt awkward directing the couple to sit there, but he would have felt even more awkward with them sitting in the front seat with him, so he opened the back door, and they both slid into the back seat without saying anything. The short ride to the coroner's office took place in total silence, and Ben couldn't wait to get the official identification of Phyllis Beaumont completed.

Ben noticed how pale Wanda Cartwright looked as he accompanied her and her husband into the coroner's office, where all three of them crowded into the tiny space, Ben standing in the doorway behind the couple. Wanda sat in the wooden chair next to Petrowski's desk while her husband stood beside her.

"I'm very sorry for your loss," Petrowski said, "and I'm sorry to have to put you through this, but we need to confirm your sister's identity."

Wanda Cartwright withdrew a white linen handkerchief from her handbag and dabbed at her eyes. Her husband gently put his hand on her shoulder.

"Unfortunately, I'm afraid it's going to be difficult. Her face—well, she went through the windshield."

Wanda Cartwright began sobbing.

"Can't we spare my wife?" Peter Cartwright asked. "I've known Phyllis for years, and I can identify her."

"No, Pete. I want to see my sister," his wife protested through her tears. "This all seems like a bad dream. Maybe if I see her, I'll realize it's real."

"All right, dear. If that's what you wish."

"Let's go down the hall then," Petrowski said, and Ben backed out of the office while the Cartwrights exited and waited for the coroner's lead. Peter Cartwright circled his wife's waist with his arm, walking beside her as they followed the coroner and Ben trailed behind.

When they entered the small viewing room, Ben saw that a white sheet covered the body. Again, he stood in the back, wishing he could make himself invisible. He held his breath as Petrowski lifted the sheet, revealing the dead woman's face.

Wanda Cartwright emitted a shriek. "I can't tell. I can't tell." She wailed as she turned to her husband who was staring at the body intently.

"I don't know for sure, either," he said, holding his wife tightly.

Petrowski covered the woman's face. "Does your sister have any birthmarks?" he asked.

Wanda Cartwright nodded. "Yes, on her left instep—it's dark pink, about the size of a fifty-cent piece. And another thing—she always wears bright red polish on her toenails."

Petrowski carefully picked up the sheet once again, exposing the accident victim's left foot, which he held up so that they could all see it.

"That's not my sister! Oh, Pete, it's not her!"

Even from where Ben stood behind the Cartwrights, it was apparent that there was neither a birthmark on this woman's foot nor any red polish on her toenails. Ben noticed the coroner examining the other foot, probably to look for the mark there in case Wanda had been mistaken about which foot her sister's birthmark was on. Petrowski quickly replaced the sheet and ushered them all back to his office.

In a frenzy of relief, Wanda Cartwright laughed and cried. Her husband, on the other hand, looked angry.

"How could this happen, doctor?"

Ben stepped in before Petrowski could answer. "We made the tentative identification based on the fact that Phyllis Beaumont's driver's license was in the glove compartment of the Cadillac, which is registered to Adrian Beaumont. A fur stole was found in the car with a monogram "PB." Also, Carol Ellis, one of the owners of the Circle E Ranch, reported that one of her guests—a Mrs. Phyllis Beaumont from Pasadena—was missing. So naturally we assumed that—"

Peter Cartwright held up his hand. "I apologize, deputy. I probably would have come to the same conclusion under the circumstances. This has been extremely upsetting, I must say."

"I'm sorry for the mix-up," Ben said.

"But where's my sister? Where's Phyllis?" Wanda cried.

"When was the last time you heard from Phyllis, Mrs. Cartwright?" Ben asked.

"About two months ago. She called and told me she and Adrian were having some problems, and she was thinking about getting a divorce. That's the reason I wasn't surprised to hear that she was in Reno."

"I doubt that she was ever here, but if, as you say, she had been thinking about getting a divorce, maybe she planned to come to Reno originally. My guess is that your sister arranged for some other lady to take her place because she didn't want to stay in Nevada for six weeks."

"That leaves us with the mystery of who died in the accident," the coroner said.

"I'll get to the bottom of this," Ben promised, tight-lipped. "I'll be in touch," he told Petrowski as he ushered the couple out of the coroner's office.

"I don't want to keep you," he told them. "I know this has been a terrible ordeal for you both. Let me drive you back to your car now. Will you be returning to San Francisco tonight?"

"No, I've booked a room at the Mapes," Peter Cartwright said. "We always stay there when we come to Reno to gamble. Now that we know my wife's sister isn't an accident victim, maybe we can have dinner in the Sky Room and catch a show."

"But what about Phyllis?" Tears sprang to Wanda Cartwright's eyes again. "This isn't like her."

"I think it's exactly like her. She's a little bubbleheaded sometimes, but I'm sure she'll get in touch with you soon. Anyway, there's not a thing we can do. We're here now, and we might as well have a night out on the town."

Wanda leaned against her husband, and Ben had a feeling that his wishes would prevail. Ben hustled the couple back to their car in record time. When he dropped them off, he asked them to notify him if they heard from Phyllis Beaumont.

In the meantime, Ben planned on doing some sleuthing. What had seemed like an unfortunate, but routine, accident had rapidly turned into a crime investigation. Ben wasn't sure exactly which Nevada statute had been violated—he'd leave that to the district attorney to specify if he decided to file charges against Phyllis Beaumont—but he knew that conspiring to perpetrate fraud was against the law. If Ben were right—and he could think of no other logical explanation for the identity switch—Phyllis Beaumont had hired or cajoled the dead girl to take her place to establish her six weeks' residency in Nevada. Then she'd planned on obtaining a divorce without ever having to "do her time." For all anyone knew, she could be living it up in Acapulco or Paris right now.

Ben was well aware that the mistaken identity of the accident victim wasn't his only problem. He'd already told the newspaper reporter that she was Phyllis Beaumont. The error would put both Ben and the sheriff's department in a bad light. Thinking about the way he'd already botched the investigation that the sheriff had entrusted to him, he cringed. The same sinking feeling in the pit of his stomach that he'd had shortly after he'd realized that he'd shared too much information with the reporter returned. Ben worried that even if the sheriff didn't fire him, he probably wouldn't call on Ben again for any special duty. Ironically, Ben hadn't realized that he wanted more from his job until the sheriff had assigned him the accident investigation. As the day went by though, he'd begun to feel more of a sense of accomplishment than he derived from his regular work as a deputy sheriff. Right up until Wanda Cartwright had burst his balloon with her revelation that the dead woman wasn't her sister, he'd felt like a competent investigator. Now he felt like a fool.

Hanging his head, he entered the sheriff's department. Anita, looking just as perky as she had in the morning, told Ben that the sheriff was still out of the office, but he'd called to say he'd been delayed at a meeting of the county commissioners. Sheriff Rogers would be back in about an hour, she told Ben. Slightly relieved that he couldn't talk to the sheriff yet, Ben made a quick phone call to the Circle E.

Then he headed south on Virginia Street for the third time that day. The woman who answered his call had told him that Carol Ellis couldn't come to the phone because she was outside, showing a new guest around the ranch. Ben felt too restless to stay in the office and wait to make contact with Mrs. Ellis by phone. He'd told the coroner that he would get to the bottom of this business, and, by God, that's exactly what he meant to do.

Chapter 4

When Mary woke from her nap, she lay in bed for a few minutes, getting her bearings in the unfamiliar guest room and enjoying the ability to stretch out and relax after her tedious train trip. She remembered dreaming that she was still on the train, swaying back and forth, walking to the club car through three other coaches and those horrible spaces between the coaches where the cars were coupled together. It had taken her an entire day to get used to the motion, but now that she was back on solid earth, she resolved to return to New York by airplane as soon as her divorce was granted.

It had been her own idea to take the train to Reno, one she had regretted only a few hours into the trip. She'd thought it might be fun to see something of the countryside, and although she'd enjoyed some of the scenery, especially the Rocky Mountains, she hadn't realized quite how cramped and uncomfortable sleeping in a reclining coach seat would be.

Straightening the rumpled chenille bedspread, she felt grateful to have arrived at her destination. During her six weeks in Nevada, she'd have time to think about what she intended to do with the rest of her life. Right at the moment, she had no idea. The last few weeks of her life had been devoted solely to plans to end her marriage, and she hadn't been able to think beyond that goal at the time.

Still dressed in her satin robe, Mary unpacked her suitcases, depositing some of the contents in the dresser drawers and hanging the rest in the closet. She stowed her empty suitcases under the bed and took her make-up case into the bathroom, where she applied fresh make-up. Then she dressed in white shorts and a sleeveless cotton blouse. After lacing up her new white Keds, she pulled them on, tying the shoelaces into little bows.

After she descended the stairs to the first floor, Mary found the living room deserted except for Carol, who was leafing through the latest issue of *Woman's Day*. Mary noticed the wooden spindle magazine holder on the floor next to the sofa brimmed with magazines.

"Well, Mary, don't you look pretty," she observed. "Would you like to take the grand tour now?"

Mary smiled and nodded. "That would be great."

"Just a second."

Carol poked her head out the front door and told the two women that Mary could see sitting on the front porch that she was going to be showing a new guest around the property.

"That's Sally and Bea out there on the porch. You'll meet them at dinner."

As Carol led Mary to the large dining room and through the French doors that opened onto a wide flagstone patio, she explained that the Circle E required references of all its guests, and drop-ins were never accepted. The guests tended to be women who'd come to Reno to establish their six-weeks' Nevada residency, but men and, occasionally, couples sometimes also stayed at the Circle E. Carol told Mary about the necessity of staying in Nevada and that she would act as her witness in court when the time came. Carol emphasized that she had to know that Mary was there every day.

"That shouldn't be a problem, Carol," Mary said. "I don't know where else I'd go, anyway."

"You'd be surprised what can happen. We're only a few miles from the California-Nevada border, so it can be tempting to take a trip to California. A couple of years ago, one of our guests decided she wanted to go sight-seeing at Lake Tahoe. She got caught in a blizzard, barely made it over to Truckee, which is in California, not Nevada, and she wasn't able to get back to Reno for several days. The lady only had a week to go before her scheduled hearing, but she had to start her six weeks all over again."

"She must have been unhappy."

"Yes, but our hands were tied. Anyway, it's usually not a problem. We ask that guests be back at the ranch by midnight if they're going into town in the evening. So if you're going to a show, it's better to go to an early one. The casinos never close, night or day, so it can be tempting to stay late. As far as driving into Reno for the evening entertainment, one of the guests often has a car and offers to take the other ladies, and both of our wranglers like to gamble, so they're usually willing to drive, too.

"For daytime business in Reno, Chuck usually makes a couple trips there every day, once around ten in the morning and again around one in the afternoon. He usually drops guests off at the Riverside and picks them up there, too, but if your lawyer or hairdresser isn't within walking distance, Chuck will take you right to their door."

"Oh, goodness, I have an appointment with my lawyer at nine tomorrow morning. Maybe I should change the time."

"No need to change your appointment. I'll take you myself."

"I don't want to be any trouble."

"It's no trouble, Mary. I'll just take along my embroidery to work on while I'm waiting for you." Carol pointed to the red rose that decorated the pocket of her plaid Western shirt. "I like to embroider flowers on my Western shirts."

Mary looked at the flower more closely. "That's beautiful, Carol. It's so detailed and realistic."

Renoites certainly dressed differently from New Yorkers, Mary thought. She was beginning to realize that most of the clothes—mainly dresses and suits—she'd brought with her from New York might not be very practical to wear around the ranch.

The patio, where Carol and Mary stood chatting, was deserted, but two women sunned themselves in lounge chairs around the gleaming swimming pool in the back yard.

"The water's still pretty cold in the pool, but it's refreshing if you can stand it," said one of the women, a young brunette with a golden sun tan, jumping up from her chair. "I'm Shirley Snowden. You must be the new girl on the block."

"Shirley, this is Mary Marchetti from New York," Carol said.

"Nice to meet you, Mary. I'm from L.A. myself."

"You have a wonderful tan, Shirley. Do you go to the beach a lot at home?"

"Oh, sure. All the time. I love the beach. We...." Shirley hesitated. "That is, *I* have a beach house on Balboa Island besides our, uh, *my husband's* home in Beverly Hills."

"I'm afraid I don't even know how to swim, and I've never tried to get a tan, but maybe I should. I don't have a swimsuit with me, though."

"I'll bet you could find a perfect swimsuit downtown at Gray Reid—it's Reno's big department store," Carol said.

"Mary, you should get one—maybe a Jantzen or a Catalina," Shirley urged. I'd be happy to teach you to swim, too. It'd be fun and help us pass the time. I just got here a few days ago myself."

"OK," Mary said after a few seconds hesitation. "I guess it's time for me to try something new, and it's very generous of you to offer to teach me."

"Great. Let's go into town in the morning and do some shopping. You'll need a cover-up, a hat, and some suntan lotion besides the suit."

"I have an appointment with my lawyer at nine. Carol's going to drive me."

"Why don't I drive you there, instead, and then we can go shopping. It shouldn't take very long at the lawyer's office. I was in and out of mine in less than half an hour."

"That sounds fine." Mary smiled and Carol nodded her approval. "See you later at dinner, Shirley, and thanks!"

Perhaps her stay at the Circle E wouldn't be so bad, after all, Mary thought, as she followed Carol toward the stable, although Mary had noticed that the other woman sunning herself on a deck chair hadn't even looked up when she and Carol approached the pool.

As though reading her thoughts, Carol told Mary that Mrs. Smythe, a wealthy Chicago socialite, had barely said a word while she'd been at the Circle E, spending most of her time in her cottage and the rest at the pool. She kept to herself and ignored the other guests, taking her meals in her cottage, too.

"Don't pay any attention to Mrs. Smythe, Mary. You're not likely to see her, except at the pool. I'm sorry she acts so aloof, but I guess it takes all kinds."

Mary hoped that the rest of the guests would be more congenial than Mrs. Smythe. Shirley had certainly been friendly and kind. Since Mary had to be in Nevada for six weeks, she thought that she might as well make the best of it.

Chapter 5

A couple of women lounged in wicker chairs on the porch of the ranch house, smoking cigarettes and drinking lemonade, when Ben parked his official car next to the flagstone walk. They stared at him curiously.

When he reached the porch, he removed his hat.

"Afternoon, ladies. Is Mrs. Ellis around?"

"Not in the house, sheriff, but I'd be more than happy to help you," one of the women, a curvaceous blond, cooed.

"Deputy sheriff, ma'am," Ben said, blushing. He'd never been good at lighthearted banter with the opposite sex.

"Never mind her, deputy," said the other woman, a plump lady of about fifty with short salt-and-pepper hair. As soon as she said it, the blond promptly stuck her tongue out at her friend and made a face. They both giggled. "Carol's showing someone around. They're back at the corral right now." She pointed down the road where Ben could see three people gathered by the fence of the corral, watching a couple of horses inside.

"Thank you." Ben tipped his hat and beat a hasty retreat back to his patrol car. He drove the half-mile down the lane and parked in front of the stable. Ben approached Carol Ellis, who was standing with a ranch hand and a pretty young woman dressed in white shorts and a white sleeveless blouse with red polka dots.

Carol turned and recognized Ben.

"Hello, Mrs. Ellis. I wonder if you could spare me a few minutes." In a low voice, he added, "It's official business."

"Of course, deputy." She excused herself, and she led him away from the others, toward an old house beyond the back of the stables. "How can I help you?"

"It seems that Phyllis Beaumont isn't the woman who died in the accident last night."

"What? Is Phyllis all right?"

"We don't know that yet, but there's been a mix-up. The woman who was staying here—the woman you knew as Phyllis Beaumont— wasn't really Phyllis Beaumont at all. I believe that your guest was here posing as Phyllis Beaumont."

"Good Lord, deputy! I don't think anything like that's ever happened here before. It's hard to believe."

"I'm afraid it's true, ma'am. I need to find out who this woman was. How did she arrange for her stay here?"

"She didn't arrange it personally. We get referrals through attorneys, and their offices usually make the arrangements. We never accept any drop-in guests. Everybody has to have references. I believe her attorney is Willis Canfield in Los Angeles, but her husband's attorney's office reserved her room."

"So when she arrived, you were expecting Phyllis Beaumont?"

"Yes. There was no reason to suspect that she was anyone else."

"I understand. I wonder if I might have a look around her room. Maybe she left some clue to her identity."

"The car she was driving was registered to Phyllis's husband. I know that for certain because Chuck took the car into Reno for her— whoever she was—to get it serviced, and he got a speeding ticket on the way home. He had to show the registration and explain why he was driving it."

"You're right. The car involved in the accident was a black Cadillac registered to Adrian Beaumont. That the one?"

"Yes, so I guess at least one of the Beaumonts arranged for the switch."

"Looks that way."

Carol pulled a set of keys from her jeans' pocket and picked a small brass key out.

"Here you go, deputy. This is the master key for the cottages. The lady was staying in Little Washoe, the cottage closest to the main house over there next to the creek." Carol gestured toward several cottages nestled in a grove of cottonwood trees.

"Would you mind looking around the cabin with me?" Ben wanted a witness with him if he was going to look at the unknown woman's possessions. There could be valuables in her room, and he had no intention of being in there alone and later having her relatives say that something was missing.

"I can do that," Carol answered. "I'll ask Jack to give our new guest a riding demonstration."

They joined Mary and the wrangler by the corral fence. Carol introduced them to Ben, who couldn't help noticing how different this guest was from the blond he'd met on the porch, not just in looks, but also in manner; one with dark, almost black hair, a contrast to her creamy white complexion, the other blond with a dark tan; one, unassuming, the other, coquettish. The blond had scared Ben with her bold approach. He felt much more comfortable with Mary's quiet way.

"Jack, I need to help the deputy for a while. I wonder if you'd mind showing Mary how you mount up and maybe give her a few riding tips so that she can decide if she'd like to give riding a try sometime."

"You bet," he answered and then told Mary, "I'll bring out Old

Paint. She's a real gentle horse, the best we have for a beginning rider."

Ben liked the way Mary unpretentiously agreed, her enthusiasm showing in the gleam in her eyes. Forcing himself back to the reason he'd come to the Circle E, he walked to the cottage with Carol and waited patiently while she fumbled with the master key, finally unlocking the cabin's door.

Glitzy costume jewelry lay on top of the dresser, which Carol identified as paste immediately, and cosmetics were strewn about the counter next to the sink in the bathroom, but nothing else appeared in plain sight.

"Let's check for a handbag," Ben said, remembering that the little white beaded evening clutch that'd he'd found in the Caddy's glove compartment couldn't hold much. His mother and his sisters always carried a purse with handles, and Ben figured most women did the same.

Carol pulled open the dresser drawers, seeing only clothing, but when she opened the drawer of the bedside stand, she found a white summer handbag. She handed it to Ben who upended it, and the contents spilled onto the bed. Carol spotted a pink linen handkerchief with Phyllis Beaumont's monogram on it while Ben sorted through the other items, coming up with two charge plates, both with Phyllis Beaumont's name on them.

"Buffum's and Bullock's?" Ben read.

"They're both big department stores in Southern California," Carol told him. "They don't have stores in Reno, though, so why would she have these with her?"

"Maybe for the same reason she had Phyllis Beaumont's driver's license—to establish herself as Phyllis Beaumont if anybody snooped around. Well, nothing else here," Ben noted, returning everything to the handbag. "Let's check the pockets of her clothing and her suitcases."

Carol opened the closet and showed Ben the luggage neatly stacked beneath several dresses hanging there. Ben took the three bags and set them on the bed, thankful the mystery woman hadn't locked her suitcases. Although he searched the lining and pockets inside the luggage, Ben found nothing of interest in any of the bags, nothing that gave him a clue to the identity of the Circle E's late guest. A quick check of her clothing and shoes didn't shed any light on her secret, either.

Glancing at his Timex, Ben knew he needed to get back to the sheriff's office right away if he wanted to update Sheriff Rogers on the unexpected developments in the accident investigation, but before he left, he felt obligated to inform Carol of the erroneous newspaper report that would be in running in tonight's *Reno Evening Gazette*, thanks to Ben. Sheepishly, he told Carol that the Circle E would be named as the place where Phyllis Beaumont had been staying, and as he'd anticipated, Carol wasn't at all happy. She informed Ben that all the owners of guest ranches tried their best to protect the privacy of their guests, many of whom were well known celebrities, although she admitted that stringers trying to dig out a sensational story often found success, especially since they maintained a wide network of contacts, usually employees or suppliers of the guest ranches.

After asking Carol to make sure the contents of the cottage remained undisturbed and promising that he'd arrange to have them picked up in the morning, Ben returned to his patrol car, which he'd left in the small gravel parking lot next to the stable. As he pulled out onto the lane, Mary turned and waved at him. Feeling awkward, he held up his hand in acknowledgement as he drove away.

"Sheriff's back," Anita told Ben as soon as he walked in the door.

Ben walked down the hall to the Sheriff's office and saw that his door was open. The sheriff was clearing his desk, as he did at the end of every day.

"I need to bring you up to date on the accident investigation," Ben told the sheriff as he stepped into his office.

"If I don't leave right now, I'll be going home to a dry pot roast and an unhappy wife. Can it wait till tomorrow?"

"No, sir," Ben said glumly. He wished his timing could have been better, but with the sheriff at the commissioners' meeting most of the afternoon, he'd had no choice but to wait to talk to him.

"OK, Ben, let's have it," he said with a sigh, motioning Ben to take a seat.

"I really messed up," Ben began, as the sheriff lit a Lucky Strike and leaned back in his chair.

The sheriff listened without interruption as Ben told him about the mix-up in the accident victim's identity and that he'd mistakenly released Phyllis Beaumont's name to the newspaper reporter. He explained that Adrian Beaumont, Phyllis's husband, was a big Hollywood director and that Cal Harris had been confident that the story would go national.

"You worried about giving the sheriff's department a black eye?"

"Yes, sir. I should have waited for a positive identification before I talked to Harris. He seemed concerned that his editor would be angry if he didn't have some details for the accident story in time for his deadline."

"So you thought you'd help him out?"

"That's about it," Ben said, hanging his head.

"Ben, I knew you were a conscientious guy when I asked you to investigate the accident, and I wasn't wrong. What you've done today was solid investigation. As for the bad publicity, we're going to take care of that. Get on the horn and call that reporter pal of yours and tell him to get over here right now. You've got a scoop for him, and tell him it's going to be an exclusive."

"Yes, sir,"

"Here. Use my phone," the sheriff said as he pushed the instrument toward Ben and rose from his chair. "I'll be back in a minute."

Ben didn't have the reporter's card with him, but he didn't want to go back to Carmine's desk to retrieve it, so he dialed the operator who connected him with the newspaper office. He caught Harris just as he was about ready to leave for the day, but, on hearing the offer of an exclusive story by the sheriff's office, he promised to meet Ben in a few minutes.

With the door open, Ben could hear the sheriff's gravelly voice and the metallic clicking of typewriter keys as he pulled his pack of Luckies out of his shirt pocket, struck a match, and lit his cigarette. He took a few puffs, but hurriedly ground it out in the large ashtray that sat on the desk when the typing ceased, and he heard the sheriff coming back down the hall.

"Read it," he said, handing Ben a sheet of paper.

Ben scanned the press release, written on official department stationery and tagged "Exclusive" along with the name of Cal Harris and the two local newspapers he represented. At the bottom of the story, Ben's name was listed as the contact person for further information, and both Ben and the sheriff were quoted in the story, which Ben recognized as a masterpiece of redirection. In the story, Ben came off as a great detective, and the sheriff's department looked just as good as its deputy.

Amazed that the same story, which would have made Ben look like a fool if he'd told it himself, could be told so differently, Ben looked up from the press release and saw that the sheriff was grinning at him.

"I can't believe. . . ."

"All in the telling, Ben. Now put your John Hancock at the bottom there, right over your typed name, and when Harris shows up, just hand him the press release. You can confirm the details, but don't say anything else. Tell him he has the inside track on the story for now, and that you're considering giving him the rest of the story."

Ben nodded. Although Ben was a novice in the world of public relations, he could see where the sheriff was going with this. He also realized that the sheriff could have taken over the entire story and not mentioned Deputy Sheriff Ben Cameron at all. Now Ben felt an even greater obligation to do a thorough investigation, one that would bring credit both to the sheriff's department and to himself. He'd always been determined to do a good, solid job, but maybe, in this case, *good* wasn't good enough. For this investigation, *good* had better be stellar.

Chapter 6

Dinner at the Circle E was a more subdued affair than usual, most likely because Carol had told each of the guests privately about the woman they'd known as Phillis Beaumont and her death in a car accident on Mount Rose Highway. Mary thought that the appearance of the deputy sheriff and the curiosity it had aroused had forced Carol to reveal the news before she was ready to share it. Carol had certainly been hesitant about telling Mary, and although Mary already knew what had happened because she'd accidentally overheard Carol talking to Chuck about it earlier, she'd pretended to be hearing it for the first time. Since she hadn't known that the dead woman had been an imposter, it wasn't difficult to act surprised.

Although the aloof Chicagoan, Mrs. Smythe, had taken dinner in her cottage, the rest of the guests of the Circle E gathered in the dining room, where Mary met Sally and Bea, the two women who had been lounging on the front porch earlier as well as the four other prospective divorcées whom she hadn't yet met: Carla, a Hollywood actress who was well past her zenith; Faye, a forty-five-year-old mother of teenagers she'd left at home with their grandparents; Lois, a stunning redhead from New York; and Kate, a sad young woman who'd arrived at the Circle E a few days before Mary.

After the quiet dinner, some of the guests drifted outside, onto the patio. Chuck set up a bar in one corner and began to serve drinks. Although wine with dinner and beer at the ranch's barbeques were included in the cost of each guest's stay, Carol had explained to Mary that other alcoholic beverages were extras, like long-distance phone calls, postage, and dry cleaning, all of which would be added to the guest's tab. Mary noticed that Chuck unobtrusively kept track of the drinks he was serving, but he was such a genial host that it was easy to forget that the women were all paying guests.

Still sipping her dinner wine, Mary joined Shirley at the bar, where Shirley ordered a martini.

"Let's go sit by the pool," Shirley suggested, and Mary walked with her down the flagstone path to the backyard pool. Even though the other guests on the patio weren't too far away, Mary felt as though she were in a different world.

"We can talk here, and they won't hear us," Shirley said, gesturing toward the group gathered on the patio. "I'm dying to hear your story, but I'm going to bore you with mine first." Shirley had been friendly from the moment Mary had met her, but Mary wasn't used to sharing secrets with strangers, and she felt vaguely uncomfortable, but she didn't protest. After all, she told herself, gossip at the Circle E wasn't likely to affect her situation, anyway. It would be nice to have a friend during her stay.

"OK," Mary said.

Sensing Mary's hesitancy, Shirley gently laid her hand on Mary's arm.

"We're all in the same boat here, Mary. I suppose Carol and Chuck have heard the old story told a thousand different ways in the years they've been running the Circle E."

"I never thought I'd be here. That's for sure."

"I guess I should have known that I would. That's what I get for marrying a man with a drinking problem."

"Your husband's an alcoholic?"

"Yep, and Dale's getting worse. The 'man in the white hat' just can't seem to control himself."

"Wait a minute. Shirley Snowden. Snowden, Snow. . . . You're not Dale Snow's wife?"

Shirley nodded. "They call him the handsomest actor in Hollywood. I guess I didn't look beyond his good looks and his movie-star, man-in-the-white-hat magnetism when I married him. Actually, he was on the wagon when I met him, and we married a few weeks later, but there'd been rumors. Of course, I foolishly ignored them."

"Wow. Dale Snow—I can't believe it."

"Believe it. He's nothing like the man you see on the movie screen. Unfortunately, he's a mean drunk. I'm still bruised from his last bender. He keeps promising to quit, but it never lasts. Finally, I wised up and realized that the six-week solution was just what I needed."

"I'm sorry, Shirley."

Wide-eyed, Mary watched as Shirley quickly drained her martini glass.

"You're wondering if I might drink too much, too, aren't you, Mary?"

"Uh, no."

"Don't worry about me. I have a strict one-drink limit. I don't even drink wine with dinner."

Mary thought that Shirley's declaration had the ring of truth. She remembered that Shirley had sipped coffee during dinner and that their waitress had removed her wine glass.

"How long were you and Dale married?"

"Ten years. I should have realized our marriage was a no-go, almost right from the beginning. Dale started drinking again a couple months after we married. It's my own fault, Mary. I was too eager to be the wife of a big Hollywood actor."

"What will you do now, Shirley?"

"Kick back for a while and get my bearings, I guess. Before I met Dale, I played a few small parts in movies—that's how I met him, on the set of *Long Trail to Santa Fe*—but it's been too many years, and I wasn't really much of an actress, anyway. I don't really have to work now, though. I suppose I'll probably get married again eventually."

"I'm not sure that I'll be able to do that."

"Why not, Mary? We may not have made the best choices the first time around, but men aren't all bad guys."

"Oh, I know, but I'm Catholic. Even after I get my legal divorce, the church won't recognize it. I'd have to have an annulment officially sanctioned by the church, and that's almost impossible to get."

"How awful. I guess I didn't realize.... I'm not much of a church-goer myself."

"Believe me, if there were any other way, I'd do things differently, but my husband makes me sick."

"You don't have to tell me about it if you don't want to, Mary. I was just kidding earlier."

"Like you said, we're all in the same boat, but at least your husband really wanted to marry you."

Shirley nodded.

"I found out that the only reason my husband married me was for political advantage. He never loved me at all. In fact, he has nothing but contempt for me and my entire family."

"That's crazy, Mary. You're a beautiful woman, and I know you're a nice one, too."

"It's true. I only found out a few weeks ago. I guess I'm still reeling from the shock. Oh, and to top it off, I also learned that he's kept a mistress the whole time we've been married."

"How awful. At least Dale didn't play around, not like lots of others in Hollywood."

"That's not the reason I'm divorcing him. If that was the only problem, I would have stayed with him."

"What happened, Mary? You said you only found out a few weeks ago."

"Yes. I came home early from a charity board meeting. One of the members wasn't feeling well, so we adjourned early. Obviously, John didn't hear me come in. He was in the study talking with Frank, his campaign manager, and they weren't especially quiet. I heard every word. John bragged about how he'd married the perfect wife."

"That doesn't sound bad."

"No, but here's the reason he said that I was perfect. 'Mary's great—half Italian and half Irish,' only he didn't say Italian and Irish, if you know what I mean. He used really ugly words I'd never heard him say before. Then he made fun of my parents and grandparents, and his tone was so contemptuous that, at first, I couldn't believe what I was hearing. Every time he had a political event, he asked them to come and always introduced all of us to the crowd. We were just pawns in his scheme to run for office. He was running for alderman when I met him, and now he's running for Congress in an Italian-Irish district."

"Oh, boy. I bet he's not happy that you're getting a divorce."

"No, he tried to talk me out of it. He even called here this morning, but the train was late, and I hadn't arrived yet. When I found out he had called, I told Carol that I wasn't going to talk to him, so she's alerted Chuck and the staff.

"I don't know why I didn't see it before, Shirley, but I was so busy attending all the events that he insisted on, I felt as though I hardly had time to breathe. There were charity fundraisers, community events, parades, and political speeches, and I was expected to show up at every single one of them. Whenever I brought up the subject of having children, he said that there'd be plenty of time for kids later."

"So you think he didn't really want to have kids?"

"I know it now. He also told his buddy that he knew we'd need to have kids so that his political career could flourish—he had to look like a good family man—but that he'd make sure they were shipped off to boarding school as soon as they were old enough."

"Good grief, Mary. He sounds like an awful jerk."

"I'm afraid so, although you'd never know it from everything he's said and done since I overheard his conversation. According to him, I misunderstood what he said, I need to come to my senses, and he's going to set up a trust fund for our future children worth millions if I come back to him. In reality, he's afraid that a divorce will hurt his political career and that he won't win the House seat he's running for in this fall's election if word gets out about the divorce. Even though he finally agreed to pay my way out here, he insisted that the train tickets and the stay at the ranch be reserved in my maiden name. He had his lawyer's office make the arrangements, just to be sure I didn't use my married name."

"He probably still thinks that he can talk you out of the divorce somehow."

"He probably does. He keeps calling my parents and grandparents and sending them gifts, begging them to try to influence my decision."

"What do they think about him?"

"They used to love him; he seemed so thoughtful, always including them in his political rallies and fundraisers, but now that they know the truth, they feel embarrassed that they were taken in by his charm routine."

"So they're on your side?"

"All the way, which is difficult, too, because we're all Catholic, but we all understand now that he was just using us to further his political career. Honestly, I don't think I could get through this without my family's support."

"You're right. I wish my family would back me, but they want me to stick it out with Dale, even though they've seen him in action when he's drunk."

"But he hurt you."

"I was too embarrassed to tell them."

"It wasn't your fault, Shirley. I think you should tell them—make them understand what you went through."

"Maybe you're right. I've been thinking about it. It's just that they've always been so star-struck by Dale, especially my sister Meg. Lots of our relatives are heavy drinkers, and they're still married, so I suppose they think that I should be able to put up with Dale's drinking."

"Hey, girls, why don't you join the club?" Bea called from the patio. "Chuck's going to serenade us."

Shirley and Mary saw that Chuck had produced a guitar from behind his portable bar, and he strummed it softly before beginning to sing a mournful version of "Red River Valley."

"Looks like we have our very own singing cowboy," Shirley commented as she and Mary joined the others on the patio.

"Kind of like in the movies," Mary said, wishing it were a movie, rather than her reality.

Chapter 7

"SWITCHEROO!" screamed the lead headline in the *Nevada State Journal*. The sensational front-page story carried the byline of Cal Harris and featured a large photograph of the Beaumonts' mangled black Cadillac. Ben saw that much of the reporter's story had been taken word-for-word from the sheriff's press release.

Carefully Ben refolded the newspaper and pushed it through the mail slot of his landlord's Virginia Street antique shop. Ben didn't subscribe to the newspaper himself, but he knew that Calvin Perry didn't mind if Ben browsed through the paper before Perry arrived to open the Truckee Treasures Antiques Emporium in the morning. In fact, on the days Ben skipped checking the paper, it frequently disappeared before the antique dealer arrived to open the store.

Ben climbed into his truck and headed downtown. The brown paper grocery bag containing his bloody pants still sat on the floor, next to the passenger's seat. Ben detoured a few blocks from his normal route to the sheriff's office to stop at the laundry and dry cleaning establishment that he patronized on a regular basis since there was no washing machine in his apartment and he didn't have the patience to wait around at a coin-operated laundromat.

"Good morning, deputy," Alice Grayson, the white-haired, eighty-year-old counter clerk, greeted Ben.

"Hello, Mrs. Grayson. I thought I'd see if you could do anything with these." Ben pulled the pants from the bag and laid them out on the counter.

"Oh, dear! I hope you didn't get hurt," Alice Grayson said as she examined the pants.

"No, ma'am. I was at an accident scene."

"We'll do our best, deputy, but I can't make any promises. This blood's already dried, and it's going to be difficult, or maybe impossible, to remove it completely."

"OK, I understand. Just thought I'd give it a try."

"I'll get these pants soaking right away, and we'll see what we can do. If I'm not mistaken, we have some laundry ready for you, too."

Mrs. Grayson disappeared into the back of the laundry and returned a few minutes later with two packages. Ben paid his bill and said good-bye to the clerk. Back in his pickup, he laid the packages on the passenger seat. One contained his freshly laundered underwear and socks and the other held five shirts, all starched heavily, just the way he liked them, and neatly folded around a cardboard insert.

Arriving at the office, Ben found himself surrounded by several other deputies who were reporting for their day-shift duty. They'd heard about the accident investigation or read about it in the morning paper, and they wanted to know whether or not Ben had found out who the mystery woman was yet. When he told them that there was nothing new on the case, they drifted away, and Ben settled himself at Carmine's desk, still under orders to pursue the investigation and report directly to the sheriff.

Anita handed him several messages, most from national newspapers and one from a network television news program produced in New York. All were inquiries about the strange accident case. Ben asked Anita to tell any other reporters who called that there were no new developments in the case. He wasn't about to become distracted by the media again. He'd made that mistake once and felt lucky to have made it through unscathed. When he learned the accident victim's true identity, he'd give Cal Harris another exclusive story. The sheriff wanted to keep the local newspaper on their side, and Ben intended to do whatever was reasonably necessary to accomplish that goal.

"Cameron, you lucked out again, didn't you, Bud?"

Ben turned around and looked at Deputy Carl Overmeyer, a man not much older than Ben, but one who had been a Washoe County deputy for eight years longer than Ben. Since the day Ben had first reported for duty, it had been obvious that Overmeyer didn't like him. According to Deputy Jergens, Overmeyer's younger brother had applied for the same deputy slot that Ben had been tapped to fill. Overmeyer disliked the new guy Virgil, too, for the same reason— Overmeyer's younger brother hadn't been hired on his second try, either.

Thus far, Ben's strategy for dealing with Overmeyer's razzing had been to ignore him, but Overmeyer wasn't always easy to ignore.

"Hey, Bud, I'm talking to you."

"Well, I'm not talking to you," Ben replied.

"Figures. Mr. High-and-Mighty can't be bothered with us little people."

"Get lost, Overmeyer," Ben said, turning his back to the taunting deputy.

Fearing that Overmeyer might try to start a fist fight, Anita was about to try to distract him when Jergens walked in with the undersheriff, and Overmeyer brushed past them, muttering under his breath as he left the office.

"Wonder what he's in such an all-fired hurry for," Al said.

"Who knows? There's no tellin' with that guy," Jergens replied with a shrug.

"Carl was giving Ben the business," Anita volunteered.

"That right, Ben?" Al asked.

"It was nothing. I better get over to the Mapes before the Cartwrights decide to head back to San Francisco. Maybe now that Mrs. Cartwright has had a chance to think about it, she can come up with some clue to her sister's whereabouts."

Al nodded. Even though Ben hadn't discussed the case with Al, he knew that the sheriff had filled Al in on all the details. Nothing happened in the sheriff's office that Al didn't know about.

Ben walked the few blocks to the Mapes Hotel and Casino and asked the desk clerk for the Cartwrights' room number.

"It's 610, deputy, but they're not in their room. I saw them go into the coffee shop about ten minutes ago."

Ben thanked the clerk and looked toward the crowded coffee shop. Ben bypassed the line outside the hostess station, earning him a few dirty looks from the patrons who were waiting for a table.

The hostess eyed Ben warily, but she relaxed when he explained that he was looking for the Cartwrights. He described the couple, and the hostess showed him which booth they occupied.

As Ben approached, he saw another couple sitting with the Cartwrights.

"Phyllis Beaumont?" Ben asked, although he had no doubt that the woman sitting across from Wanda Cartwright was her sister Phyllis.

"Yes, I'm Phyllis."

"We were coming in to clear up this matter right after breakfast, deputy, but since you're here now, pull up a chair," Peter Cartwright said.

Ben grabbed a chair from a nearby table and pulled it up to the booth. The man sitting on his right, next to Phyllis, extended his hand.

"Bill Mead. I'm Phyllis's fiancé," he said as he and Ben shook hands. "Look, we didn't mean any harm. We just wanted to avoid press coverage. We were staying at my ranch in the valley when we heard about the accident."

Ben frowned. How had they heard the news so quickly? It had just hit the local paper a few hours earlier.

Before he could say anything, Wanda Cartwright nervously offered the answer. "I started calling around to Phyllis's friends in Los Angeles, and I finally found out where she was staying." She glanced ruefully at her sister.

"I didn't tell you because I knew you wouldn't approve. You would have tried to talk me out of it."

"You're darn right I would have. Now look at the mess you've caused!"

"Honey, I'm sorry you thought I'd been killed," Phyllis told her sister. "I know it was a shock."

"You can say that again," Wanda agreed, as she wiped away a tear. "It was an awful feeling. Honestly, Phyllis, I don't know how you keep getting yourself into these scrapes."

Ben had heard just about all of this breakfast conversation that he could stomach. It was time for him to take charge. He held up his hand and cleared his throat.

"Folks, I need to get to the bottom of this matter, and this isn't the place to do it. Mrs. Beaumont, I need you to come back to the Sheriff's Department right now."

"Am I under arrest?"

"Do you want to be?" an exasperated Ben asked, "Because I can certainly arrange that."

"No," Phyllis mumbled.

"All right, then. I suggest you come along now."

"Can't I drive Phyllis to your office, deputy?" Mead asked.

"OK. In that case, I'll be going with you."

"Fine," Mead said, rising and tossing some cash on the table.

"We're coming, too," Wanda said, motioning for her husband to get up.

"There's no need, Mrs. Cartwright, unless you know something you haven't told me already."

"No, I don't, but I want to be there for my sister."

"Suit yourself, but I'll need to question Mrs. Beaumont by herself."

A glum Phyllis sat silently in the front seat next to the man who claimed to be her fiancé while Ben sat in the back seat and gave him directions to drive to the Sheriff's Headquarters, just a few blocks away. Once there, he grabbed a yellow legal pad from Carmine's desk and asked Bill to wait while he led Phyllis to a conference room where he sat across the table from her.

"Smoke?" he offered, tapping out a Lucky Strike from his cigarette pack.

"Thanks, I have my own," Phyllis said, and pulled a pack of Kools from her brown alligator handbag. "I like the menthol," she said, pulling one of the ashtrays that sat on the table toward her.

"Mrs. Beaumont, I want to know who took your place at the Circle E. She had your driver's license, your husband's car, and some of your credit cards. I assume you set up the impersonation yourself, or you had somebody else do it for you."

"It was my idea," Phyllis admitted. "I didn't want to spend six weeks at a dude ranch in Nevada. I wanted to be with Bill—we're going to be married just as soon as my divorce is granted—and he has to go on location in Arizona next week. I didn't see the harm. These divorces are pretty much automatic, aren't they? It's kind of a sham from what I understand."

"I'm not sure that the district attorney would agree with you, Mrs.

Beaumont, but be that as it may, who was the woman who took your place?"

"Candice Martin, a friend of mine." Phyllis said with a sigh. "I'm devastated that she had an accident and was killed. I met her when we both had bit parts in a movie a long time before I met Adrian. Everybody kept commenting that we could have been twins, so I looked her up, told her that I had an acting job for her, and she agreed to take it."

"She was going to appear in court and claim to be you?"

"Yes."

"That would be fraud, Mrs. Beaumont, and conspiracy, too."

"I really didn't mean any harm," Phyllis said softly. "And I know that Candice needed the money. She hadn't worked in months."

"Are you able to identify Miss Martin? I don't want her relatives to have to go through what your sister did yesterday at the coroner's."

Phyllis hesitated. "Do I have to?" she asked.

"No, you don't have to, but your cooperation might be considered favorably by the district attorney."

"I guess so," she reluctantly agreed, nervously stubbing out her cigarette.

"Let's take care of that now."

"Can Bill come with me?"

"All right," Ben said as he stood and motioned toward the door. They stopped briefly to tell Bill and the Cartwrights, who had shown up while Ben was questioning Phyllis, where they were going.

"I never want to see that place again," Wanda Cartwright declared with a shudder. "We'll wait for you at the Mapes," she told her sister.

Within an hour, Phyllis had confirmed Candice's identity, based on her unusually tiny shoe size, the same as Phyllis's, and an inconspicuous mole behind her left knee. Besides, at the time of her death, Candice had been wearing a custom-made silver gown Phyllis had given her for the impersonation, and the gown fit her every bit as well as it had fit Phyllis. In looks, stature, and figure, Candice and Phyllis could have been twins, which was the reason Phyllis had selected Candice as her double in the first place.

After warning Phyllis not to leave town and fulfilling the unpleasant duty of contacting Candice's Southern California relatives, Ben told the sheriff about the latest development in the accident case. Realizing that the case could turn into a public relations nightmare, Ben knew that the decision about whether or not to arrest and charge Phyllis Beaumont with fraud had to be left to the sheriff and district attorney. The case had already received national publicity, and Ben was fairly certain that the district attorney wouldn't want the public to think he was being too tough on the beautiful Hollywood starlet.

After a brief phone conversation with the district attorney, the sheriff asked Ben to set up a late-afternoon meeting with Phyllis Beaumont at the district attorney's office. He said that Bill and the Cartwrights could come, and he wanted Ben to be there, too. Immediately, Ben put in a call to the Cartwrights' suite at the Mapes and arranged the meeting. He had to leave the disposition of Phyllis's case to the higher-ups now, but if he had his way, he would throw the book at her. Her little charade had ended up costing a woman her life, all because Phyllis was too self-centered to do what she should have done in the first place—spend the required six weeks in Nevada in order to get a legal divorce.

The rumble in Ben's stomach reminded him of more mundane things. Ben hadn't eaten any breakfast, not even a cup of coffee, and he felt half-starved. He told Anita that he was going out for lunch and would return in an hour. He popped into his truck and headed to the A & W drive-in, where the carhops roller-skated to the customers, who stayed in their autos, to take their orders, then delivered the food and drinks on a tray that attached to the driver's window.

It was early for lunch when Ben arrived, just as the drive-in opened. A cute teenager took his order—two chili dogs, large French fries, an order of onion rings, and a tall mug of root beer—and quickly returned with a tray piled with his food. Ben ate the first chili dog in record time, although he was careful not to spill anything on his clothing. He had a feeling that he'd have to buy new pants to replace the blood-stained pair that he'd dropped off at the laundry, and he didn't want to ruin any more clothes. A deputy sheriff's salary was adequate, but hardly princely, and when any major expenditure came up, it always threw a monkey wrench into Ben's budget. He realized that he probably shouldn't have splurged on the top-of-the-line tires that were now on his truck, but it was too late for regrets on that score.

Figuring that he should be pleased that the accident investigation was nearly wrapped up, Ben tried to relax as he alternately munched French fries and onion rings, but the nagging feeling that he'd missed something wouldn't go away. He'd left his notes on the case back at the office, or he would have read through them while he was eating. Just as well, he thought. He probably would have gotten grease all over his paperwork if he'd done that, anyway.

Ben dug some coins out of his pocket and left them on the tray as he signaled the waitress that he was finished. Although several more cars had arrived while Ben was eating, the busy waitress promptly retrieved Ben's tray and cheerfully pocketed the tip he'd left her.

Back at the office, Ben filled his mug with coffee and sorted through his case notes. He wasn't looking forward to typing the report on Carmine's beat-up Underwood, especially since he was excruciatingly slow with his two-finger typing method. Deciding to write out the report by hand first, Ben ripped his page of notes from the yellow legal pad he'd used earlier and began writing his report. He started with a factual description of the accident. As he was noting the names of the couple who had witnessed and reported the accident, Ben remembered that they had both said that the driver hadn't slowed before the crash. Now that Ben had learned the accident victim was in Reno to do a job—at least that's the way she and Phyllis had looked at the impersonation act—he was more certain than ever that she hadn't committed suicide. The coroner had confirmed that she hadn't been drinking, which would have led Ben to the natural conclusion that she had fallen asleep at the wheel, except for the fact that she had swerved around the witnesses' car. She couldn't have done that if she'd been asleep at the wheel. Ben realized that his investigation wasn't finished quite yet. The facts now led him to believe that a mechanical problem had caused the accident.

Writing wasn't exactly Ben's forté, and he struggled to find the right words as he continued his work on the report. After a couple of hours, he glanced at his watch and saw that he'd struggled with his paperwork far longer than he'd meant to. He worried that he'd be late getting to the district attorney's office until he saw the sheriff coming down the hallway from his office. Sheriff Rogers motioned to Ben, and Ben rose to join him.

The sheriff surprised Ben by insisting on driving the short distance to the meeting.

"This'll be one meeting down and another one to go today. Sometimes I think I won't be able to stand another meeting," the sheriff groused, rather unconvincingly. Ben knew the man loved his job, meetings and all.

"Tip off your buddy Harris at the paper that you IDed the girl?"

"Yes, sir, and I told him that I might have some more news for him later today. I haven't informed him yet that Phyllis Beaumont has turned up—only that we've identified the accident victim as Candice Martin of Long Beach, California."

"Good thinking, Ben. The district attorney's going to want to get in on the act."

Ben frowned. "He's not going to file charges, is he?"

"Nope. If I know Lawrence Korel, he won't let this opportunity slide by. I'd guess magnanimous is the way he'll play it. He can look chivalrous, help the damsel in distress—all that. He's up for election this fall, and it won't hurt his chances to have his picture on the front page of the paper, right next to a good-looking Hollywood actress."

"It's not right."

"Can't say that seeing the world in black and white is a bad trait for a lawman, Ben, but things don't always pan out in a clear-cut way. Plea bargains and other compromises happen every day. You did your job. Now the ball's in the DA's court, and no harm done."

"But harm has been done," Ben protested. "A woman's dead because of Phyllis Beaumont and her impersonation scheme."

"Phyllis Beaumont didn't cause the accident, Ben."

Despite Ben's offended sense of justice, he agreed with the sheriff's assessment. "I guess not. Nobody would wish that kind of death on a friend."

"Here we are. Let's get this over with, and I can go on to my next meeting. At least, they'll be serving dinner at that one."

Sheriff Rogers and Ben entered the building that housed many of the county offices and took the elevator to the third floor, where the district attorney and his assistants had offices. Ben had never been in the DA's office before, and he was surprised to find it rather luxuriously appointed, compared to the sheriff's smaller and much more modest office. An imposing wooden antique desk featuring elaborate scrollwork and a matching wooden chair dominated the far side of the room, where several bookcases filled with law books sat on either side of two enormous draped windows. Closer to the door, a plush leather sofa, two cordovan leather chairs, a coffee table, and a couple of end tables were placed. Several large paintings of Western scenes completed the suite. District Attorney Korel greeted the sheriff, who introduced him to Ben. As they were shaking hands, the Cartwrights appeared with Phyllis and Bill, and there were introductions and greetings all around. Korel disappeared for a minute, returning with two chairs he'd borrowed from his next-door conference room, and the group sat around in a circle, waiting to find out what the district attorney would say.

Phyllis's somewhat flippant attitude had undergone quite a change since Ben first spotted her at breakfast earlier in the morning. Looking at a corpse will have that effect, Ben thought, as it should have. The fact that, earlier in the day, Ben had reminded Phyllis that she had committed a crime probably had something to do with her chastened frame of mind, too.

Phyllis nervously pulled her pack of Kools from her handbag, extracted a cigarette, and held it while Bill eagerly lighted it for her. She took a few puffs as she listened to the district attorney slowly reciting the facts of the case, but she visibly relaxed when it finally became clear that he had no intention of filing any charges against her. By the end of the meeting, the Californians were laughing and joking with the district attorney while an incredulous Ben looked on, and the sheriff surreptitiously checked his wristwatch.

After agreeing to appear with the district attorney the following day for a brief announcement and photo, Phyllis left to return to the Mapes with Bill and the Cartwrights. Korel asked the sheriff not to brief the press before he made his appearance with Phyllis, and Ben knew, without being told, that he'd have to put off feeding Harris more information about the case until the district attorney had his say, not that Ben felt especially eager to talk to the reporter, anyway.

Deciding to walk back to the office, Ben declined the sheriff's offer of a ride, but by the time he'd gone a couple of blocks, he began to regret it. The late afternoon sun felt hot, and his clothes were damp with perspiration by the time he arrived. The office wasn't much cooler than the street outside. Two creaky fans blew warm air around, and the odor of stale cigarette smoke permeated the place. Ben decided that he could finish his report the next day. There was one thing he needed to do before he completed writing it, anyway, but that would have to wait until tomorrow.

Chapter 8

"Good morning, Mrs. Garrison," Mary's elderly, silver-haired lawyer greeted her as his secretary showed Mary into the attorney's office and gestured toward a chair across from the old man's desk.

Shirley had driven Mary into Reno from the Circle E, just as they had arranged the day before, and although Mary wasn't looking forward to the meeting with her lawyer, she was looking forward to shopping with Shirley, who waited for her in the small reception room that doubled as the legal secretary's office.

"I'm using my maiden name again now—Mary Marchetti. I hope that's all right, Mr. Cooper."

"Of course. Just as you wish. And you want to legally change your name back to Marchetti, I presume."

"Yes, I'd like to do that."

"I'll make sure the name change is stipulated in the divorce decree. Let me note that in your file."

Mr. Cooper picked up a folder from the corner of his desk, opened it, and jotted down some notes.

"Now, Mrs.—uh—may I call you Mary?"

She nodded.

"Mary, before we go any further, I'd like to ask you the same question I ask every client of mine: are you absolutely certain you want to proceed with a divorce?"

"Yes, I'm sure."

"No chance of reconciliation?"

"No. My mind's made up."

"Very well, then. Let me explain the procedure—it's a fairly simple one, but you will have to appear in court and take the witness stand. Also, you'll need to bring a witness with you to verify your six-week residency in Nevada."

"Yes. Mrs. Ellis will be my witness."

"Of the Circle E?"

Mary nodded.

"A very reliable lady. You can count on her."

Mr. Cooper spent half an hour briefing Mary about the types of questions she'd answer when she took the witness stand and told her to call him if she needed anything. He said that his secretary would be in touch with her to give her the date and time of her court appearance as soon as it was put on the court's calendar.

Mary left, feeling confident that the legal details of her upcoming divorce were in good hands.

"Everything go OK, Mary?" Shirley asked after they'd left the lawyer's office.

"Fine. Mr. Cooper seems very efficient. I guess it's all a routine matter around here."

"Oh, it definitely is. Just look at all the guest ranches that cater to people like us, who've come here to establish residency. They say thousands of people have gotten a quick divorce in Reno."

"There's one thing I'm not too clear on. Maybe your lawyer mentioned it to you, too. Mr. Cooper said that he would ask me if I intend to stay in Nevada permanently. Then he said that I must answer 'yes' to that question, even though he knows that I'm planning on returning to New York as soon as my divorce is granted.

Somehow, that doesn't seem right."

"I see what you're saying, Mary. I'm planning on going right back to Balboa Island as soon as mine's final. I don't remember my lawyer mentioning that, but he may have. I was a little bit upset the day I saw him, and he suggested that I check in with him again about a week before we go to court. I thought the six weeks was all we needed to establish Nevada residency."

"Well, it must be, or I guess people wouldn't come here for a divorce. I just thought it was odd. You know, Mrs. Ellis was so adamant about her guests staying in Nevada and that she wouldn't lie if someone wasn't in the state every day, but then we have to say that we're planning on making Nevada our permanent homes, when we all know that we're not."

"I guess we'd better play the game if we want our divorces. After all, we're staying the required six weeks, and once the divorce is granted, it's a done deal."

"I suppose so."

"Don't worry about it, Mary. I'm sure your lawyer wouldn't steer you wrong. Anyway, enough of the serious stuff. Let's go find you a nice swimsuit. I think I'll leave the car here if you don't mind walking a few blocks."

"Sure, let's do that."

"With your fair skin and dark hair, I think you'd look great in a red bikini."

"Oh, no. I couldn't possibly wear a bikini!"

"Well, OK, we'll just have to find you a fabulous one-piece, then."

A few hours later, Mary and Shirley, each carrying a couple of large shopping bags, emerged from Gray Reid. Mary hadn't intended to spend so much on her new swimwear, but Shirley's infectious enthusiasm had rubbed off on her, and she'd purchased two swimsuits, a flowery cover-up, a wide-brimmed sun hat, a couple of beach towels, a bathing cap, and a large straw beach bag. She rationalized that she'd need some way to keep busy for her six weeks in Nevada, and since the Circle E had a nice pool and Shirley had offered to teach her how to swim, it made sense to buy swimwear.

"All you need now is some suntan lotion," Shirley said. "We'll stop at a drug store on our way back to the ranch and pick some up. Right now, I'm starting to feel hungry. Why don't we stop for lunch at one of the casino restaurants? By the time we get back to the Circle E, lunchtime will be over. It's usually just soup and sandwiches set out as a buffet at noon anyway. At the ranch, the big meal of the day is always dinner."

"Casinos have restaurants, too? I thought they were only for gambling."

"Most of them are hotels as well as casinos, and usually they have at least a couple of restaurants. They have big-name entertainment, too. Frank Sinatra played the Sky Room at the Mapes a couple of months ago, and Tony Bennett sang there just last month. Of course, it's not New York or L.A., but, for a town this size, it's something."

"I didn't realize that. Every time I've heard about Reno, it's always been in connection with a divorce, and now here I am to get one myself. I can't quite believe it."

Shirley and Mary lingered over a long lunch in the bustling coffee shop at the Riverside. Walking through the casino had been like a trip through a foreign land for Mary as she gazed in amazement at the crowd of gamblers playing table games and slot machines. The gambling didn't stop in the casino, either. It spilled into the coffee shop, too, where patrons could play keno while they were enjoying their meals. Short, stubby pencils and packs of keno forms were on every table in the coffee shop, and keno runners in black and white garb came by the tables periodically to collect the keno forms that customers were going to play or to return them after the numbers had been verified. Shirley, who had played the game before, explained to Mary how it worked. It was as simple as choosing numbers on the form that resembled a bingo card, then hoping that the numbers the house drew matched. Winnings could range from a dollar to several thousand dollars, depending on how many numbers were played and how many numbers matched those that the house drew. In every casino game, losers outnumbered winners, but gamblers' optimism that they'd beat the house kept the Nevada gaming business healthy.

Shirley lost several dollars before giving up, but Mary won enough to pay for their lunch and leave their waitress a generous tip. Gathering up their shopping bags, they left, satisfied with Mary's small winnings.

As Mary and Shirley emerged from the Riverside, they were surrounded immediately by a large crowd of tourists who had evidently just arrived by bus. They sidled their way through the crush—they were leaving while the tourists were clamoring to enter the casino. Finally, the tourists all passed, and the two women paused to recover from the jostling for a moment. The onslaught wasn't over yet, though, as another tourist bus pulled up to the curb, and its passengers began streaming from the bus. Hoping to cross the street to get away from the throng, Shirley and Mary hurried to the corner where they had to wait for the red light to change. Mary turned to look for Shirley, but she didn't see her new friend. Somehow, they'd become separated when the big group of tourists mingled with the locals outside the casino.

The temperature had risen considerably since Mary and Shirley had left the Circle E in the morning, and Mary thought it must be well above ninety degrees by now. She squirmed in her beige raw silk suit, which was stylish, but too heavy to wear in hot weather. The shopping bags felt like lead weights, and her girdle felt constricting, as beads of sweat popped out on Mary's forehead. People kept bumping into her, and she began to feel as though the whole world were closing in on her. Assuming that Shirley would catch up to her on the other side of the street, Mary inched her way forward until she stood right on the edge of the curb, and there was nobody between her and the street. Fighting lightheadedness, she took a deep breath. The red light seemed to stay on forever. If only she could reach the other side of the street, if only she could escape from the crowd, if only she could get out of the hot sun. The seconds ticked away, seeming like an eternity to Mary.

Suddenly, she felt a blow on her back, and she pitched forward, into the busy intersection. She heard screams, maybe from herself, maybe from Shirley or other people on the crowded sidewalk as a taxi screeched to a halt just inches from her. People rushed to help. The cab driver leaped from his taxi and picked up the scattered contents of Mary's shopping bags while Shirley and a couple of cowboys held onto Mary as she struggled to stand. Throbbing scrapes covered her knees and forearms, and she had a large bump on her forehead. Her silk stockings were in shreds.

"Lady, you're lucky you weren't killed," the cabbie said. "I sure burned rubber trying to avoid hitting you."

Looking as though she might pass out at any moment, Mary moaned and swayed.

"Can she sit down in the cab?" Shirley asked. "She's about ready to faint."

"Oh, sure. Sorry, lady." The cabbie flung open the taxi's back door, and the cowboys guided Mary onto the seat.

"Lie down, Mary," Shirley said. "You'll feel better."

Shirley turned to thank the two ranch hands who had helped, but they'd already disappeared into the crowd.

"Where you wanna go, lady? It's on the house," the cabbie said. "Maybe we should take her to the hospital," he said to Shirley.

"I'll be OK," Mary said. "I felt like I was going to pass out for a few minutes back there, but I'm starting to feel better."

"Are you sure you don't want to see a doctor, Mary? You have quite a bump on your head."

"No, let's go back to the Circle E. I don't want to be a bother."

"All right." Shirley gave the cab driver directions to her car. When they arrived, she offered to pay him, but he refused to take any money, repeating that the ride was "on the house."

Shirley's car felt stuffy, but at least it had been parked in the shade. Shirley and Mary rolled down the windows and enjoyed the rush of air, even though it was hot, as Shirley drove back to the Circle E. She whizzed past a drug store without slowing down before she remembered that she'd intended to stop so that Mary could buy some suntan lotion.

"Oh, shoot. I meant to stop at the drug store. I guess we'll have to come back tomorrow. You'll need to get those scrapes cleaned up as soon as we get back, anyway. I bet they really hurt, don't they?"

"Oh, boy, do they! It reminds me of when I was a kid and fell off a curb while I was roller skating. I was really banged up then, too."

"I'm sorry our shopping trip came to such a bad end, Mary. We were having fun until you fell and nearly got run over by that taxi."

"Shopping was fun, but I didn't fall. I was pushed."

Chapter 9

At eight sharp, Ben pulled up in front of Virgil's house, a small bungalow just off North Virginia Street, half a block west of the University of Nevada's campus. As Ben had arranged the previous evening with Al, Virgil would be earning a few overtime hours assisting Ben. Virgil must have been watching for Ben because he came out on the front stoop as soon as Ben turned into the driveway. Virgil motioned for Ben, and Ben hopped out of his truck and joined Virgil, who insisted that Ben come in for a cup of coffee.

Virgil led Ben inside, through the house, and into the kitchen at the back. A toddler sat in a high chair fiddling with a spoon and a bowl of cereal, while a pregnant young woman removed a muffin pan from the oven. Virgil introduced Cindy, his wife, and Tommy, his son, to Ben.

"Pleased to meet you," Ben said, politely removing his hat.

"Ben, won't you have some coffee and muffins before you boys take off?" Cindy offered.

To Ben, who hadn't had his first cup of the day yet, the muffins smelled heavenly, and so did the coffee.

"Don't mind if I do," he said, sitting beside Tommy's high chair. "Thank you, ma'am."

"None of that ma'am business now, Ben. Call me Cindy," Virgil's wife said, setting a steaming mug of coffee and a plate of warm muffins in front of him.

Ben promptly sampled a muffin. "Blueberry—my favorite. This is delicious, Cindy."

"Glad you like it."

"I sure do. Say, I'm sorry to take Virgil away on his day off, but this job shouldn't take too long."

"Think nothing of it, Ben," Virgil said. "We can always use the overtime with another baby on the way, right, honey?"

"That's right."

"I don't know what I would have done if I hadn't gotten hired on as a deputy. At my last job, I never knew whether my paycheck would bounce or not. Owner had a gambling problem, and he spent more time in the casinos than he did at Mac's Motors, his own garage. The guy's still in business, but just barely."

"I was happy to get a good, steady job myself when I got out of the army a couple of years ago. It's not always easy for a vet to find a job. Well, I guess we'd better be shoving off," Ben said, tousling Tommy's hair. The toddler giggled as Ben made funny faces at him. Ben drained his coffee mug and thanked Cindy. Virgil kissed his wife and son and grabbed his hat before he and Ben left the little house. Someday, Ben wanted what Virgil already had—a sweet wife, children, and a cozy home, but that would have to wait until he increased his savings account. He'd expected to be married by now himself, but after his fiancée had sent him a Dear John letter a couple of months before his tour in Korea ended, he hadn't had much luck with the ladies, and he'd spent all his extra funds on his truck.

Ben hoped that he could clear the accident case within the next few hours. If all went well, he'd finish his report and submit it to the sheriff by the end of the day. Although it would be a relief to close the unusual accident case, Ben felt a twinge at the thought of resuming his regular duties. Investigating the accident had made him realize that not only was he capable of carrying out an investigation, but he also liked the work better than his routine job as a deputy on patrol.

What Ben had told Virgil was true. When he had been hired as a Washoe County deputy sheriff after a ten-year stint in the army, he'd been pleased to have a steady job, one with benefits. Ben's plan was to stick with it until he retired. He'd never wanted more, not until Sheriff Rogers had put him in charge of the accident investigation.

"Where are we headed, Ben?" Virgil asked.

"Out West Fourth Street to the department's impound lot. It's in a corner at Joe's Junkyard. Most of the vehicles towed there have been in accidents, but some of them were abandoned in our jurisdiction."

"What are we looking for?"

"The Cadillac that was involved in the accident up on Mount Rose Highway the other night. I want you to examine it for any mechanical problems that might have caused the accident. I remembered Al telling me that you're an ace mechanic, so I thought you'd be the right man for the job. I asked him if you could take a look at the wreck, and he approved your overtime."

"I'll do my best. I been working on cars since before I could drive."

"Here we are," Ben said, as he made a right turn into the main entrance of Joe's. One of the yard workers saw his pickup truck and signaled for him to stop. Ben pulled up beside him.

"Oh, sorry, deputy, I didn't see your uniform. Go right on ahead."

Ben waved and continued to the impound lot in the corner of the junkyard. It was fenced with heavy steel wire, and the wide gate was secured with a large padlock. Ben jumped out of his truck, unlocked the padlock, and opened the gate. Virgil spotted the Caddy right away and pointed Ben in its direction. Ben parked in back of the mangled vehicle, and they both got out and walked toward it, remembering the last time they'd seen the car.

"Witnesses said that the Cadillac went around their car, but the Caddy didn't slow down at all before going off the mountain."

"Sounds like the steering worked, but the brakes didn't. Let's have a look," Virgil said, pulling out his regulation flashlight and crawling under the car. It was several minutes before he emerged, dusting himself off. Ben mentally kicked himself for not thinking to tell Virgil, who was in his deputy's uniform, to wear old clothes, but, luckily, the ground where the Cadillac rested, had been hard and dry, and there didn't seem to be any damage done to Virgil's clothing.

"What do you think, Virgil? Did the brakes fail?"

"They failed, all right. This car was tampered with by someone who knew what he was doing. He rigged it so that the brakes would work for a few miles before giving out."

"You're absolutely sure?"

"No doubt about it, Ben. Looks as though you've got a homicide on your hands."

"Good Lord! A murder! This case keeps getting stranger and stranger. When we came out here, I was trying to make sure I'd covered all the bases before I finished writing my report. I really thought you'd find a mechanical failure. Nothing else seemed to make sense because the driver hadn't been drinking at all and there was no reason to think she might have been suicidal."

"What's your next step?"

"I guess we'd better head back to the office, and I'll tell the sheriff what you found. I'm going to tag the wreck as evidence and tell Joe to make sure nobody disturbs it. Could you put what you've found in writing—you know, the technical details?"

"Sure thing."

"We should shoot some photos of the damage, too. Camera's back at the office."

"I can take care of that. I know what to look for, and I'm a fairly decent photographer. I've used the department's camera before."

"Looks like I may have fibbed to your wife, Virgil. I told her this job wouldn't take very long."

"Don't worry about it, Ben. I'll call her from the office. She'll be happy for the extra overtime pay."

"We'd better get a move on. I need to talk to the sheriff before the D.A.'s announcement this morning."

As soon as they entered the office, they encountered Overmeyer, who was on his way out.

"Oh, look who we have here—it's Mutt and Jeff. Ain't they a pair?" Stepping directly into their path, Overmeyer blocked them from proceeding past Anita's desk and on into the bullpen area of the office.

"Get out of the way, Overmeyer," Ben said. "We have business to attend to."

"Yeah, I bet. Monkey business."

"I mean it, Overmeyer."

Virgil looked around nervously. It was Anita's day off, and they were alone in the office with the pugnacious deputy.

"So you want me to get out of your way, huh?"

"Yes, I do."

"Make me."

"If you insist." Quick as a viper, Ben grabbed Overmeyer's wrist and twisted it until Overmeyer winced, lost his balance, and fell heavily to the wooden floor. Ben and Virgil brushed past him and went down the hall that led to the sheriff's office, leaving Overmeyer swearing as he picked himself up.

"I'll get you for that, Cameron," he called, but Ben ignored him and kept walking. Virgil and Ben heard the office door slam, and evidently the sheriff heard it, too, because he came out of his office and looked toward the bullpen.

"What the hell was that?" he asked.

"Oh, Deputy Overmeyer just had a little accident," Ben said. "Nothing serious."

The sheriff looked speculatively at Ben, then at Virgil.

"Uh, huh."

Neither Ben nor Virgil said anything.

"Were you looking for me, Ben?" the sheriff asked.

"Yes. There's been another new development in the accident case. I thought we'd better fill you in before the press announcement at the D.A.'s office."

Fifteen minutes later, the three men emerged from the sheriff's office. Ben had imagined that the sheriff would probably take him off the case, now that it had turned into a homicide, rather than an accident, investigation. Although several of the other deputies had more seniority than Ben, the sheriff told Ben to stay on the case and to continue to report directly to him.

They had discussed the possibility that Phyllis might be in grave danger if she had been the intended victim of the killer. The sheriff promised Ben that he would make sure the district attorney's statement about Phyllis's future plans would be deliberately vague. If someone was trying to kill the would-be divorcée, they didn't want to tip off the person as to where Phyllis would be staying. Ben wanted her to stay in Reno long enough so that he could question her again, in light of his discovery, but he had no real power to detain her. He hadn't intended to go to the brief press conference at the district attorney's office, but he knew now that he'd have to attend and try to talk to the starlet as soon as the news photographer finished with the pictures.

The thought of the district attorney's public relations gambit turned Ben's stomach. Even if the man didn't intend to press charges, did he have to make it look as though Phyllis were a heroine? Nevertheless, shallow and flighty as she seemed, Phyllis could be in real danger, and it was Ben's duty to warn her. Despite his low opinion of the beautiful actress, Ben's protective nature kicked in, and he was very concerned that an attempt might be made on her life. If the accident had been staged with Phyllis as its target, someone still wanted her dead.

While Virgil stayed at the office to write his report, promising to take photographs of the damaged vehicle when he was done, Ben and Sheriff Rogers headed to the district attorney's office, where they persuaded him to alter his statement so that Phyllis's plans for the future would seem up in the air. Once Harris, along with a photographer and a few stringers who worked as independent contractors, showed up, the brief press conference began. It consisted primarily of a photo shoot featuring the district attorney shaking hands with Phyllis, followed by a brief statement expressing shock and sorrow at the accident and downplaying Phyllis's role in the switched identity scheme to the point that she now claimed that she'd never intended for her friend Candice to go through with a Reno divorce, but just to impersonate her so that Phyllis herself could get away for a while. After that whopper, the district attorney announced that Phyllis would be seeking a Nevada divorce at some time in the future. As the sheriff had requested, the D.A. didn't give any details.

Afterwards, Harris approached Ben and reminded him that he'd promised to give the reporter more news about the story. Ben didn't want to reveal that the accident had really been a murder, not yet anyway, so he told the reporter that he didn't have anything to add to the district attorney's statement. Harris didn't seem upset, though, especially since the news photographer he'd brought with him had been able to get several good shots, one of which would be running on the front page of the *Reno Evening Gazette*, right next to the reporter's latest story about the case.

While Harris had been talking to Ben, Phyllis and her fiancé Bill left the building. The Cartwrights hadn't attended the short press conference, and Ben surmised that they might have returned to San Francisco.

Rushing outside, Ben caught up with Phyllis, who had paused to allow Bill to light her cigarette.

"Mrs. Beaumont," Ben called, and the woman looked directly at him before turning away.

He ran to catch up with the two, but Phyllis ignored him and kept walking. Finally, Ben was able to persuade Bill that he had something vital to tell Phyllis. Ben suggested that they come to the sheriff's office with him, but Phyllis refused, so they settled on a meeting in the Cartwrights' room at the Mapes. Ben wasn't about to let either of them out of his sight as he trailed behind them back to the hotel-casino and up to the sixth floor. The Cartwrights' suitcases sat beside the door to their room. Evidently, they were waiting for Phyllis to return before they checked out of the Mapes and returned home. They looked surprised when Ben followed Phyllis and Bill into their room.

"What's going on, deputy?" Peter Cartwright demanded when he saw Ben. "I thought this business had been all settled with the district attorney."

"Yes, sir, it has. I'm here on another related matter."

"If you're planning to drum up some other charges against Phyllis, you can forget it. It's clear to me that your D.A. has no interest in prosecuting her," Cartwright continued.

"I understand that, but new evidence has come to light." He turned and gazed at Phyllis. "Mrs. Beaumont, I don't want to frighten you, but you could be in grave danger. That car crash was no accident."

"What are you saying, deputy?" Bill asked.

"I'm saying that the Beaumonts' Cadillac was tampered with, the brakes rigged to fail as it went down the mountain. We're looking at a murder here, and the intended victim may have been you, Mrs. Beaumont."

At that, the men's faces registered shock, Wanda Cartwright began wringing her hands, and Phyllis fainted dead away.

Chapter 10

"Pushed? How awful! Why would anybody do such a horrible thing?"

"Oh, I didn't mean that someone deliberately pushed me. I'm sure it was an accident. The people in the crowd closed in on me, and I felt like I couldn't breathe. I had to get out of the crush, so I wiggled my way through until I reached the curb, but people kept surging forward. I felt a thump on my back, and, all of a sudden, I ended up in the street."

"Thank goodness you weren't hurt any worse. It's bad enough that you're all scraped up. I'll bet you'll be black and blue by morning."

Shirley's prediction turned out to be correct. Mary awoke the next morning to find ugly, dark bruises on her arms and legs. When she and Shirley had arrived back at the ranch the day before, Carol had wanted to apply mercurochrome to Mary's scraped skin, but Mary had refused the ugly orange tincture, preferring to use rubbing alcohol as a disinfectant instead. Shirley had fussed over her all evening, and Carol had insisted on bringing Mary dinner in her room so that she could relax and recuperate. Although she felt sore, Mary had no intention of staying in her room any longer. She took a warm bath and gingerly washed her wounds again. Mary donned a pink cotton sundress, although it didn't hide her bruises, and went downstairs to the dining room, where she poured herself a cup of coffee and doctored it with a generous dollop of cream and a couple teaspoons of sugar. Lingering over her coffee, Mary sat at the long dining table for several minutes slowly sipping the hot brew until one of the ranch's cooks emerged from the kitchen to clear the breakfast buffet. Mary decided that she wanted a little something to go with her coffee. She quickly helped herself to a sugar-and-cinnamon-topped cake doughnut and a second cup of coffee before the cook began to remove the food from the sideboard where the buffet was set up.

Mary took her coffee and doughnut out to the patio, where she carefully set them down on a small table. She pulled a white wicker chair over and sat down next to the table. Alone on the patio, Mary could see a couple of the other guests lounging poolside. Down the lane, past the pool next to the stables, the two wranglers were each leading a horse and rider into the corral while some of the guests stood along the fence watching. It was too far away for Mary to be able to tell who the riders were, but it was obvious that they were beginners. While the wranglers circled the corral, they held the reins, and the women who were riding simply sat astride the horses, their hands clutching the saddle horns, and allowed the wranglers to control the horses.

As Mary observed the scene, Shirley burst through the French doors, carrying her purse and a small paper bag.

"There you are, Mary," she said, grabbing another wicker chair and pulling it around so that she could sit next to Mary. "Feeling better?"

"I'm OK, just a little bit sore."

"Oh, boy, Mary. Those are some bruises you have, and, I can tell you from experience, that it's going to take a while for them to fade."

"I must look like a wreck."

"Oh, no, Mary. I didn't mean that. Just don't expect those bruises to clear up right away. It takes time."

"I wish I could hide them, but I sure didn't bring the right clothes to do it. All I have with me are some suits, a few sundresses, and a couple of pairs of shorts, and the blouses I brought to wear with the shorts are both sleeveless, anyway."

"Say, I have an idea. What about buying some Western clothes—you know, like Carol and some of the other ladies wear around the ranch? Jeans and a long-sleeved Western shirt would cover those bruises very nicely, and you'd look like one of the locals, too."

"Well, I don't know."

"It would be fun," said the irrepressible Shirley enthusiastically. "You could go all out and get a Stetson hat and leather boots like the cowboys wear, and maybe some turquoise and sterling silver jewelry to complete the look."

"Do you really think so?"

"I do, Mary. And I'm going to buy a Western outfit for myself, too. We can pretend that we're cowgirls."

At that, both Mary and Shirley giggled. Both city girls, neither had ever been near a cow, and neither could ride a horse, but that didn't need to prevent them from dressing the part.

"Here, Mary, I bought you something." Shirley handed Mary the paper bag, and Mary reached inside.

"Suntan lotion," Mary exclaimed as she pulled the bottle out of the brown paper sack. "Thanks, Shirley!"

"Why don't we make good use of it and start your swimming lessons as soon as you've finished your coffee? And don't worry about those bruises showing in your swimsuit. You can wear your cover-up to the pool, and nobody will notice."

The swimsuit cover-up Mary had purchased the day before was a colorful, long, kimono-like robe with wrist-length sleeves, and Mary agreed it would be perfect for hiding her bruises.

"I'm ready if you are," she said. "I'll go change right now and meet you at the pool in fifteen minutes."

By the time Mary had put on her new pink strapless swimsuit and the vibrant floral cover-up that went with it and arrived at the pool, Shirley, a strong swimmer, had already done several laps in the pool. Placing her beach towel on a lounge chair, Mary greeted Carla and Faye, who waved languidly and returned to sunning themselves. Mary slipped out of her cover-up and left it at the edge of the pool while she began slowly to descend the steps into the water at the shallow end. Sensing Mary's hesitancy, Shirley assured her that they would never go in water so deep that Mary couldn't stand up in the pool with her head entirely out of the water.

Before asking Mary to try to float, Shirley demonstrated her technique. After a few panicky false starts, Mary succeeded in floating face down for several seconds. Back floating didn't go so well, though, and Mary struggled, trying to maintain her body on top of the water and breathe at the same time. Shirley suggested that Mary keep trying to float on her back several more times before she switched to practicing her front floating technique, and she watched patiently, giving Mary gentle guidance and encouragement.

While Mary watched from the edge of the pool, Shirley disappeared under the water, and, several seconds later, she popped up in the deep end, where she executed a series of acrobatic maneuvers à la Esther Williams. Then she disappeared again and shot up from under water right in front of Mary. Delighted at the impromptu show, Mary applauded her friend's antics. With a grin, Shirley pulled herself out of the pool and bowed.

"Wow, Shirley, what a great performance! I can see that my teacher really knows what she's doing."

"Dale always did say that I was half fish and half show-off." A shadow passed over Shirley's face, and she said quietly, "We did have some good times."

"You're not considering getting back together with him, are you?"

"Not for a second. Nostalgia kicks in once in a while, but I'll never forget why I need to divorce Dale. No doubt about it. My mind's made up. That's why I'm here."

"Ditto."

"We'll do what we need to do and get on with our lives, but while we're here, we might as well make the best of it."

"I guess so," Mary agreed with a sigh.

Chapter 11

As Phyllis wobbled, her knees buckling, Bill caught her before she crashed to the floor. Then he scooped her up in his arms and deposited her gently on the bed, where she lay moaning. Bill, Wanda, and Peter crowded around Phyllis until Wanda tucked some pillows behind her, and Phyllis eventually sat up.

Feeling somewhat guilty for provoking such a reaction, Ben proceeded carefully, explaining step-by-step what his investigation had uncovered. His matter-of-fact demeanor calmed the group, although they were all shocked at the suggestion that anyone would want to kill Phyllis. Ben pressed ahead with his questioning.

"Now, Mrs. Beaumont, please understand that it's possible that Candice Martin was the intended victim, but, since she was posing as you at the time of her death, it's also possible that you were the target."

"It's totally unbelievable!" Wanda protested. "My sister may be a bit impulsive, but she's a good person, and she doesn't have any enemies."

"Maybe we should let Mrs. Beaumont speak for herself," Ben said. "You two haven't lived in the same city for how many years?"

"Well . . . about five years."

"So maybe you don't know everything that's happened in your

sister's life. You didn't know that she wasn't at home in Pasadena, and you didn't know that she was planning to divorce her husband."

"You're right, deputy," Wanda said, hanging her head.

Ben turned his attention back to Phyllis, hoping that perhaps he could finally get some answers, but Phyllis denied having any enemies and claimed that she couldn't imagine who would want to hurt her.

"What about your husband, Mrs. Beaumont?"

"Oh, Adrian." Phyllis waved her hand dismissively. "He wouldn't hurt a fly."

"You've already made a property settlement with him?"

"Our lawyers took care of all that. Adrian didn't object. He told his lawyer to give me anything I wanted."

"It's true, deputy; I heard him," Bill claimed.

Without Adrian Beaumont there to confirm or deny the story Phyllis was telling, Ben decided to switch gears.

"All right. What about Candice Martin, Mrs. Beaumont? She was a friend of yours, wasn't she?"

"A good friend once upon a time, but I hadn't seen her much in the past couple of years."

"Can you think of any reason someone might want to harm her?"

"No, I really can't."

"Did she have a boyfriend?"

"No, she told me that she broke up with her boyfriend a few months ago."

"Do you know his name?"

"Sure. It's Billy Littleton. He's a two-bit clarinet player with the Les Brady Band."

After asking Phyllis to keep him informed as to her whereabouts and suggesting that she might consider hiring a bodyguard, Ben left the hotel room, feeling that he'd only managed to scrape up one lead—Candice Martin had a former boyfriend, and it was just possible that he'd held a grudge against Candice. Since Littleton played with a well-known band, it shouldn't be too hard to track him down, but questioning him might be another story. The man could be any place in the country.

Ben hoped that he'd frightened Phyllis and Bill sufficiently that they would take the possible threat to her life seriously. Shocking as it had been for them to learn that a murder had taken place and that Phyllis might have been the intended victim, Ben wasn't too sure that the couple truly grasped the nature of the threat. They'd both dismissed Adrian Beaumont as a suspect, but Ben figured that Beaumont was rich enough to have arranged the accident and smart enough to have made sure that he was on another continent when the accident happened.

Beaumont could have a motive, too. Evidently he knew that Bill was in the picture, and Ben didn't know any husband who wouldn't be jealous and enraged, given that his wife had a new love interest. Money could be another factor. If the Beaumont divorce were granted, Adrian Beaumont undoubtedly stood to lose a good deal of money. Ben found it difficult to believe Phyllis's assertion that Adrian didn't care about their financial settlement.

With two possible suspects—neither immediately available for questioning—and no way of knowing which woman, Phyllis or Candice, had been the intended murder victim, Ben decided to work the case from another angle. He drove out to the Circle E to find out who had known about Candice's plan to drive to the Cal Neva at Lake Tahoe the night she was killed. Someone at the ranch might have known more about Candice's plans than Carol Ellis had.

This time when Ben arrived at the ranch, none of the guests were outside, on the porch. Through the front screen door, Ben could see Carol chatting with a couple of other women in the living room. Ben tapped on the door frame, and Carol called to him to come in. Before he could explain that he'd come to question the guests and the ranch's staff, Carol told him that she was expecting two new guests the following day, and she wanted to be able to have the cabin where Candice had stayed prepared for occupancy.

"I don't need to keep the cabin off limits any longer, do I? What should I do with the clothes she left, deputy?"

"You can go ahead and use the cabin, Mrs. Ellis. I'll take her belongings back to the office and see that they go to the right place." Just exactly where the right place might be, Ben didn't know. Some, maybe all, of the clothing might belong to Phyllis, but whether or not she'd want it returned, under the circumstances, he had no idea.

"I can have one of our housekeepers pack her suitcases if you'd like."

"Yes, thanks." Ben nodded his agreement. "The reason I'm here today is that I need to talk to all your guests and employees to find out if Candice shared her plans. Did she tell anyone where she intended to go the night of the accident?"

Carol hesitated, and Ben understood that she wasn't happy about his disrupting life at the ranch, but he had a job to do.

"I hate to disturb the guests," she said. "I've already told you that Phyllis, or rather Candice, just mentioned to me that she planned to visit a friend at the Cal Neva in Incline Village, but that's all she said."

"She may have given someone else more information. I really need to talk to everyone who was here that day. Could you make a list of names for me?" Ben's persistence didn't allow refusal, and Carol reluctantly agreed to provide him a list. While she moved to the small desk next to the front door and began writing names on a sheet of Circle E stationery, Ben turned to the others in the room and asked them whether or not they'd talked to the woman who'd gone by the name of Phyllis Beaumont before she drove up the mountain to Incline Village.

Although Ben realized that it was far from ideal to question the women together, they had already heard his conversation with Carol, so they knew why he was there. Ben drew a small spiral-bound notebook and a pen from his shirt pocket to take notes. Unfortunately, the two guests, Faye Cannon and Carla Reilly, knew less about Candice's plans than Carol. Neither of them had spoken to Candice that day. Ben jotted the ladies' names in his notebook, along with a brief note to that effect.

Before Carol finished with her list, Mary appeared. After her swimming lesson, Mary and Shirley had gone upstairs to their rooms in the ranch house to change their clothes. Mary put on shorts again since the day promised to be as hot as the day before. Coming downstairs, Mary paused when she spotted Ben. The two women Ben had just questioned waved to Mary and disappeared into the dining room.

"Looks like you started your riding lessons," Ben observed, making an assumption that he almost instantly regretted.

For a moment, Mary looked confused. "No, not yet," she replied.

Now it was Ben's turn to look confused. "Oh, I thought, uh. . ." Ben realized that he probably shouldn't have said anything, but it was too late now, so he plunged ahead. "Did you have an accident?" Ben asked, feeling awkward.

"She sure did," Shirley answered, bouncing down the stairs two at a time. "She's lucky to be alive. She was pushed off a curb yesterday in town, right in front of the Riverside."

"Pushed?"

"An accident, deputy," Mary assured him. "There was a big crowd waiting to cross the street, and the people were all jostling about. I just happened to be in the wrong place at the wrong time."

"I'm sorry you were hurt, ma'am," Ben said.

"She came within inches of being struck by a cab. I'm telling you, my heart was in my mouth;I was so horrified," Shirley declared dramatically.

"Well, thank goodness it's over now. I'm sure the deputy has more important things to do than listen to my troubles."

Mary smiled, and Ben couldn't think of a word to say. As he stood there, tongue-tied, Carol interrupted with the list she'd made, and then Ben got back to business, asking both Shirley and Mary if Candice had mentioned her plans to them. Mary explained that she hadn't arrived in Reno until after the accident. Although Shirley remembered talking to Candice that day when they were both at the pool sunbathing, she didn't remember Candice's mentioning a word about her planned excursion to the Cal Neva.

Ben began to think he was wasting his time, but a thorough investigation demanded that he talk to everyone at the ranch, so he pressed on. After tracking down everyone else on the list, except for a guest named Arlene Smythe, Ben hadn't picked up any new information at all. His last stop had been at the corral where the two wranglers had paused for a smoke break, joined by Bea and the flirtatious Sally. This time, Ben was relieved to find that Sally's attentions had been focused on Buster, the younger wrangler, a handsome man in his thirties who seemed to enjoy Sally's playful teasing. Sally pointedly ignored Ben, which suited the deputy just fine, and when he asked her if she knew anything about Candice's trip to Lake Tahoe, she shook her head and began fiddling with Buster's bolo tie.

Ben drove back up the lane to the ranch house, found Carol still in the living room, and asked her where Arlene Smythe was, only to learn that the woman had left that very morning to return home.

"She told me that she was reconciling with her husband," Carol informed Ben. "Come to think about it, that was odd because, the whole time she was here, she didn't receive one single phone call or a letter, and that went both ways. She didn't call or write anyone, either."

"And that's unusual?"

"Yes. In my experience, when a couple decides to put their divorce on hold and get back together, there's usually a lot of communication back and forth. But I guess Mrs. Smythe could have changed her mind, and maybe she knew her husband would want her back, although I wouldn't know why he'd want to be married to such a stuck-up woman."

"I guess I'd better trouble you for her address. I may need to contact her."

"All right." Carol went to her desk and rummaged through her files. "All I have on her is her lawyer's name and address in Chicago. All the arrangements were made through his office."

"That should do," Ben said, as he wrote the information in his notebook and scanned the list Carol had made for him one more time. Ben realized that Carol hadn't listed her name or her husband's, a natural oversight since the deputy knew that they owned the ranch.

"Mrs. Ellis, is your husband around? I haven't talked to him yet."

"Oh, goodness. I didn't think to put him on your list. He's back in our apartment right now. Would you like me to get him?"

"If you don't mind."

"Be right back."

When Carol returned with Chuck, she introduced him to Ben, and the two men shook hands.

"Sad 'bout that poor gal, deputy. How can I help you?"

"Did Candice Martin mention anything about her plans before she left for Lake Tahoe?"

Chuck scratched his chin and looked down at the floor as though he were trying to remember.

"Seems like. . .oh, yeah, now I recollect it. I picked up the mail on the way back from town—took a couple of the gals in to get their hair done." Chuck said. "Mailbox is out by the highway there," he added, jerking his thumb in the direction of the lane that led from the highway to the Circle E. "I sorted out the mail and took it around to everybody."

"Candice Martin received some mail here?"

"Uh, no, can't say as she did. I still think of her as Phyllis, ya know."

Ben wished that Chuck would get to the point, but he could see that hurrying the old man probably wasn't a good idea.

"Yes, sir. Any mail addressed to Phyllis Beaumont that you remember?"

"Nope, she didn't get no mail, that day or any other day. That's for sure. Most of the gals—well, they get a lot of mail, send a lot, too, far's that goes. Not Phyllis, though. Not that Smythe woman, either. Real unusual, if you ask me."

Chuck seemed to have lost his train of thought, so Ben prompted him.

"Go on, Mr. Ellis."

"Oh, yeah. Well, I was takin' the mail to the gals in the cabins, and, like I said, Phyllis, she didn't get none. But she come out of her cabin when I was walkin' by, real gussied up in a flashy silver dress, and called me over. Said she needed a man's opinion and could I come in, so I said 'sure.' She had two of them little perfume bottles on her dresser, and she told me to sniff them and tell her which one I liked the best. Well, I picked one that was real pretty smellin' and told her I liked that one. That was about it."

"She never mentioned her plans at all?"

"Nope, but she didn't hafta. She was plannin' on meetin' a man. No doubt about it."

Based on Chuck's account of his encounter with Candice, Ben

believed that Chuck had guessed correctly: Candice had planned to meet a man that night, a man with whom she'd had a romantic relationship. But who? This bit of information didn't get Ben much closer to solving the puzzle of who had rigged the Cadillac's brakes to fail.

"I'd like to thank you folks for your cooperation," Ben said. "I know this hasn't been easy. I wonder if I could trouble you for one more thing."

When she heard that Ben wanted something else, Carol didn't look especially happy, but the voluble Chuck had no such qualms.

"Sure thing, deputy," Chuck said.

"I need to make a phone call." Seeing Carol's frown, Ben quickly added, "It's a local call."

"Phone's right over there," Chuck nodded toward the desk that sat next to the front door of the ranch house. "Help yourself."

After he called the sheriff to let him know that he was headed to the Cal Neva at Incline Village to continue his investigation and wouldn't be back in the office for the rest of the day, Ben left the ranch with more questions than answers. Stowing the suitcases the housekeeper had packed with the belongings left in Candice's room, Ben drove back to the highway, turned right, drove another few miles, and turned right again, this time onto the Mount Rose Highway.

Despite his reason for driving up the mountain to Lake Tahoe, Ben enjoyed the ride. He rolled down his window and let the air wash over his face. Down below in the Truckee Meadows, the air felt hot and dry, but as he drove up the winding road, the breeze became cooler, almost refreshing.

Ben liked to drive, and his enjoyment of the open road had served him well because Washoe County comprised an area of sixty-six hundred square miles, bordering both California and Oregon, and the sheriff's office was responsible for enforcing the law in the entire area with the exception of the cities of Reno and Sparks. Since Washoe County touched the northeast corner of Lake Tahoe, it encompassed Incline Village, a small resort town on the lake where the Cal Neva Lodge and Casino straddled the border of California and Nevada.

Ben frequently tooled around in his truck on his days off. His route often took him home along the shores of Lake Tahoe and through the mountains to Placerville, a town in the Sierra Nevada known as the heart of the Mother Lode, about forty-five miles from Sacramento, where he'd grown up in a rambling old Victorian house. His parents still lived in the same home. Ellen, his younger sister, lived with her husband Andy and their two boys a couple of blocks from his parents' house, and Connie, the baby of the family, still in high school, lived at home. Early in his childhood, as the only boy and the oldest child, Ben had developed a heightened sense of responsibility, assuming the role of protector for his younger siblings.

Today, though, Ben's mind focused on the case he was investigating. Unless he broke the case soon, Ben doubted that he'd make it home to Placerville for Sunday dinner this week. Tenacious as a bull dog, Ben would keep at it until he either solved the case or completely ran out of leads. As he approached the scene of the accident, Ben thought about stopping again but decided against it. He'd already gleaned as much information as he could from the scene, so he kept driving until he crested the mountain and looked down on the deep blue lake, sparkling in the summer sunlight. He turned right and drove the few miles to the Cal Neva. Bypassing the valet parking stand in front of the casino, he drove to the parking lot, where he left his pickup.

Inside the casino, the jingle of change in the slot machines provided a constant background clatter, feeding the patrons' hopes that the next big jackpot would be theirs. In most cases, that hope was a futile one. The odds always favored the house, and Ben had quickly learned to avoid gambling, although he'd succumbed to temptation a few times shortly after he hired on as a deputy sheriff. After losing more than half of his first paycheck and a good chunk of his second, Ben had decided that he'd limit his future wagers to no more than a few dollars. When he'd come out of the army, he'd had just enough money saved to buy a brand new pickup truck. He'd needed to build a nest egg, and depending on gaming winnings wasn't a viable way to achieve his goal.

The rumbling in Ben's stomach heightened his awareness that he hadn't eaten since Virgil's wife had given him some of her homemade blueberry muffins. He felt half-starved as he made his way across the casino floor to the coffee shop, where he wasted no time ordering a hearty early dinner. After refueling with a T-bone steak, a baked potato, green beans, a couple of rolls, and a big slice of apple pie, Ben felt ready to resume his investigation, and he didn't have to go far to begin.

When the waitress brought his check, he asked her if she had worked on Tuesday evening, the night Candice had come to the casino. Ben asked her if she remembered seeing a young blond woman wearing a sparkly silver evening gown and carrying a silver fur stole and little white beaded purse. The waitress didn't remember seeing her, and neither did the hostess and other waitresses who had worked the evening shift on Tuesday. Ben wished he had a picture of Candice to show the employees, but he thought that people might remember seeing a beautiful woman in such an eye-catching dress. The coffee shop probably wasn't a place where a woman dressed in formal attire would have dined, but since Ben was there anyway, he didn't think it would hurt to ask.

After paying his bill, he drifted out onto the casino floor, threaded his way through the throng of gamblers, and went to the office of

Paul Knudson, the Cal Neva's chief of security. Knudsen looked more like a college mathematics professor than a security chief, with his thinning gray hair and thick spectacles, but Knudson recognized Ben, who'd been dispatched to the casino a couple of times in the past year, the first time because of a body found in a parked car in the casino's lot and the second because of a rowdy gambler who had been detained by casino security agents and held until the sheriff's deputies could arrive.

"Hello, Deputy. . ."

"It's Cameron, sir."

"Right. What can I do for you, Deputy Cameron?"

Ben explained his mission and said he'd like to question some of the casino employees who might have run into Candice Martin on Tuesday night. With the caveat that Ben shouldn't keep the employees away from their posts too long, Knudson agreed and sent for an agent who would shuffle the employees back and forth from the casino floor to the office, where Ben could talk to them. Knudsen remained in the office, too. When the employees came in, they understood that their employer was on board with the deputy's investigation, making Ben's job a little easier. Witnesses often weren't forthcoming, many preferring not to get involved when a crime had been committed, even though they might have some knowledge about it.

After talking with a waiter and one of the bus boys from the casino's steakhouse, Ben confirmed that Candice Martin had indeed visited the Cal Neva on Tuesday evening. And she'd dined with a man. Unfortunately, neither of the waiters could describe the man, although they had no problem at all remembering Candice, who'd made quite an impression in her spangled gown and silver fur stole.

Chuck had been right that Candice had been planning to meet a man that evening, but that knowledge didn't bring Ben any closer to identifying the mystery man or to learning if Candice had been the killer's intended victim.

After he finished questioning the casino employees, Ben asked Knudson for a list of any second-shift employees who'd worked Tuesday night, but weren't at work today. The list proved to be a short one with only five names on it. Knudson provided addresses for all of them and phone numbers for two. Ben assumed that the other three didn't have a phone. Although Ben intended to follow up with the absent casino employees, he didn't have much hope that they'd be able to provide any new information.

Ben thanked Knudson for his help and exited the casino, but he'd gotten turned around in the confusion of slot machines and table games, and when he emerged, he realized that he was in the front of the casino, standing right next to the valet parking stand. He didn't remember questioning any valets, so he asked the young guy who'd just returned a car to a patron if he'd worked Tuesday evening. Although he'd worked that evening, he hadn't seen Candice. Ben waited until the other valet returned to the stand driving a big red-and-white Buick Century. The couple who had been waiting next to Ben went to the car, and Ben watched as the man handed the valet a dollar and the valet held the passenger door open for the man's wife and closed it after the woman had settled herself in the front seat. As they drove off, the valet pocketed his tip and smiled. Not too many people gave him such a big tip. Most people tipped him a quarter; a few gave him only a dime. A lull in activity gave Ben a chance to ask the valet if he'd parked a black Cadillac for a young, blond woman on Tuesday evening. The valet remembered her immediately.

"Sure did, deputy. She was a looker, that one. I told her she ought to be in the movies, and she said that she had been in some movies. She told me which ones, but I never heard of any of 'em."

"Were you here when she left?"

"I was here all night, but Ernie must have run for her car when she left. I'd have remembered if I saw her again. That perfume she was wearing. Wowee!"

"You don't happen to remember exactly where you parked her car, do you?"

"Right over there; right on the end of the first row." The valet pointed to an empty parking spot.

"That lot's all valet parking, right?"

"Yup. Nobody else can park there."

Ben thanked the valet and walked over to the place, now empty, where the Beaumonts' Cadillac had been parked. He examined the pavement, which was dotted with oil spots, and he thought he saw a glint of metal. He stooped down for a closer look and found some tiny metal shavings lying on the pavement. Ben took out his pocket notebook and ripped a page from it, carefully folding it twice. Then he scooped up the shavings, made another couple of folds in the paper so that the shavings wouldn't fall out, and tucked it into his pocket, behind the notebook.

Returning to the valet stand, Ben waited while the valet who'd told him that he'd seen Candice parked a car.

"Did you see anyone in the valet lot Tuesday night?" asked Ben after the valet returned and Ben caught his attention. "Someone who shouldn't have been there?"

The man shook his head. "Can't say that I did."

He turned to the other valet. "Say, Ernie, you see anyone messing around in the lot here on Tuesday night? Deputy wants to know."

"No. Sorry." With that, Ernie turned to greet a customer who had driven up and parked in front of the valet stand. Ernie gave him a valet ticket, and the man handed Ernie his car keys.

With no witnesses to the tampering with the Cadillac that Virgil had discovered, Ben reckoned that the valets couldn't tell him much more.

"Just one last question," he said. "Did anyone else work the valet stand on Tuesday night?"

"Nope. Just me and Ernie."

"OK, thanks."

On the way back to Reno, Ben thought about all the tangled details of the strange case and what his next steps should be to investigate it. By the time he arrived back in town, it was early evening, and there seemed to be no reason to return to the office when he could just as easily sort out his notes at home. He found his usual parking spot on the side street next to the door that led upstairs to his apartment and pulled in. He didn't realize how tired he was until he trudged up the steps to his second-floor apartment.

As soon as he walked into his one-room apartment, he took off his uniform, stripping to his underwear. Although he'd left the windows open, the air in his apartment felt hot. Ben turned on his electric fan, grabbed a Bud from the tiny refrigerator, turned on his radio, and tuned in a baseball game. The New York Yankees were playing the Chicago White Sox in Chicago. As usual, Ben wished there were a Western team to root for. All the major league teams were either in the East or the Midwest, and, to the native Californian, now a Nevada transplant, that didn't seem fair. With the ball game on the radio and familiar sound of the announcer's voice as background, Ben thought about what his next move should be. He retrieved his notebook and the folded paper with the metal shavings enclosed and placed them on his turquoise Formica-topped kitchen table. Then he ripped another page from the notebook and began writing down everything he knew about the case and what he needed to learn. He outlined the next steps in his investigation, and, by the time the low-scoring ball game ended with a 1-2 loss for the Yankees, Ben had determined what to do next.

Chapter 12

The wolf whistle came, low and long, from a grizzled, old cowboy as Mary was showing Shirley the jeans she'd just tried on.

"Lookin' mighty fine in those Levi's, ma'am," the old cowhand said.

Mary's face turned red as she fled back into the dressing room at Parker's Western Wear, the downtown Reno store on Center Street, where real cowboys and dude ranch visitors alike purchased their Levi's, Western boots, and Stetson hats.

Before the cowpoke's whistle, Mary had already decided to purchase the jeans, but his reaction confirmed her own opinion that she looked good in them. Even so, Mary felt embarrassed by the cowboy's attention, and she cautiously opened the dressing room door a crack to peek out, hoping that he'd left the store. She scanned what she could see of the shop, but the old man was nowhere in sight, so she emerged from the dressing room, carrying the Levi's and a light blue Western shirt with mother-of-pearl snaps on it.

Mary joined Shirley in trying on leather Western boots, but Mary found the boots she chose too weighty, and she walked awkwardly in them.

"Don't worry, Miss. You'll get the hang of them boots," the sales clerk who was assisting them said. "Just like your friend here."

Mary glanced at Shirley, who appeared to walk easily in the boots she was trying out.

"I think I'll buy this pair," Shirley announced, looking at her reflection in the mirror the store provided for its customers. "What do you think, Mary? Do I look like a cowgirl?"

"You really do. These boots I have on don't seem to fit right. Maybe I should try a different size."

The sales clerk pressed on the boots Mary wore and then helped her take them off before he measured her feet for the second time.

"Yup, you're right, Miss. Let's try a smaller size."

After trying on a few more pairs, Mary settled on a snazzy pair of pointed-toe cordovan Lucchese boots. By the time they'd left Parker's, both women had bought Levi's, a couple of Western shirts, a leather belt, boots, and a Stetson hat.

"Well, we made quite a haul there. Now that we have the right clothes, we can start our riding lessons tomorrow," Shirley said.

"I can't take a lesson tomorrow. I need to go to Sunday Mass."

"Oh, yeah. I forgot tomorrow's Sunday. I don't think the wranglers usually give lessons on Sunday, anyway. I guess we'll have to put it off for a day. Say, as long as we're downtown, how about getting some jewelry to go with our outfits? Everybody around here wears turquoise and sterling silver."

"That sounds like a great idea. Where can we get some?"

"Carol told me to check Newman's Silver Shop if we want to look at Western jewelry. I think it's on Second Street."

After an hour of browsing at Newman's, Mary and Shirley each selected a turquoise and sterling ring. Shirley bought a matching cuff bracelet to go with her ring, while Mary chose dainty turquoise drop earrings, set in silver.

The two women enjoyed the carefree day, deliberately putting aside any thoughts of their soon-to-be ex-husbands and life after their upcoming divorces. They lingered over a long lunch at Harold's Club, then tried their luck with the one-armed bandits before leaving the casino. Shirley won a cupful of quarters, which she exchanged at the cashier's cage for folding money, but luck hadn't smiled on Mary, who lost several dollars in a slot machine before she stopped pulling its handle, but she rationalized that, between the two of them, they hadn't lost any money.

As soon as they arrived back at the ranch, Mary and Shirley donned their new Western duds and modeled them for the other women, who applauded their approval. Carol looked pleased to see her guests all "duded up," and Mary earned her second wolf whistle of the day from Chuck.

Mary's sky-blue Western shirt with its long sleeves and her denim Levi's covered her ugly bruises completely, so even though the day was a warm one, Mary opted to wear her new outfit as the guests gathered on the patio for cocktails before dinner.

Mary noticed that, true to her vow, Shirley drank only one martini during the cocktail hour before switching to club soda, and she sipped water during dinner.

Several of the guests planned to go into Reno with the ranch's wranglers after dinner to gamble, but Mary and Shirley skipped the excursion, since they'd already done all the wagering they were going to do for the day.

They spent the evening with Carol and Chuck on the patio. Chuck tuned his guitar and began singing, giving an impromptu performance that would have done any country singer proud. A soft breeze came up, and the air felt pleasantly warm as it lightly brushed Mary's face and rustled her hair. Far away, they could hear the howl of a coyote, and, for a moment, it seemed to Mary as though she were inhabiting a dream world, one very unlike her real life in New York. She almost wished that she could remain in a kind of suspended animation so that she wouldn't have to face re-making her life after she returned to New York as a divorced woman. Eventually, she would have to face it and decide what she was going to do, but tonight she willed herself to get lost in the music, the setting, and the freedom of indecision.

Chapter 13

The day after his trip to the Cal Neva, Ben planned to allow himself the luxury of an extra hour of sleep. After all, it was Saturday morning, and he had no definite schedule now that he was charged with investigating what he'd come to think of as the Beaumont case. Despite his intentions, he woke well before his alarm clock sounded its raucous call and decided not to dawdle since he had so much work yet to do. After a quick shower and a cup of coffee, he left his apartment and headed downtown to the sheriff's office.

The nature of law enforcement work dictated that the sheriff's office never closed, and neither did the near-by jail, which also came under the sheriff's authority, although, for the most part, Sheriff Rogers left its management in the capable hands of one of his assistants. When Ben entered the office, an older couple stood at the reception desk, but the room was otherwise empty. Ben assumed that the weekend receptionist, a known slacker, was probably lounging in the back room, but rather than go to search for her, Ben asked the couple what they needed. After they explained that their son had been picked up on a drunk driving charge the previous evening and they had come to pay his bail, Ben directed them to the jail next door. He'd always hated delivering prisoners, many of whom got into trouble because of their out-of-control drinking, to the jail to be booked, but he accepted that it was a necessary part of the job. He shuddered to think what life must be like for a prisoner confined behind bars, and he didn't understand why any man in his right mind would commit a crime that would land him in jail.

As the couple departed, Al came down the hallway from his office and greeted Ben.

"Ben, just the man I was looking for. I called your apartment, and when you didn't answer the phone, I hoped you'd come in today. There's someone here to see you, and he says he won't talk to anyone except the sheriff or you. Mark took his wife to San Francisco for the weekend, so I guess you're elected. Come on back to my office."

Soft snoring noises emanated from the man who was waiting for Ben. His head resting awkwardly on the back of the chair he was sprawled in, his mouth half-open, the man looked like a hobo with his mussed hair, several days' growth of beard, and his rumpled linen suit. However, the suitcase beside him told a different story. Even though Ben was no connoisseur of fine leather goods, he could tell that the brown alligator bag was an expensive piece of luggage. The large diamond ring, set in gold, on the man's finger and the gold watch on his left wrist confirmed Ben's impression that the sleeping man was no hobo.

Al cleared his throat loudly, and the man stirred, stopped snoring, and opened his eyes.

"Sir, this is Deputy Cameron."

The man rose to his feet unsteadily and stuck out his hand, which Ben shook.

"Hello, deputy. I've come to take my wife home. I'm Adrian Beaumont."

"Well, I'm not sure about that, Mr. Beaumont. Her fiancé's with her."

"Good lord, man. Mead has no right to bury her. I'm her husband."

Instantly, Ben realized that Adrian Beaumont had received only the first telegram sent to him by his secretary—the one that informed him that his wife Phyllis had died in a car accident. As soon as Ben had learned that a mistake had been made in identifying the victim, he'd contacted Beaumont's secretary at Excelsior Studio and asked her to send a second wire. She'd promised to dispatch it immediately. Ben had assumed that Beaumont had received the second telegram and no longer believed that his wife had died in an auto accident, but, clearly, that wasn't the case. Obviously, Beaumont had been traveling for the last several days, which explained his disheveled appearance.

"Mr. Beaumont, please sit down. I have some good news for you. Your wife's very much alive."

"But the telegram from my secretary. . ."

"I'm sorry about that. I had her send you another telegram as soon as I realized that the woman who was driving your Cadillac wasn't your wife. I apologize for the mix-up," Ben said, but the look of joy on Adrian Beaumont's face told him that Beaumont was thinking only about Phyllis and that she was still alive.

"My God! Where is she? Where's Phyllis now?"

"I believe she's still in town. Let me make a quick call to confirm that, and then I'll take you to her."

Ben wasn't at all sure that Phyllis would welcome a visit from the man she planned to divorce, but, considering that Beaumont had traveled thousands of miles to make her funeral arrangements, and, judging from his reaction to the news that she was still alive, Ben thought that perhaps Adrian Beaumont really cared for the beautiful, young woman.

Ben phoned the registration desk at the Mapes and learned that neither Phyllis Beaumont nor Bill Mead had checked out. Ben had asked the couple to keep him apprised of Phyllis's whereabouts, but he couldn't force their cooperation, and it wouldn't have surprised him to find that the two lovers had left Reno.

On the short drive to the Mapes, Ben filled Beaumont in on the details of the accident that had taken Candice Martin's life. He asked Beaumont if he'd ever met Candice, but the director claimed he didn't know her. He also insisted that nobody had any reason to kill his wife.

"What about you, Mr. Beaumont? You stood to lose a lot of money if your wife divorced you. She says that you told her she could have whatever she wanted. That's hard to believe."

"Maybe, but it's true. By the time I said that, things had gone too far, and I'd resigned myself to her leaving me. It was my own fault in a way. I was busy—too busy to pay any attention to Phyllis—and I neglected her. When I trusted Mead to take her to a couple of parties while I was out of town, I made a big mistake. You know the rest."

Ben held his tongue. This movie director didn't act like any man Ben knew, but maybe rich, famous people behaved differently than ordinary mortals. Ben hadn't warned Phyllis that her husband was on his way to see her because he wanted to observe their interaction. As far as Ben was concerned, there was a fifty-fifty chance that Beaumont had hired a hit man to do away with his wife while he established an ironclad alibi for himself half a world away from the scene of the crime. Although Beaumont played the part of the grieving husband well, he could have been acting, and now that he'd arrived in Reno, Beaumont could finish the job that his hired gun had bungled.

Although most of the Mapes' gamblers paid no attention to Ben and Beaumont as they crossed the casino floor on their way to the elevators, Beaumont's unkempt appearance drew stares from a few of the hotel's patrons.

Upstairs, Phyllis opened the door to her room just as Ben raised his hand to knock. Dressed in a pink-and-white striped sundress and wearing pink high heels, a white straw handbag dangling from her wrist, the beautiful starlet appeared to be on her way out.

"Oh, deputy, you startled me. I was just about to leave."

Ben stepped aside, and she caught sight of her husband. Before Phyllis had an opportunity to say anything, Beaumont swept her up in his arms.

"Phyllis! My darling! My beautiful darling!"

"Adrian! I thought you were in Africa."

"I got word that you'd been in an accident," he said, still holding her tightly.

"And you thought I was dead?"

Beaumont began sobbing. "Thank God! Thank God! You're all right. I didn't know until a few minutes ago." As the couple clung to each other, Phyllis began to cry, too.

For two people on the verge of divorce, they seemed awfully chummy, Ben thought. Beaumont had begun kissing away Phyllis's tears, and soon she was returning his kisses with her own.

Just then, Bill Mead burst through the open door into the room.

"Phyllis, I've been waiting for you." He stopped short when he saw Phyllis locked in an embrace with her husband. "Hey, what's going on here?"

"I'll tell you what's going on here. This is what's going on here." Beaumont disengaged himself from his wife long enough to deliver a roundhouse punch to the handsome actor's jaw, knocking him to the floor.

"What the hell did you do that for, you idiot? Get me some ice, Phyllis. Quick. Before my jaw swells up."

Phyllis didn't move, and Mead's face contorted with anger.

"Phyllis, help me out. You know they'll be shooting my first scene Monday."

"You're worried about how you'll look?" Phyllis asked.

"Damn right. There's only so much a make-up artist can do. I'm the star of the picture. I have to look good."

"Take a hike, Mead." Beaumont looked at his wife. "OK with you?"

"OK with me."

Holding his jaw and glaring at the Beaumonts, Mead staggered to his feet. "To hell with you both!" he shouted.

"Right back at you," Phyllis said, slamming the door hard as her ex-fiancé stormed out of the room.

A silent observer of the dramatic scene that had just unfolded, Ben wondered whether the players were sincere or whether they were acting. Or maybe a little bit of both. And who were they playing to—Ben or themselves? With Hollywood types, Ben was learning that he couldn't tell for sure.

After giving the Beaumonts the same caution he'd delivered to Phyllis and Bill the day before, Ben slipped out of the room, gently pulling the door closed. From the looks of things, the reunited couple couldn't wait to be alone.

As Ben drove back to the sheriff's office, he thought about another possibility—one that seemed too fantastic to consider. What if Phyllis had demanded a divorce, consulted a lawyer, agreed to a financial settlement, planned the accident, and hired someone to rig the Cadillac's brakes—all in a desperate bid for her husband's attention? He'd admitted to neglecting her, and maybe, at first, she'd hoped her affair with Mead would be enough to make Adrian jealous and attentive. When that didn't work, she could have gone on with a more elaborate scheme, one that pivoted around the murder of her look-alike. Ben couldn't quite discount this theory, but, at the same time, he found it difficult to believe that a beautiful young woman like Phyllis could hatch such a plan, let alone execute it. Even so, Phyllis now occupied a place on Ben's mental list of suspects, whether she deserved it or not.

Chapter 14

"What a perfect day for a picnic," Shirley exclaimed, as she pulled her car off to the side of the road. "This looks like the spot Carol told us about."

Shirley and Mary got out of the front seat while Bea, Sally, and Faye piled out of the back. Shirley opened the trunk of her car and handed a beach umbrella, blankets, towels, and beach bags to Mary and Faye. Then she removed the wicker picnic basket while Bea and Sally grabbed the portable cooler that they'd borrowed from Chuck, each holding one side of the unwieldy box that held the beer and sodas they'd brought with them, and struggled to carry it.

Once they'd left Reno behind and driven north on Highway 445, they'd arrived at their destination on the shore of Pyramid Lake in less than an hour. They headed down a well-traveled path to the lake and staked out a spot near the shore. Even though Mary wore sunglasses, she held up her hand to shade her eyes and looked out over the lake. The sunlight glazed the sheer surface of the water. An unusual pyramid-shaped formation jutted up from the lake, forming a small island. Several boats dotted the water, but they floated too far away for Mary to make out whether their occupants were fishing or simply enjoying a cruise on the lake.

Several yards away, a half-dozen Paiute youngsters splashed in the water. Mary waved to them and received shy smiles in return. At first, she didn't see any adults supervising the children, but after scanning the area, she spotted an old man with long, white hair lingering in the shade of a large boulder, his eyes focused on the children. She waved at him, too, but he didn't respond unless his almost imperceptible nod counted as an acknowledgement.

"Carol told me that there's a guest ranch up here at the lake," Bea said. "It seems kind of odd because the whole lake's on the Paiute Reservation."

"I wouldn't want to stay this far from Reno myself," Faye said. "I think a lot of women who bring their kids with them for their six weeks like it up here, but I'm sure glad I didn't bring my Sammy and Lucy with me. Thank goodness, Mom and Dad volunteered to watch them while I'm gone. This is the first vacation I've had in twenty years. My husband always said we couldn't afford to take a vacation. Then I find out he's squirreled away a fortune. I have to hand it to my lawyer—I never would have known about Len's secret bank accounts if it weren't for him. Now it's share and share alike."

"You wanted to get a divorce, I take it?" Bea asked.

"Sure did. The man was never home, even for the kids' birthdays. It was always work, work, work, or so he said."

"Well, I suppose he must have been working some of the time or he wouldn't have accumulated all that money he was hiding."

"I guess." Faye sighed. "I don't think life without Len will be much different than life with Len. Sometimes I wonder if Sammy and Lucy even know they have a father."

"That's a shame. I guess I'm the only one here who doesn't want to get a divorce," Bea said.

"Bea, I don't think anyone really wants to get a divorce. It's just that sometimes circumstances . . ." Mary said.

"I understand, Mary. Really, I do. I guess my case is different. My husband wants to get rid of me, and he's willing to pay big bucks to do it. Unfortunately for me, I still love the jerk."

"Maybe you could get back together. Maybe go to a marriage counselor," Shirley said.

"I tried everything I could think of. The truth is that he just doesn't love me anymore."

"Oh, come on, Bea. It's more than that, and you know it," Sally interjected. "He's having an affair."

"I don't know that for sure."

"Bea, you're deluding yourself," Sally said.

"Ladies, ladies, can't we get away from the divorce talk for a few hours?" Shirley asked. "We came to the lake to have a good time."

"I guess," Sally said.

"Let's promise not to mention our husbands for the rest of the day. How about it?"

The women murmured their agreement, although Sally didn't seem especially happy about it. Mary thought that it was strange that Sally had been goading Bea, because she thought they were friends. The two of them hung out together most of the time, but Mary surmised that the prospect of their impending divorces might be taking a toll.

Shirley spread one of the blankets they'd brought with them on the ground, and Mary laid out the other one. While Sally handed everyone a drink, Shirley began unpacking the picnic basket filled with fried chicken, potato salad, rolls, and giant chocolate chip cookies, all prepared for them by one of the ranch's cooks. Mary passed out plates and utensils wrapped in paper napkins, and, as the women piled food on their plates and began to eat, they chatted about the new Marilyn Monroe movie, *The Seven Year Itch*, the film that they'd all gone to see the previous evening. Although the film's subject came perilously close to paralleling Bea's experience with her husband, the picnic had lightened their mood, and they kept the conversation as frothy as the comedy had been, especially since Marilyn Monroe's white halter dress inspired as much interest as the movie's plot.

After lunch, Faye shed her sundress, revealing her black, figure-flattering, one-piece swimsuit underneath, and announced that she was going swimming. Bea protested that she should wait an hour after eating to avoid getting cramps, but Faye laughed and said that was an old wives' tale. As it turned out, Faye didn't do much real swimming, anyway, but she splashed around in the water for a while, always staying close to shore.

Although the Paiute children had disappeared by the time they finished their picnic, the women from the Circle E were no longer alone. Several guests of the Pyramid Lake Dude Ranch had shown up, and many of them had brought their children along with them. Some of the newcomers lolled on the beach as the kids played nearby. While others swam or joined Faye in wading, Shirley, Mary, and Sally all ventured out into the lake, and despite her protests, even the reluctant Bea took a dip.

It had been a week since Mary's first swimming lesson. She still couldn't execute a respectable back float, but she'd learned to swim using the crawl stroke, and she was able to swim several yards, although she hadn't yet quite gotten the hang of breathing without taking on water. Her dip in Pyramid Lake would be her first time swimming in a natural environment, rather than in a pool.

All week, Mary had occupied herself with swimming and riding lessons, along with shopping and tours around the Reno area, so that she'd had little time to reflect on her current situation or to think about what she would do after the judge granted her divorce.

After Mass on Sunday, she'd phoned her parents, and the three of them had spent as much time crying as talking. Mary was happy to hear that John Garrison, her husband, had stopped calling her parents in an attempt to mend fences and persuade them to influence their daughter to go back to him. He'd stopped badgering her grandparents, too. On the other hand, Mary's divorce wouldn't be recognized by the Catholic Church, and her family was concerned that the church wouldn't annul the marriage. If not, Mary would be left in a religious limbo that would prevent her from ever remarrying. Even so, nobody in Mary's family had tried to dissuade her.

Cautiously, Mary waded out from shore while Shirley began her Esther-Williams routine—diving, swimming underwater, and making acrobatic maneuvers. Mary watched her for a few minutes before wading deeper into the water. She didn't want to swim in water that would cover her head if she stood. When she'd gone into the lake far enough that the water lapped at her waist, she began to swim a few yards at a time. Then she'd stop, stand up, and catch her breath before repeating the process. She knew that she should be practicing the proper method of breathing, just as Shirley had demonstrated over and over during the past week, so, finally, Mary tried to swim and take a breath while she swam.

Her first attempt left her sputtering and choking on lake water. Mary's look of surprise when she tasted the water prompted one of the guests from the Pyramid Lake Dude Ranch who was paddling nearby to tell Mary that Pyramid Lake was a salt-water lake. Mary had noticed that she felt more buoyant in the lake than she did in the swimming pool at the Circle E, and she guessed that the salt water probably accounted for the difference.

Continuing to practice, Mary felt encouraged when Shirley gave her a thumbs-up signal before swimming away. Growing bolder, Mary ventured out farther from shore, until the water rose almost to her neck, before she resumed swimming.

Suddenly, she felt a hand on her ankle, a hand with a firm grip, and then she was pulled under the water. Frantically, Mary shook her leg and tried to stand, but she couldn't touch the lake bed under her feet. In a full-blown panic, she flopped around, splashing violently, and managed to catch a breath of air before she was pulled under the water once again. This time she felt the bottom of the lake, but not with her feet. Her head had been forced down, and she hit her forehead against a rock. She couldn't open her mouth to scream without swallowing the salty lake water. As Mary helplessly thrashed about, growing weaker by the second, she fought to maintain consciousness, but she could feel herself beginning to drift away.

A great calmness enveloped Mary as she found herself moving away from the lake and into a narrow tunnel, inching toward a bright, beautiful light. Mary saw her little brother, Tony, beckoning to her and heard her Aunt Emilia calling her name. Polio had taken Tony from the family when he was just four years old, and Mary's Aunt Emilia had succumbed to a heart attack in March. Yet here they were, welcoming Mary. Tony held out his small hand, and Mary took it in her own as Aunt Emilia put her arm around Mary. They all drifted together, toward their destination at the end of the tunnel. Blissfully bathed in the brilliant light, Mary's heart filled with joy.

Surrounding her in the water, none of the other swimmers recognized her predicament as Mary peacefully floated on the water's surface.

The swimmers did take notice, though, when the old man Mary had seen earlier, watching the Paiute children as they played in the lake, dashed from behind a huge rock, yelling bloody murder, and shedding his clothes as he ran to the beach, entered the water, and swam toward Mary.

When he reached Mary, the old man grabbed her arms and crossed them, flipping her over so that her head no longer hung in the water, and then he began towing her toward the shore. Several yards away, Shirley finally noticed the unfolding drama and swam over to help pull Mary out of the water. Shirley screamed for help, and several people waded out to meet them, but it was the old Paiute who lifted Mary in his arms and carried her onto the sandy beach.

"I'm calling for an ambulance and the lake patrol," one of the guests of the Pyramid Lake Dude Ranch shouted, running toward the road. She'd have to drive a few miles to the tiny reservation town of Sutcliffe to make the calls because there was no telephone close to the picnic area.

Faye and Bea looked on in horror as Shirley leaned over Mary and announced, "She isn't breathing."

Immediately, Shirley tried to revive Mary, but her body lay still as death.

As if by rote, Shirley began the resuscitation procedure she'd learned when she'd trained for a job as a lifeguard the summer before her senior year in high school. She rhythmically alternated pressing on Mary's chest and pulling on her arms.

"Stop that!" Sally shouted, as she threaded her way through the onlookers, pushed Shirley aside, and knelt next to Mary.

Sally opened Mary's mouth and blew into it as the stunned crowd that had gathered anxiously watched. Sally raised her head, breathed deeply, and once again put her mouth to Mary's.

"Mommy, what's wrong with the lady?" a freckled-faced little girl asked.

"She's hurt, honey."

"I bet she's dead," whispered a towel-draped teenager, her eyes brimming with tears. Softly she murmured, "Holy Mary, Mother of God, pray for us sinners now and at the hour of our death."

Chapter 15

Ben sat in his patrol car, writing a short report about a burglary at a house where the owners had returned from vacation to find that a couple of rifles and some tools had been stolen in their absence. Thankful that he could fill out the paperwork by hand on a short official form, rather than typing a lengthy report, required in more complex cases, Ben painstakingly copied the descriptions of the missing property from his pocket notebook to the form. He'd alert the local pawn shops and keep an eye on the classified ads in the newspapers, in hopes of tracking down the stolen items. He also planned to stop by the flea market to see whether one of the vendors might be trying to sell them.

When Ben had reported to work Monday morning, Sheriff Rogers had called Ben into his office and told him that Carmine's condition had improved, but since he wouldn't be returning to work for a few weeks, Ben should take over Carmine's work on a temporary basis. In addition to the Beaumont case, Ben would be investigating cases pending at the time Carmine had had a heart attack as well as some of the new cases that might crop up. The sheriff's department had only two investigators, and Fred Barton, the other detective, had his hands full tracking down the men behind a dangerous cattle rustling operation, so the sheriff advised Ben that he'd funnel most of the routine cases his way.

His new responsibilities meant that Ben couldn't spend all his time investigating only one case, and in the week since Phyllis Beaumont had reunited with her husband, Ben hadn't made much progress on the murder investigation. Although he'd tried to contact the Cal Neva's employees who hadn't been working on the day he'd driven to the Lake Tahoe casino, he'd succeeded in talking to only a couple of them, and neither had remembered seeing a woman in a silver, spangled evening gown.

Although he'd persuaded the coroner to wait to release his official report, which would list the cause of Candice Martin's death as homicide, he couldn't stall much longer, and he feared that alerting the murderer would drive him to either make a desperate move, assuming that Phyllis, who had stayed in Reno to enjoy a second honeymoon with her husband, had been the intended victim, or cause him to disappear, in which case Ben might never uncover the murderer.

As Ben double-checked the official report form to make sure he'd filled out all the necessary information, the radio in the patrol car crackled and the dispatcher's voice came through the static, reporting a drowning at Pyramid Lake and requesting the closest deputy to respond. Calculating that he was part way to the lake already, Ben called in and reported his location, and the dispatcher confirmed that he should proceed to the south picnic area at the lake.

After securing his paperwork, Ben made a wide U-turn in the gravel driveway where he'd parked and pulled onto Highway 445, leaving a cloud of dusty Nevada dirt in his wake. As soon as the tires of the patrol car hit the pavement, Ben turned on his lights and siren and drove north toward the lake. Ben knew that he'd arrive at the scene before the ambulance, which would come from Reno. He increased pressure on the gas pedal until the powerful cruiser reached a speed of ninety miles an hour. He passed few cars along the way.

Most of the drivers heard his siren and pulled over to the side to let him pass, but the driver of a beat-up, old blue Chevy stayed on the road, blocking Ben's way. With an oncoming car in sight, Ben was forced to brake hard to avoid hitting the Chevy. Cursing, Ben swerved around the Chevy as soon as the car in the other lane passed, and he drove the rest of the way to the picnic area without incident.

Several cars lined the road adjacent to the picnic area. Ben parked behind the truck of the Pyramid Lake Patrol, an all-volunteer organization of tribal members who were trained in search-and-rescue operations, and headed down the path leading to the picnic area on the lake's shore. A few yards down the path, Ben encountered Jim Smith, one of the patrol members, a man Ben had met during a search for some missing hikers, coming up the path to the road.

"Thought I'd go up to the road and signal the ambulance," Smith said.

"What's the situation down there?" Ben asked.

"Not the worst, but not the best, either. The victim's breathing on her own now, but she wasn't breathing when she was pulled out of the water. She has a big gash on her head, and she's unconscious."

"How old?"

"Early twenties, I'd guess."

Each man continued on his way, Ben to the picnic area and Smith to the roadside. When Ben came to the end of the path, he could see a crowd gathered close to the water.

"Excuse me," Ben repeated several times, as he edged his way through the crowd until he could see the drowning victim lying on the ground. Smith's partner, a young Paiute man, was urging the crowd to stand back, but they didn't seem inclined to move.

"Stand back!" Ben bellowed. "Please move back and give us some room here," he said in a lower voice until the crowd fell back several yards. "Rubber-neckers," Ben muttered as he exchanged a look with the young Paiute patrolman.

"How's she doing?" Ben asked him and received the same information Smith had given him.

Ben hadn't really taken a good look at the woman who was lying on the ground because two other women were leaning over her, their backs toward Ben, but, as he knelt beside them, he recognized them all as guests from the Circle E. He felt a sickening lurch in the pit of his stomach when he saw Mary. He remembered her name but not the names of the other two women, although he knew that one of them had flirted with him the first time he had gone to the ranch.

"It's Mary, isn't it?" Ben asked.

"Yes," Sally said, her demeanor serious. "She's breathing on her own now, but she hasn't come to."

"What happened?"

"We don't know," Shirley said, "but that's a nasty looking gash on her forehead. Maybe one of the kids threw a rock and hit her by accident."

"You didn't see anything then?"

"No, I didn't realize that she was in trouble until that old Indian man started towing her to shore." Shirley looked around. "I don't see him right now, but maybe he saw what happened."

"You see him?" Ben asked the Paiute patrolman.

"Yeah, he's Smith's great-uncle. Smith'll know where to find him."

"OK, thanks."

The wail of the ambulance's siren alerted them to its arrival, and this time, the patrolman had no problem clearing the way for the two ambulance attendants and Smith. While one of the attendants performed a quick examination, the other one laid out a litter beside Mary; the patrolmen and attendants hoisted Mary onto it; and, one at each corner, they lifted the litter and carried it to the waiting ambulance. In a few minutes, siren screaming, the ambulance left. The women from the Circle E piled into Shirley's car and followed. They had agreed to meet Ben at the hospital in Reno.

Before the crowd dispersed, Ben needed to make sure that he'd gathered all the pertinent information. He called the crowd together and told them to give their names and contact information to him or to one of the patrolmen. The three then proceeded to filter through the crowd, taking notes as they went. Then the people in the crowd dispersed, no longer in the mood for swimming after seeing a victim of a near drowning..

"I understand your great-uncle was the one who pulled Mary out of the water," Ben said to Smith.

"You know the victim?" Smith asked, surprised.

"Slightly," Ben said before quickly changing the subject back. "Where can we find your great-uncle? I'd like to talk to him."

"He'll be at my grandmother's house, but he won't talk to you."

"Doesn't he speak English?"

"He pretends not to, but he understands it all right. He's a stubborn old man. He'll talk to me, though, as long as I speak in Paiute."

"That'll work."

Ben followed the Pyramid Lake Patrol truck about a mile up the road to a small home situated in a grove of cottonwood trees. Smoking a cigarette, an old man sat in a white Adirondack chair near the front cement stoop of the house. A lone cow, a reminder that the entire area was open range, wandered through the side yard, but the old man paid it no mind.

Ben got out of his cruiser, but Smith suggested that he wait by his car while Smith talked to his great-uncle, and Ben agreed. The young patrolman waited with Ben while Smith greeted his uncle, then sat on a step and conversed with him in Paiute. After a few minutes, Smith returned.

"Did he see what happened?" Ben asked.

"He says he saw the woman flailing around in the water before she went under. When she came up, she didn't gasp for air, but floated face down. He realized that she was in trouble, and that's when he ran out to help her."

"Sounds like an accident."

"Her friend told me that she was just learning to swim. It could be that she went out too far."

"What aren't you telling me?"

"You aren't going to believe this."

"Try me."

"He says he knew something bad was going to happen."

"How could he know that?"

"Because he heard the cries of an owl and a coyote coming from the shore last night."

"I don't get it."

"Bad omens."

"You believe in that stuff?"

"I don't know, but he believes in it. It happened to him once before—the night before his son was killed in a boating accident five years ago. That's why he insisted on going to watch over his grandchildren when they wanted to play at the beach. After his daughter-in-law took them home, he stayed to keep watch."

"Hmm. Well, I guess it's a good thing. Nobody else seemed to notice that Mary was in trouble. Did you thank him for pulling her out?"

"Uh, no."

"Mind if I try? I know he might not talk to me, but I want to thank him."

"Suit yourself, but don't be surprised if he ignores you."

Ben strolled up to the front stoop and stood in front of the old man.

"Sir, I'd like to thank you for saving the young woman today. I don't know if she's going to make it, but if she does, she owes you her life." Ben stuck out his hand, but the old man paid no attention. Slowly, Ben lowered his hand. "Well, I'd better go now. I need to get to the hospital." He turned and began to walk back to the road.

"She will live," the old man called, but by the time Ben turned to look at him, he'd disappeared into the house.

"Well, I'll be damned," Smith said. "I've never heard him speak English before. For that matter, I've never heard him talk to a white man before. No offense."

Ben grinned. "None taken, and I hope he's right."

Chapter 16

Mary's lids fluttered as she gingerly opened her eyes. There was a bright light in the room, but rather than the bright, beautiful light she'd seen earlier, this light seemed cold and clinical. She looked around her at white everywhere—white sheets, white walls, white floor. The permeating odor of disinfectant hung in the air, and Mary realized that she was lying in a hospital room. She closed her eyes again. Mary could hear voices in the hallway. One of the voices sounded familiar, although she couldn't place it. She had never heard the other voice before.

"How's she doing, doc?" she heard the familiar voice ask.

"Her vital signs are good, but she hasn't regained consciousness. I'd say that's due to a concussion. It's difficult to know how serious it is right at the moment. She could wake up at any time, or . . . We just don't know."

"Mind if I look in on her?"

"All right. Ring for the nurse if she shows any signs of waking up."

Confused, Mary realized that the two men were talking about her, and even though she knew now that she was in the hospital, she struggled to remember the reason. Then it came to her. She'd been swimming at Pyramid Lake and then—.

Mary could hear someone entering the room. He came closer, and she opened her eyes and looked straight at him, recognizing Ben as the deputy sheriff she'd seen on two different occasions at the Circle E. No wonder his voice had sounded familiar.

"I saw heaven," she whispered.

Ben bolted from the room and yelled, "Doc! She's awake!"

"Wait here in the hall, please." Mary could hear the doctor telling Ben. "I'll need to examine her."

"Mrs. Marchetti, I'm Dr. Kohl," he said, entering her room. "How are you feeling?"

"My head hurts."

"I should think it would. That's quite a bump you have there, and it's caused a concussion. Now let's have a look-see." After a brief examination, the doctor stood back and declared, "I'm going to admit you overnight for observation, Mrs. Marchetti, just to be on the safe side, but it's a good sign that you've regained consciousness. If there are no more symptoms by tomorrow afternoon, I'll discharge you."

Mary nodded.

"Your friends are waiting in the lobby to see you. You gave them quite a scare. Are you up to having some company?"

"Oh, yes, please."

"I'll send them in."

While she waited, Mary stacked the pillows behind her so that she no longer lay flat on her back. She thought that she must look a fright. Now, not only did she have bruises on her arms and legs, but she also had a gash on her head and, no doubt, another bruise there, too. As she smoothed her hair in an ineffectual attempt to straighten it, a few strands caught in her mouth, and she tasted salt. She remembered swallowing salty water just before she was pulled underwater at the lake.

"Thank God you're all right," Faye said as she, Shirley, Bea, and Sally crowded around Mary's bed.

"Mary, I'm so sorry. I should have been keeping a better eye on you. Instead, I was playing around, doing my water nymph routine," Shirley said. "It's my fault you almost drowned out there."

"Oh, Shirley, don't blame yourself," Mary said. "I'll be fine. Better than fine."

"What are you talking about, Mary?" Bea asked. "You're in the hospital!"

"I saw my little brother," Mary said.

The women glanced at each other in confusion.

"Your brother was here?" Sally asked.

"No, not here. You don't understand. He died when he was four years old, but I saw him today. He took my hand. I saw my Aunt Emilia, too. She died a few months ago."

"Mary, it sounds as though you visited heaven," Faye said.

"I did, Faye, and I didn't want to come back."

Chapter 17

After Mary's friends from the Circle E left, Ben cooled his heels while two orderlies moved Mary to a private room on the fourth floor of the hospital. Once she was settled and he'd received the go-ahead from Mary's nurse, Ben popped into her room.

"Hi, Mary. Do you remember me?"

Mary nodded. "You're the deputy sheriff who came out to the Circle E last week. But why are you here now?"

"The sheriff's department responds to accidents at Pyramid Lake. You almost drowned, Mary. I understand that Shirley and Sally revived you there on the beach, after an old Paiute man pulled you out of the water."

"My goodness! I didn't know that. Shirley and Sally just left, and they didn't say a word about reviving me. I need to thank them and the Paiute man, too."

"All in due time, Mary. You'll have a chance to thank everybody after you're discharged from the hospital. The doctor told me that you'll probably be able to leave tomorrow. Can you tell me what happened at the lake, Mary?"

"Well, I remember some of it."

"Go on."

"I was practicing breathing while I was swimming—Shirley's

been teaching me in the pool at the Circle E—and then I felt something pulling me. I tried to shake it loose, but I went under the water. I remember thrashing around, and I was able to come up for air for a few seconds, but then down I went again, and that time I hit my head. The next thing I knew, I was going through a tunnel, toward a bright light. I was in heaven, deputy. I'm sure of it. And I remember that I wanted to stay there, but suddenly I was back, right here in this bed."

Ben cleared his throat. Although he was something of a skeptic himself, he understood that many people believed in the supernatural. Both the old Indian man and Mary had experienced something mystical at the lake, and they both believed in a spiritual explanation for what had happened. Despite Ben's logical take on the events—he figured that the bad omens were mere coincidences and that Mary's vision of heaven was probably a dream based on her faith—Ben didn't want to upset Mary by suggesting a different explanation than the one she clung to. If she believed, who was Ben to contradict her?

Rather than engage Mary in a discussion about her religious experience, Ben decided to direct their conversation back to the realm of the physical.

"OK, Mary. You said that you felt something pulling you while you were swimming. Could you be more specific?"

"It's a little hazy, but let me think." Mary closed her eyes for a moment. "The pulling—it was like somebody was tugging at my ankle."

Shocked, Ben asked, "You think somebody deliberately pulled you under?"

"At first, I thought maybe one of the kids was playing a joke on me."

"And what do you think now?"

"It was no joke because whoever it was, he wouldn't let go."

"You said 'he.' Did you see a man?"

"No, honestly, I didn't see anybody. I . . . I had my eyes closed the whole time."

"Hitting your head—do you remember how that happened?"

"After I came up for air, I could feel hands grabbing me again, and I was pushed. I know there were rocks on the bottom because I remember feeling them whenever I stood up. Whoever it was, he must have pushed me into a rock. I'm not really sure."

"Mary, could anyone in Nevada want to harm you?"

"Why, no. I don't think so. I've been here less than two weeks."

"How about back home? Is there anyone who's angry with you?"

"Only my husband."

"Figures," Ben muttered, but Mary didn't hear him. Ben didn't know Mary well, but, for the life of him, he couldn't imagine anyone wanting to hurt a young woman as lovely as Mary. Her husband seemed the only logical suspect.

"So your husband doesn't want you to get a divorce? Is a big financial settlement involved?"

"No, only a small settlement and no alimony. I really don't want my husband's money, but my lawyer in New York insisted on negotiating a lump-sum payment."

"Maybe your husband's jealous. Is there another man in the picture?"

Mary's pallor turned to a pink blush. "Of course not!"

"I apologize for having to ask that question, Mary. You say that you can't think of anyone, other than your husband, who's angry with you. I'm simply trying to understand why your husband might be so angry that he'd want to kill you."

"I can't believe that! He's from a prominent family, he's rich, and he's running for Congress. He doesn't want a divorce because he thinks it'll hurt his political career, not because he wants me." A note of bitterness crept into her voice. "He never wanted *me*."

"Have your plans to divorce Garrison been made public yet?"

"No. He wanted me to use my maiden name for the train ticket out here and my stay at the Circle E. I was more than happy to go by Mary Marchetti again, instead of Mary Garrison."

"All right, Mary. I'm sorry if I upset you. I'm going to do my best to get to the bottom of what's going on. In the meantime, we'll post a deputy outside your room to keep you safe."

After Ben left Mary's room, he headed straight to the nursing station and asked to use the phone. He made two calls before he borrowed a chair from an empty room and stationed himself outside the door to Mary's room while he waited for reinforcements. Half an hour later, Virgil appeared. After Ben explained the situation to him, Virgil took over guard duty while Ben went to search for Dr. Kohl.

Ben had a plan, not only to protect Mary, but also to catch a would-be killer, but he knew that he was cutting it close. He only hoped that Harris had been able to convince his editor that a miraculous ending to a near-drowning incident at Pyramid Lake justified the extension of the deadline for the evening newspaper, long enough so that Harris could write the story with all the details that Ben had provided him.

At first, Harris had been reluctant; that is, until Ben promised him an exclusive—a sensational story about a new development in the Beaumont accident case. Ben knew that the coroner couldn't hold his report much longer. Since the coroner's finding of homicide would go public, anyway. Ben didn't see the harm in funneling the information Harris's way before it was officially released. Once tantalized by the prospect of another exclusive, Harris had jumped on the bandwagon, but the reporter couldn't promise his editor's cooperation.

Now Ben needed to put the next step of his plan into motion. He had to convince Dr. Kohl to fudge some paperwork and arrange for an ambulance to transport a patient—one Margery Kaminsky—from Reno Regional Hospital to St. Mary's.

Once Virgil had been briefed, he could accompany Mary on her ambulance ride to St. Mary's and guard her room there after she was moved.

Whether or not the plan worked would depend on Mary's attacker. All Ben could do once he'd set his plan in motion was to wait for the man to strike. He'd arranged for back-up so that he wouldn't be the only law enforcement officer present if the would-be killer took the bait. When he'd called Al from the fourth-floor nursing station, Ben had requested a second deputy to assist him, and once he'd explained the situation to Al, the undersheriff had agreed to send another man to Reno Regional Hospital after visiting hours ended. He'd ask for a volunteer for overtime when the shifts changed, but he told Ben that if nobody volunteered—an unlikely scenario since most of the deputies jumped at the chance to earn some extra pay—he'd assign someone who already had night-shift duty to the job.

Although Ben doubted that the attacker would be bold enough to make a move while the hospital still bustled with activity, he felt relieved when Mary, alias Margery Kaminsky, had been whisked away by ambulance, accompanied by Virgil, to St. Mary's Hospital. Once visiting hours ended, Reno Regional Hospital would lapse into nighttime quiet. During those late-night hours, Ben hoped that the man would try to attack again. If he did, Ben would be ready for him. If not, Ben knew he'd face a difficult task in trying to identify whoever had tried to drown Mary. Now he believed that the same person had been lurking in the crowd outside the Riverside Hotel and Casino when Mary had been pushed into the street. The incident, which she'd brushed off as an unfortunate accident, no longer looked like an accident to Ben. Someone was out to get Mary. He'd come close to succeeding the first time, but since she had survived the fall in front of the taxi, the attacker had tried again. Both times, he'd made what happened look like an accident.

Even if he caught the hit man, Ben knew he'd have only one of the men responsible for trying to murder Mary. Ben thought that Mary's husband was the only logical suspect, but he wouldn't sully his hands by doing the job himself. He'd hire someone to do it for him. Unless Ben caught the attacker and persuaded him to talk, it would be extremely difficult to tie Mary's husband to the attack, and she might still be in danger.

Ben carefully arranged the bed in Mary's former room, stashing a rolled blanket beneath the top sheet so that it appeared as though a woman were lying in the bed. He turned on the light in the tiny bathroom that adjoined Mary's room and cracked the bathroom door just enough so that he could see if anyone entered the room. Ben planned on stationing himself in the tiny closet to wait for the killer.

He'd pulled the shades earlier so that someone who knew Mary's room number couldn't see anything from outside the building. With Dr. Kohl's assistance, Ben had made sure that the hospital's switchboard and receptionist freely gave Mary's room number to anyone who inquired. The night nurses on the fourth floor had also been briefed and warned to steer clear of Mary's room. Restless, Ben paced up and down the hallway before one of the nurses told him that she was going on a break and asked him if he'd like her to bring him some dinner or coffee. He turned down food and drink, instead asking her to bring him a copy of the *Reno Evening Gazette*.

When the nurse returned fifteen minutes later with the newspaper in hand, Ben eagerly scanned the front page, and there it was, a short article, but one with a noticeable, bold headline, about a woman who had almost drowned at Pyramid Lake. According to the article, the victim was recovering in Reno Regional Hospital. Amazed that Cal Harris had persuaded his editor that the story should be on the first page, Ben surmised that Harris must be in the editor's good graces now. He remembered the first time he'd met Harris and how worried the reporter had been because his editor was hounding him. Ben had to hand it to Sheriff Rogers. The man had certainly been right about maintaining good rapport with the press. Almost everybody in Reno read the evening paper. Ben hoped that the man who'd tried to drown Mary wouldn't be an exception.

By nine o'clock, Ben was wondering who Al had sent as back-up and where he was. Al had told Ben that he'd have a deputy report to Ben at the hospital by eight o'clock. Ben was dialing the phone at the nurse's station to check on the deputy's whereabouts, fearing that he might have gone to St. Mary's by mistake, instead of Reno Regional Hospital, when he heard the whine of the elevator, and Carl Overmeyer stepped out. Of all the deputies in the department, Overmeyer was the last one Ben wanted to see, let alone work a stakeout with. Not only was the man a jerk, but, in Ben's opinion, he was a marginally competent law officer.

Ben nodded toward the room where he planned to spend the night, watching the bed where Mary had lain just a few hours earlier.

"In here." He motioned to Overmeyer, who sauntered down the hallway and leisurely entered the room.

"You're late. You were supposed to be here an hour ago."

"What's the big deal? A guy has to eat, doesn't he?"

Ben ignored that comment and proceeded to fill Overmeyer in on the basics of the operation. He didn't bother to go into any details, revealing just enough information so that Overmeyer would know what to do. While Ben lay in wait, hidden in the hospital room's closet, Overmeyer's job consisted of waiting in the vacant room across the hall, observing, and coming to Ben's aid if the hit man showed up.

"Sounds like a waste of time to me," Overmeyer said.

"Nobody asked your opinion. Just go across the hall, keep the light out in there, and do what I told you."

"You're sure getting a big head on you, Cameron. You're not really a detective, you know."

"I don't have time to argue with you. Get on over there!"

Grumbling, Overmeyer went on his way while Ben concealed himself in the tiny closet. He'd placed a chair there earlier so that he wouldn't have to stand up all night while he maintained his vigil. He opened the closet door a couple of inches and positioned himself so that he could see both the door to the room and the bed clearly in the dim light that shone from the bathroom.

Ben waited. Occasionally he heard the low voices of the nurses, and once he started when a patient yelled for a nurse, rather than using the call button. Otherwise, quiet reigned until midnight when the nurses made their rounds, checking on each patient on the floor and dispensing medicine from a rolling cart. Figuring that the killer wouldn't do anything while the nurses were bustling about, Ben took the opportunity to use the bathroom before wedging himself back in the closet. His arms and legs felt stiff from the confinement. He could barely move in the small space, and when he did, he banged into the walls so he forced himself to stay still.

Despite the cramped quarters, it wasn't the most uncomfortable place Ben had ever been forced to lie in wait. That designation would have to go to the many foxholes Ben had occupied in France and Korea. Ben's present dilemma qualified as a cake walk compared to the misery he and his fellow soldiers had suffered, burrowed in the mud, waiting for the enemy to strike.

The nurses finished their rounds, and several more minutes passed. Soon Ben heard snoring and hoped it was coming from one of the patients and not from Overmeyer. More time passed, and Ben began to think about what he would do if the killer didn't show up. It would be extremely difficult to investigate the attempted murder from the New York end, which is where Ben thought it originated, with Mary's husband hiring a hit man. He'd need to involve the New York City Police Department, and he doubted that he'd find much of a spirit of cooperation there, given the political connections that a Congressional candidate was bound to have.

Suddenly, barely audible footsteps alerted Ben, and the door to the room opened slowly. A figure clad in a white lab coat entered, his face hidden in the shadows, and stood still for a minute, orienting himself in the dark. From what Ben could see in the dim light, the light-haired man, a stethoscope dangling from his neck, carried a clipboard, probably in an attempt to look like a doctor. As Ben had hoped, the man didn't reach for the light switch next to the door. Positive that the intruder didn't work for the hospital because Dr. Kohl had designated Room 412 off-limits to all personnel, Ben held his breath and waited for the man's next move.

The man stared at the bed Mary had occupied just a few hours earlier. Reaching into his pocket, he withdrew a syringe and advanced toward the bed. Ben had seen enough. He burst from the closet, intending to tackle the man, but the noise of Ben's chair bumping the closet wall when he jumped to his feet startled the man, and he fled into the hallway, slamming the door in Ben's face. It hit Ben square on the nose, stunning him. He felt a wave of nausea and dizziness as he clung to the door handle in an effort to stay on his feet.

"Overmeyer!" Ben shouted, calling for back-up. "Overmeyer, front and center!"

Ben pulled the door open and looked into the deserted hallway. There was no sign of the intruder, but his calls had alerted the nurses and awakened many of the patients, some of whom wandered into the hallway to find out what the shouting was about.

Ben hadn't heard the familiar whine of the elevator, though, so the man had either secreted himself in one of the patients' rooms on the fourth floor or he'd descended the stairway at the end of the hall. Avoiding the gawkers in the hallway, Ben rushed to the door that led to the stairwell and looked down. Nothing. Then he looked above him, at the steps leading to the upper floors of the hospital. Nothing. Ben realized that by the time he could reach the main floor, the intruder would have had ample opportunity to escape if he'd taken the stairs. He slammed his hand against the wall next to the stairwell. Overmeyer, who was supposed to have been watching from the opposite room, still hadn't made an appearance.

Ben stalked back down the hall and into the room where he'd told Overmeyer to wait. Ben flipped the light switch as he entered, revealing the snoring deputy sprawled on a hospital bed, his mouth open.

Ben moved closer to him and tapped him on the ankle, none too lightly.

"Huh, what?"

"Overmeyer, what the hell do you think you're doing?"

"Guess I must have fallen asleep." The deputy sat up, blinked, and looked at Ben, who glowered back.

"While you were sleeping, our man got away from us. Didn't you hear me calling for you?" Ben asked, realizing what a stupid question it was. Obviously, Overmeyer had slept through the entire incident, instead of watching the door to the room Ben had staked out for unauthorized visitors. "You don't deserve to wear that badge."

"Hey, you're not gonna report me, are you? Anybody can make a mistake."

Solely tempted though he was to report that Overmeyer had been sleeping while on duty and may have been responsible for the failure of the stakeout, Ben felt just as guilty for letting the killer get away from him. He should have blocked the door, preventing the man from exiting, instead of trying to jump him.

"You're a sorry excuse for a lawman," Ben said, deliberately leaving Overmeyer's question unanswered. It wouldn't hurt to have Overmeyer's foul-up to hold over his head. "I want you to search every room on this floor. Now!"

Ben stood in the hall and watched while Overmeyer entered each room in turn, and exited a few minutes later. When he finished, Overmeyer looked at Ben and shrugged.

"Get out of my sight," Ben said in disgust.

Overmeyer didn't waste any time hightailing it to the elevator. A few seconds later, Ben could hear the elevator doors open and close, as the deputy left the floor. After repeating the same search that Overmeyer had just conducted, Ben returned to Room 412. A cursory glance around showed nothing out of place, but when Ben bent down to peer under the hospital bed, he saw the syringe the killer had dropped when Ben surprised him by jumping out of the closet.

Ben left the syringe under the bed while he went to the nurses' station and asked the night supervisor, a woman in her sixties with gray hair peeking out from under her white nurse's cap, for an envelope.

"Deputy, I hope we're not going to have any more disruptions tonight." The buttons of her white uniform strained across her ample breasts as she put her hands on her hips. "My patients need their rest."

"Sorry, ma'am. Unfortunately, the man I was hoping to trap got away. I'll be clearing out of here in a few minutes. By the way, the man wore a white lab coat and carried a stethoscope as a disguise. I'll be checking with hospital security and maintenance to let them know I'm looking for those items. Could you notify me if you or any of your nursing staff come across them?"

"All right, deputy," she said, handing him a large brown envelope.

Ben returned to Room 412, scooped up the syringe without touching it, and sealed the envelope. If he ever succeeded in finding the man who had brandished it and if there were any fingerprints on the syringe, they could be used as evidence, although Ben believed that the chances of that happening were slim.

On his way out, Ben contacted the head custodian, who promised to relay Ben's request to be on the lookout for a stray lab coat and stethoscope. Tired and discouraged, Ben drove home, hoping to catch a few hours' sleep. If not for his own ineptness, he might have caught the man who had tried to drown Mary, and he mentally kicked himself all the way to his apartment. The realization that his plan still might have worked had Overmeyer not slept through the entire incident didn't make it any easier to swallow, but disgusted as he was at Overmeyer's failure, he felt even more disappointed at his own.

Chapter 18

"The doctor's going to let me check out of here in a few hours. I called Shirley to bring me some clothes, and she's going to drive me back to the Circle E."

"I'm not sure that's a good idea, Mary. You're still in danger." Ben had filled Mary in on the killer's appearance in Room 412 the night before. "What's to prevent the same man from trying to attack you at the Circle E?"

"I feel safe at the ranch, deputy, with Carol and Chuck and the girls. Besides, I don't have any other place to go. My room's paid in advance, and I'm afraid that I'm getting a little low on cash."

"I'm sure we could make some arrangements for you," Ben said, although he wasn't at all sure how far the department could go in trying to protect Mary. As far as he knew, they hadn't dealt with a similar situation.

"No, no. I'll be fine. You forget, deputy. I've seen the next world, and I'm not afraid to go there."

"Don't take this lightly, Mary. That man who sneaked into your room last night came for one deadly reason—to end your life."

"I'm sorry, deputy. I know you're trying to do your job, and I'm not making it any easier, but really don't you think I'll be safe at the ranch?"

"I wish I knew. What I do know is that whoever attacked you will be back. He's already made three attempts."

"Three?"

"The accident you had in front of the Riverside, pulling you under water at the lake, and showing up with a lethal syringe at the hospital."

Mary frowned. "I guess I hadn't put that together. So you think someone pushed me in front of the cab?"

"I'd bet on it."

"Woo hoo! I brought your clothes." Holding a garment bag folded over her arm, Shirley burst into Mary's room, followed by Carol, who rushed to Mary and gingerly gave her a hug.

"Oh, Mary, we're so glad you're all right." Carol stood back and stared at the large bandage on the right side of Mary's forehead and the purple bruise that extended beyond the bandage. "You gave everyone quite a scare yesterday."

"Thanks for coming." Mary's voice caught in a sob. "It's so nice of both of you."

"Here's your yellow sundress and your sandals." Shirley shot a look at Ben, who took the hint and asked to speak to Carol out in the hallway.

As soon as the door closed, Shirley said, "Of course, I brought undies, too. I didn't want to say anything in front of the deputy. He seems so serious, but he's kind of cute, don't you think?"

Mary giggled. She admired Shirley's lighthearted approach to life. "I guess so," she agreed. "Now that you mention it, he does look a little bit like a young Gary Cooper."

"Let's get you dressed now and back to the ranch. Staying in the hospital's such a drag. How come they moved you to St. Mary's, anyway?"

Mary shrugged. "Doctor's orders." Ben had cautioned her not to discuss the murder attempts or the reason for her transfer from Reno Regional to St. Mary's with anyone, not even her family members or close friends. "Back in a second."

Mary slipped into the bathroom that adjoined her small private hospital room. Two private rooms at two different hospitals—she knew that would cost a pretty penny. She'd meant it when she'd told Ben that her funds were dwindling. She'd been far too extravagant on the shopping trips that she and Shirley had taken, and she'd need to cut back severely, or she'd run out of money before her day in divorce court. She knew that her parents would wire her money if she needed it, and she'd be able to pay them back from the small settlement she would receive from her husband, but Mary thought that she'd already put her parents through too much grief as matters stood. When she returned to New York, she planned on going home to live with them, and she also planned to insist that they accept rent money from her. As soon as she arrived in the city, she'd start searching for a job so that she could pay her own way.

Mary, who'd told Shirley that she didn't know what she'd do after her divorce, realized that she actually did have a plan, if only she lived long enough to put it into action.

Chapter 19

Ben opened the door of Carol's wood-paneled station wagon for Mary, and she slid into the back seat.

"Take care," he said as he closed the door and stepped back onto the sidewalk outside St. Mary's Hospital, hoping that Mary would stay safe at the ranch. He'd confided to Carol that Mary could be in danger, and he'd asked her to keep a close eye on her guest and to report any strangers who might show up at the ranch.

He'd winced at the sight of the yellow bruises on Mary's arms and legs, as if the large bandage covering the gash on her forehead weren't enough. The poor girl! Nobody deserved such treatment, and although he suspected that Mary's husband wanted her out of the picture permanently, Ben still had a hard time thinking of Mary as a killer's target. She had a sterling quality about her. He thought about that quality, trying to pin it down. Self-possession, maybe. A kind of innocence and modesty, certainly. But it was more. Mary was good, good in an almost holy, other-worldly way.

Shaking off his reverie, Ben decided to turn his attention to another case for a few hours. He intended to swing by the Saturday flea market, where vendors paid a small fee to set up in a large field south of the city limits. That put the flea market in the Washoe County Sheriff's jurisdiction, and Ben had directed traffic and patrolled the area more than a few times since he'd joined the sheriff's department. He jumped into his pickup, headed out of the hospital parking lot, drove east on Fourth Street, and turned right, onto Virginia Street. Driving through downtown, under Reno's "Biggest Little City in the World" arch, he proceeded south several miles until he came to the flea market. He pulled off, parked on the side of the road, and hiked half a mile to the field, where the vendors had set up.

He stopped near the entrance and bought a bottle of Coke and a couple of hot dogs, which he slathered with mustard and pickle relish, from one of the food vendors. Sitting at a picnic table in front of the vendor's booth, Ben pulled out his notebook and reviewed the list of missing property from the burglary he'd investigated the day before. Then he checked his notes on other hot-sheet items that had been reported stolen in the county during the past week. Satisfied that he had a pretty good idea of what to look for, Ben ate the hot dogs, washing them down with Coke, and began his trek through the flea market, starting on the right side and working his way up and down the grassy aisles. The flea market was laid out in a grid pattern. Vendors set up back-to-back, in long rows, with wide grassy aisles providing plenty of space for shoppers. Some of the vendors used tents, others had tables, and still others, like the food vendors, had permanent structures that served as mini-stores. A few simply put out their wares on blankets or on the grass, in hopes that a passerby would stop to make a purchase.

After an hour of working the area, Ben spotted some tools and several tabletop radios laid out on a khaki army blanket. As he approached, he could see that a few rifles and a case containing watches and jewelry were sitting on a card table in back of the blanket. A young man with greasy hair and tattooed arms sat next to the table in a red canvas lawn chair.

"Help ya, mister?"

"Could I take a look at that rifle?" Ben pointed to the weapon that lay on the back of the card table.

"This one?" Ben nodded, and the greasy-haired man handed the rifle to Ben. "She's a beauty, ain't she? A Winchester model '94 .30-.30—just what you want for big game."

Ben examined the rifle and saw that it matched the description of one of the missing guns that the vacationing homeowner had reported stolen the day before. Still holding the Winchester, he leaned over the table for a closer look at the other rifles.

"How much for the Winchester?"

"Well, now. . ." The vendor stood and paused, scratching his chin.

"I'm looking for a deal." Ben laid the rifle next to the others on the card table. "What's your best price?"

"OK, mister. I'd take $100."

"I bet you would," Ben said grabbing the man's right wrist and spinning him around so that Ben could grab his other wrist, too. Ben snapped on handcuffs before the man realized what was happening. "You're under arrest."

"Hey, mister, who the hell do you think you are?"

"I'm the deputy sheriff who's arresting you; that's who I am."

"I ain't done nothin'."

"Save it for the judge. Right now you're going to jail."

Several passersby had stopped to watch the action, and since he wouldn't be able to load his prisoner in his pickup along with all the stolen property displayed, he'd need some help. As he looked at the crowd, hoping to spot someone he knew, Ben saw a barrel-chested, middle-aged man pushing his way through. From his picture on the flea market sign, Ben recognized him as Jake Johnson, the organizer of the flea market.

"What's going on here?"

Ben flashed his badge. "Washoe County Deputy Sheriff Ben Cameron, sir. This man's under arrest. He's selling stolen property."

"Good lord!" Johnson turned toward the crowd. "Move along, folks. It's all over. Move along now." As the crowd slowly dispersed, Johnson looked at Ben. "Not too good for business. Can I help you get him out of here, deputy?"

"Sure thing. I could use some help. My pickup's parked at least half a mile down the road, and I'm going to have to confiscate all this merchandise as evidence. If you could keep an eye on everything, I'll take the prisoner to my truck and then drive back here to load up."

"Will do."

"Appreciate it."

It took Ben over three hours to walk the sullen man with the dirty hair back to his pickup, return to stow the stolen property in the bed of the pickup, question his prisoner, fill out paperwork, deposit the thief at the jail, and log the stolen property into the evidence room, a cubbyhole off the hallway that led to the sheriff's office fitted with shelves running from floor to ceiling. Although the man hadn't admitted to any burglaries, his story about selling the merchandise for his sick grandfather didn't hold up, and Ben believed that he'd confess to his thefts before his case ever went to trial. As Ben logged in each item, he ticked it off his hot sheet or the list in his notebook. All in all, he'd cleared four burglary cases with one arrest—not a bad afternoon's work and especially satisfying since he hadn't made any real progress on either Mary's case or the Beaumont case.

Ben poured himself a cup of muddy coffee, dumped in an ample amount of cream, and drank a swig. Despite the addition of cream, the coffee tasted terrible. He set it down on the desk and reached for the messages that peeked out from under Carmine's large black ceramic ashtray. Carmine's love of a good Cuban cigar hadn't endeared him to Anita, who coughed every time he lit one, although none of the sheriff's deputies had ever objected. From what Ben had heard, Carmine's doctor had forbidden his patient to smoke anymore, but, as a smoker himself, Ben knew how difficult it would be to give up the habit. Thinking about Carmine and his cigars reminded Ben that he hadn't smoked himself for a couple of hours. He pulled out his pack of Lucky Strikes, tapped out a cigarette, lit it, and inhaled a deep drag while he looked at the messages—two from the homeowner who'd reported his rifles and tools missing and one from the head custodian at Reno Regional Hospital.

Ben returned the burglary victim's phone call first. The man explained that he stored a few old tools in a metal tool box in his basement, and he had discovered that they had also been stolen, along with the tool box, although he hadn't realized it when he'd first reported the theft to Ben. When Ben heard the description of the tools, he knew that at least a couple of them had been among the items displayed at the flea market and now sitting in the evidence room. Ben told the homeowner that he'd located most of his stolen property.

"You found it? Already? Well, I'll be. . ."

"Yes, sir. We were lucky."

"More than luck involved, if I don't miss my guess. That's great work, young fella. When can I get everything back?"

"Depends on the disposition of the case. Could be a couple of days or a couple of months. We may have to hold onto the stolen property for evidence at trial or the district attorney may ask you to swear out an affidavit. The case may not even go to trial if we can get a confession."

"OK, young fella. Guess I'll have to be patient for a while longer. You tell your boss he's got a fine deputy. I sure do thank you."

"Just doing my job, sir." Ben meant what he said, but, even so, he appreciated receiving kudos from a citizen of Washoe County.

Despite his failure to capture Mary's attacker in the early-morning hours, Ben felt that he'd at least accomplished something worthwhile in this day's work

Next he called the hospital and asked for the head custodian. After waiting on hold for several minutes, Ben finally connected with the custodian, who told him that he'd found a large brown paper grocery bag wedged behind the hospital's dumpster. He'd noticed it because the end of a stethoscope was peeking out of the top of the paper bag, which someone had twisted in an attempt to close.

Ben told the custodian that he'd come to pick up the bag right away. He doubted that it would contain anything other than the white lab coat and the stethoscope, but if he apprehended Mary's attacker, those items could be used as evidence, along with the syringe Ben had recovered from under the bed.

As soon as he arrived at Reno Regional, Ben asked the receptionist who presided over the lobby to page the head custodian. When he showed up at the reception desk a few minutes later carrying the brown bag, Ben took possession of it and asked the custodian whether any of his staff had noticed someone discarding it.

"Nope. I just happened to see it because I moved the dumpster. It looked like what you said you were searching for last night, so I hung onto it and called you."

"Have you opened the bag?"

"Nope. That's just the way I found it. Like I told you on the phone, part of that stethoscope was hanging out of the top there." The custodian yawned, and Ben noticed that he had dark circles under his eyes.

"I appreciate your help. I'm surprised you're still here this evening. Kind of a long day, wasn't it?"

"Yup, and it's not over yet. I'm doing a double shift to cover for one of my guys who called in sick. Being a supervisor's not all it's cracked up to be, let me tell you. Well, I better get back to it."

As the custodian returned to his duties, Ben saw Dr. Kohl getting off an elevator. The doctor spotted Ben at the same time and hailed him.

"Deputy, the nurses tell me that you had a visitor last night."

"I'm afraid so. I could kick myself for letting him escape. I tried to tackle him, but he got away. He'd disguised himself as a doctor, dressed in a white lab coat like the one you're wearing with a stethoscope draped around his neck. In fact, the head custodian may have found what he wore. I just picked up this bag from him."

"Mind if I take a look? I might be able to tell whether the coat and stethoscope belong to the hospital."

"Sure thing." Ben hadn't tried to preserve any fingerprints that might have been left on the bag, not only because the custodian had handled it but also because he knew that its rough surface made the chances of getting identifiable fingerprints very low. Ben untwisted the top and, using a handkerchief, lifted out a stethoscope and a white lab coat. Handing them to the doctor, Ben cautioned him not to touch the stethoscope itself. He upended the bag and out dropped something that looked like a small, furry animal. Ben bent to pick it up, holding the thing gingerly. He turned it over in his hand and realized that it was a toupee. Curled on the hairless side of the rug, Ben found a stretchy, thin cap.

In the meantime, Dr. Kohl examined the other items. "Both of these came from our Pediatrics Department. See." He pointed to labels on both the coat and the stethoscope. "Your night visitor must have lifted these from one of the doctors' lockers."

"I found something else, too. I guess someone would notice if he was missing this." Ben held up the hairpiece, and the doctor chuckled.

"You're right, but I can tell you for sure that it doesn't belong to any of our doctors. Anyone wearing a rug around here would be laughed right out of the hospital." The doctor paused. "What's that?" Dr. Kohl asked. "Looks like a bathing cap."

"Yes, but a lot thinner. It must go under the toupee. Whoever sneaked into Room 412 last night sure wanted to disguise himself."

"I find it incredible that someone would want to kill that poor girl. She's just a little slip of a thing—I can't imagine anyone wanting to hurt her. Dr. Davis, over at St. Mary's, told me that he released her this afternoon. I hope she'll be safe."

"So do I, doctor. So do I."

Chapter 20

Mary knelt on the wooden prayer bench, worn smooth by the knees of thousands of supplicants over the years. The previous Sunday, her first in Reno, she'd attended Mass at St. Thomas Aquinas Cathedral on Second Street, sitting in the same pew a few rows from the back of the church, while Chuck had waited for her outside. The large crucifix behind the altar, the colorful mural depicting Biblical scenes, the life-sized replica of Michelangelo's Pieta, and the stained-glass windows all added to a sense of Catholic familiarity that Mary experienced the minute she entered the cathedral.

Although beauty surrounded her, Mary felt much more troubled than she had just a day earlier. She'd tried to downplay the accidents she'd had. She'd even told herself and others that she didn't fear death, but, despite her glimpse of what she thought was heaven, now that she'd come back, she wanted to stay. If only for an hour, she'd wanted to forget her worries, safe in church, but even that hope was dashed when Deputy Cameron had insisted on accompanying her, rather than letting Chuck drive her to and from the cathedral.

The deputy sat directly behind Mary, and although he'd told her to ignore him and pretend that he wasn't there, she found that her awareness of his watchfulness interfered with her prayerful concentration. She also felt embarrassed to be one of the few worshipers who did not go forward to take communion. It was obvious to Mary that the deputy wasn't a Catholic—he hadn't crossed himself on entering the sanctuary, nor had he kneeled in the aisle before seating himself—but, even so, he must have wondered why she didn't heed the call to communion.

When the Mass ended, the white-robed priest made his way down the aisle to the back of the church. A loud burst of organ music sounded as light from the door he'd opened shone inside, and Mary could see that the priest had stationed himself directly outside the front door of the cathedral, so that he could greet the parishioners as they filed out. Mary rose and joined the congregants surging toward the door. Ben followed close behind her. When they reached the narthex, Mary veered to the left, opening a side door, and exited, bypassing the priest at the front.

For Mass, Mary had dressed in a way that wouldn't call attention to her bruises. She wanted to be as inconspicuous as possible. She'd replaced the large bandage from the hospital with a smaller, less noticeable one, and, with Shirley's help, she'd trimmed her hair so that she now had bangs that covered the bandage. She'd carefully brushed the bangs into just the right position on her forehead before putting on her little white hat. The jacket of the aqua silk shantung suit she wore had long sleeves that totally concealed the bruises on her arms. To hide her other bruises, she'd applied foundation and powder to her legs, then donned her light-tan silk stockings. She never would have thought of using make-up on her legs if Carol hadn't told her about how she'd used leg make-up, rather than wearing hosiery, during World War II, when a shortage of silk, nylon, and rayon made sheer stockings almost impossible to buy. By the time Mary had pulled on her white cotton gloves, slipped into her white leather pumps, and picked up her small white purse, she'd decided that she'd done a good job of covering up her bruises so that she'd remain inconspicuous among the worshipers.

However, dressed as she was, gracefully getting into the deputy's pickup truck had proven impossible, and she'd wished that she hadn't agreed to his suggestion that he should drive her to church. He'd called a few hours after she left the hospital to plead with her not to leave the ranch. When she'd told him that she planned to attend Mass and that Chuck would take her, as he'd done the previous Sunday, the deputy insisted on doing it himself, saying that he was better equipped to protect her. When he'd called for her at the ranch, she'd struggled to get into his truck, finally hoisting her narrow skirt and pulling herself up, to swing into the seat. The deputy had offered to assist her, but she'd already felt awkward, and she'd refused.

Now after Mass, as they walked toward his truck, parked a block from the cathedral, she wished that she didn't have to repeat the ungainly maneuver again, but this time, the deputy solved the problem by producing a wooden crate from his truck bed and placing it beside the open passenger door. He held out his hand to help her balance, and she was able to climb into the truck without another embarrassing performance.

"Oh, thank you!"

"You're welcome." Ben grinned. "I should have realized what a big step that is for a little lady."

"No wonder you didn't realize what a big step it is for me. You must be about seven feet tall," she said as Ben settled himself behind the wheel.

"About six and a half, actually." Ben started the motor. "Would you join me for breakfast, Mary? I haven't had my morning coffee yet, and there's a new place in Sparks I'd like to try."

"Well, I don't know. . ."

"Have you already had breakfast?"

"No, just coffee."

"Well, how about it, then? You're not going to let us starve, are you?"

"No, I guess not." Mary smiled. "Do you always get your way, deputy? You're very persistent."

"Not always, and please call me Ben."

"All right, Ben." Mary wasn't too sure that she felt comfortable calling the deputy by his first name, but she knew he'd given up his day off because of her, and she didn't want to seem rude. The deputy had surprised her with his teasing, especially since he'd always seemed to be a serious guy, and she'd surprised herself by responding to his banter.

The Nugget occupied a spot on a corner of B Street, not too far away from the railroad tracks, in downtown Sparks, a small town that bordered the east side of Reno. A large sign with a curved arrow announcing CAFÉ pointed downward, to the Nugget sign. Inside, the busy restaurant bustled with waitresses hurrying about, serving customers. The clink of coins from slot machines that were paying off sounded above the customers' conversations and the clatter of dishes.

"Slot machines in a coffee shop?" Mary asked after they'd been seated and placed their orders. Mary hadn't seen the one-armed bandits anywhere in Reno except in the casinos.

"That's Nevada for you."

"Are you a native, Ben?"

"No, I'm from California—Placerville, a little town in the foothills of the Sierras not too far from Sacramento. It's about 130 miles from Reno. My family still lives there, and I visit every couple of months, when I have a few days off."

A wave of homesickness surged over Mary as Ben spoke, and she closed her eyes as she thought about her own family. She struggled to hold back her tears, but one drop escaped and rolled down her cheek. She hastily dabbed it with a paper napkin, but when she looked up, Ben's panic-stricken gaze told her that he had noticed and that, like most men, he hated to see a woman cry.

"Sorry," she whispered.

"You have nothing to apologize for, Mary. In fact, after everything you've been through, I'd say you're a real trooper."

"Here we are." Their waitress set their plates in front of them, poured them both another cup of coffee, and hurried off as quickly as she'd arrived.

Ben looked at his breakfast—a chicken-fried steak, three scrambled eggs, a couple of slices of toast, and two side orders of hash browns—and then at Mary's. She'd ordered a poached egg on toast. He shook his head in mock distress.

"That's hardly enough to keep a bird alive."

Mary smiled, knowing that she could never eat a meal the size of Ben's. "I'm not very hungry."

"Well, I'm famished," Ben said, digging in with relish. "A bowl of soup for dinner doesn't quite make the grade."

A few minutes later, a dapper man not much taller than Mary approached. Dressed in a charcoal gray suit, a white shirt, and a striped tie, he'd been circulating around the coffee shop, stopping to chat with customers at each table.

"How is everything, folks?" he inquired.

Mary glanced at Ben, who'd just shoveled a huge bite of steak into his mouth. "Wonderful!" she said, as Ben swallowed and looked at her gratefully.

"Glad to hear it."

"It looks as though business is booming," Ben said.

"It's been good," the man agreed. "Come back and see us again."

"We'll do that," Ben said.

"He must be the owner," Mary speculated when the man had gone on to the next table.

"He's the manager, but, according to our undersheriff, he's a real dynamo. With his drive, he probably will own his own place someday. His name's John Ascuaga."

"An unusual last name."

"It's Basque."

"What's that? I've never heard of it."

"Basques are people who come from a mountain area that's partly in Spain and partly in France. There are quite a few of them in Nevada. Mostly, they're sheepherders, but there are lots of Basque restaurants and hotels around the state, too. I'd never heard of Basques, either, until I signed on here as a deputy sheriff a couple of years ago."

"I guess there's more to Nevada than just a place to go to get a divorce. I should have paid more attention in Sister Anne's geography class."

"I probably should have paid more attention in all my classes. All I cared about in high school was playing baseball."

"As tall as you are, I pegged you for a basketball player."

"I played basketball, too, but baseball's my game. I was just an average player, though, not big-league material."

"So, you're a baseball fan."

"Big fan of the Yankees. I wish we had a big-league team on the West Coast, though. I might just have to switch my loyalty."

"The Yankees? You mean the Dodgers, don't you?"

"No, ma'am. I do not!"

They both laughed at Ben's vehemence. She was beginning to see a different side of the deputy, a human side. Granted, he took his job very seriously, but his badge didn't completely define him.

And, as Shirley had said, he was kind of cute in a Gary-Cooper-in-*High-Noon* kind of way.

Chapter 21

"Well, if it ain't the wanted man," Overmeyer said, as Ben entered the office on Monday morning.

Ben glared at him. He had half a mind to report that Overmeyer had been sleeping on duty Friday night.

"What's he talking about?" Ben asked Anita, as she returned from the break room.

"Oh, Ben, I'm glad you're here. Everybody's been looking for you. I put all your messages on Carmine's desk."

"I didn't see them."

Anita frowned, as she searched the top of the desk. "I know I put them right here, right under the ashtray, like I always do."

"This what you're looking for?" Overmeyer asked in a mincing tone as he held up several slips of paper. "You want 'em, Cameron, come and get 'em."

Ben grabbed the messages out of Overmeyer's hand, ripping a couple of them in the process. "I told you once, and I'll tell you again: get out of my sight." Ben's tone left little doubt as to the consequences that would follow if Overmeyer didn't comply, and the deputy bolted from the office, slamming the door as he left.

"Wow," Anita said. "I wonder why he backed down."

Ben shrugged. He knew that he'd have to have it out with

Overmeyer, once and for all, but he had too much work to do today to give it much thought. He'd just begun glancing at the messages when Al and several deputies came in.

"Great bust Saturday, Ben," the undersheriff said. "I see from your report that the guy you arrested burglarized several houses."

"Yeah, we have all the evidence we'll need to put him away. He was set up at the flea market, trying to sell all kinds of stuff that he'd stolen—everything from rifles to diamond rings. He claimed that he was selling it for his grandfather, but it all matches descriptions we have for property reported stolen right here in Washoe County. Some of the tools even have the owner's name engraved on them, and the guy still denied stealing them."

"It sounds like he's not exactly a criminal mastermind. Maybe a few years in the state pen will make him realize that he's not cut out for a life of crime. Say, Ben, let's go back to my office for a minute."

Ben followed Al down the hallway, into his office. Leaving the door open, Al gestured for Ben to take a seat.

"I was sorry to hear that you weren't able to apprehend your man at the hospital stakeout Friday night."

"Yeah, I blew it." Ben held up his right hand, indicating half an inch between his thumb and his forefinger. "I was this close to catching the guy who tried to drown Miss Marchetti. I'm sure he's the same man who pushed her into the street, too."

"I take it Overmeyer wasn't much help."

"Not much," Ben said glumly, not trusting himself to say more on that subject. "Al, I'm really worried about that young woman. I'm not at all convinced she's safe at the Circle E."

"The attacks both took place away from the ranch, right?"

"Right. So far, anyway. I suggested she move because whoever's after her obviously knows where she's staying, but she says she's low on money and can't afford it. She's all paid up for her six weeks' stay at the Circle E. Don't we have any kind of a contingency fund that we could use to help her out?"

Al rubbed his chin. "Well, there's the Sheriff's Benevolent Fund, but there's only about a hundred bucks in it right now. We usually use it to help out for emergencies and scholarships for deputies' kids."

"Nothing in the regular budget to cover something like this, I suppose."

"No, I'm afraid not."

"I told her to stay at the ranch, and I asked the owners to keep an eye on her and let me know if they saw any strangers lurking around the place, but this guy's bold. He just might try something there, especially when he realizes that she's staying put. I'll check in on her every day, but I can't be there all the time."

"No, you can't, and we don't have the manpower to offer her round-the-clock protection. I don't like it, but that's the way it is."

Anita poked her head in the door. "Sorry to interrupt, but there's a man on the phone demanding to speak to Ben right away. He wouldn't give me his name, and he wouldn't take no for an answer."

"You can transfer the call in here, Anita." Al pushed his black desk phone toward Ben as Anita returned to her desk. When the buzzer rang, Ben picked up the receiver.

"Deputy Cameron."

"Cameron, this is Adrian Beaumont. I've left several messages for you. Why the hell didn't you call me back?"

Puzzled, Ben said, "I'm sorry, Mr. Beaumont, but I didn't get any messages from you."

"Damned inefficient office you have over there, but I don't have time to argue. Phyllis and I are on our way to Nairobi. We're at the airport right now. I'm calling to give you a heads-up to expect a letter with a check in it for Candice Martin's funeral expenses. Phyllis feels bad about the accident, even though it wasn't her fault. And,

Cameron, I made the check out to you. Take care of it, will you?" Before Ben had a chance to reply, Beaumont continued. "And you can dispose of the clothes Phyllis lent Candice, too. Throw them out, donate them, give them away—I don't care."

Ben heard a click as the line went dead. Beaumont had hung up without waiting for a response from Ben.

"What an ass!" Ben told Al what Beaumont had said. "He may be a big Hollywood director, and he's obviously used to giving orders and getting his own way, but I don't work for him."

"You gonna return the check?"

Ben sighed. "No, I'm sure the Martin family can use the help. Candice's body is still at the morgue here. The family hasn't been able to raise the money to transport her body back to Southern California for burial yet. I'd like to endorse the check over to the Sheriff's Benevolent Fund as soon as it comes in, and we can disperse the payment through the fund if that's all right with you."

"That's fine, Ben." Al nodded in approval. "Maybe you could check with Anita about donating the clothes. She'll know what to do."

"OK. Uh, Al . . . maybe she'd like to have the fur and the beaded bag herself. Beaumont said we could give the stuff away."

"You're not sweet on Anita, are you, Ben?" Al teased.

"That's not it, Al," Ben protested a little too vehemently. "But I can sure see how someone would be. Anyway, she works hard, she's all alone—a widow with kids to support—and she's always willing to help out. If it weren't for Anita, my reports would never get typed."

Al laughed. "She's a good gal. Sure, I don't see why not. Why don't you call her in here right now, while I go retrieve them from Mark's office?"

Anita had just answered the phone, and another line was ringing when Ben went to her desk. He signaled Virgil, who had just come back from the jail after depositing a prisoner.

"Could you man the phone lines for a few minutes, Virgil? Al wants to see Anita in his office."

"Sure, Ben."

Anita looked startled at the request. "I'll be right there," she told Ben, as she pulled her handbag out of a desk drawer, drew out a small round compact, and hastily dabbed some powder on her nose.

By the time Anita came into Al's office, he had placed the silver stole on top of his desk.

Al explained that they'd like her to handle the arrangements for donating Phyllis Beaumont's clothing.

"Oh, sure. Any particular charity you have in mind?"

"No, we'll leave that up to you," Ben said.

Anita looked at the fur. "Is that stole part of the donation?"

"No, it's yours if you want it," Ben said.

"Seriously?"

"Yes, ma'am. What do you say?"

Anita lifted the fur from the desktop and cradled it. She stroked the soft fur as though she were petting a cat. "What a beautiful mink." Tears sprang to her eyes. "I've never had anything so gorgeous!"

"Try it on," Ben said, taking the fur and draping it over her shoulders. She hugged it close and twirled around.

"You'll want to have your own monogram in the lining," Al told her. "Take it to Gray Reid and tell them you're with the Sheriff's Department. It'll all be arranged."

"Thank you so much!" Anita's eyes twinkled with excitement.

"We'd like you to have this, too." Ben picked up the beaded clutch and handed it to Anita, who looked at it closely.

"Oh, my goodness. What exquisite glass beads, and they're so tiny!" She opened the purse and peeked inside, peering at the tags attached to the white silk lining. "Made in France, Hand Made," she read. "Freddy, 10 Rue Auber – Paris, Tel.Ric 78-08."

"I guess that's good," Al said.

"The very best!" Anita beamed. "I can't thank you enough, both of you."

"What was that you told Anita about the monogram, Al?" Ben asked, after Anita had gone back to her desk.

"Gray Reid has a fur salon. I bought my wife a coat there a couple of years ago. That's how I know about the monograms. There was a twenty-dollar bill left in this purse. I'm going to use it to arrange for Anita to get her own monogram."

"That never would have occurred to me."

"It would if you were married, especially if you'd been married as long as I have."

"How long have you been married, Al?"

"Forty-two years, although sometimes it seems like a thousand." Al sighed deeply and then grinned. "Just kidding. You ought to be thinking about getting hitched yourself."

"Yeah, maybe," Ben mumbled.

"You could do worse than Anita."

"Kind of a left-handed compliment, isn't it, Al? Any man would be lucky to have Anita as his wife."

The undersheriff raised his eyebrows and smiled.

"Well, I better get back to it," Ben said. "I need to run up to Tahoe to clear up some loose ends."

On the drive up the mountain, Ben thought about the contribution toward Candice Martin's funeral expenses that Adrian Beaumont had promised. He had a hard time believing that the flighty Phyllis cared much about Candice's death, and evidently her husband shared her view. Ben remembered that he'd made a point of saying that the accident wasn't Phyllis's fault, but he'd also stated that

Phyllis felt bad about it. Could her conscience have given her a twinge? With Phyllis, Ben could never tell. He always had the feeling that she was acting. Now she'd left for Africa with her husband, the very man who may have hired someone to kill her; that is, if Phyllis, not Candice, had been the intended accident victim.

Although he was on his way to question the few employees of the Cal Neva he'd missed during his last trip to Lake Tahoe—the ones he hadn't been able to contact by phone in the meantime—he doubted that any of them could add much to what he already knew about Candice's visit to the casino. It had been almost two weeks since the fatal accident, and even if the employees had observed something significant, they might have forgotten it by now. The thought of possible leads, no matter how slim, going unexplored pushed Ben to follow up, rather than the hope that one of those leads might pan out.

Ben had called Paul Knudson to confirm that the employees he wanted to question were on duty, and he went straight to the security chief's office as soon as he arrived at the Cal Neva. The first two people he questioned didn't recall seeing Candice Martin, but Ben hit pay dirt with the third, a waitress who'd been serving drinks in the showroom the evening that Candice Martin had visited the Cal Neva. Not only did the waitress remember the blond woman in the glitzy silver evening gown, but she also remembered the man who had joined her several times during the evening.

"So she stayed for the first two shows, you say?"

"Yeah, I remember she left right before the late-late show started. She'd been in the showroom for hours by then, drinking nothing but ginger ale the whole time." The perky waitress fluffed her hair, tossed her head, and pulled a blue-and-black package from her apron pocket. She popped a stick of Black Jack chewing gum into her mouth before offering Ben a stick. He shook his head. He seldom chewed gum, and he'd never developed a taste for the licorice-flavored stuff.

"Can you describe the man she was with?"

"Sure. Handsome guy. Tall, but not as tall as you are. Maybe six feet. Dark hair. Black, I think."

"Did the two of them seem to be getting along?"

"Yeah, real cozy, if you ask me. But they squabbled some, too."

"Could you hear what they were saying?"

"Nah, every time I came around, they got real quiet. Well, she did, anyway. He was kind of loud after he'd had a few." The waitress cracked her gum as if to emphasize her point. "He was drinking martinis. I don't know how he was able to keep playing by the second show, but he did."

"What? He was in the show?"

"Yeah, didn't I tell you that? He was in the band—played clarinet, I think."

"Do you remember the name of the band?"

"Nah. It was a one-night stand. The showroom manager would know. He books all the acts."

Ben lost no time tracking down the showroom manager, who checked his records and told Ben that the band playing the evening of Candice Martin's visit to the Cal Neva showroom was the Les Brady Band, on a tour of several Western states. The name sounded familiar. Ben checked his notes and confirmed that Candice Martin's boyfriend, Billy Littleton, was a clarinet player with the band. Ben asked the showroom manager for the name of the band's booking agent in Hollywood so that he could track down Littleton.

Ben felt almost elated as he drove back down Mount Rose. At last, he thought he'd developed a solid lead in the Beaumont case. Or maybe he should start calling it the Martin case because, after what he'd learned, he had good reason to believe that Candice Martin, rather than Phyllis Beaumont, had been the intended victim of the accident, after all. During one of the band's breaks, Littleton could have slipped out into the parking lot and tampered with the Cadillac's brakes. According to Virgil, it wouldn't have taken very long for someone who knew what he was doing to rig the brakes to fail. Ben had no idea whether or not Billy Littleton knew anything about auto mechanics, but he should be able to find out. As for Littleton's motive, perhaps he wanted to rekindle his relationship with Candice, but she had other ideas, maybe a new man in her life. Love or the loss of love could be a powerful motive. This murder hadn't involved heat-of-the-moment passion, but rather cold, calculating, ice-water-in-the-veins planning. The thought of it sent shivers up Ben's spine.

Chapter 22

Mary swam slowly across the shallow end of the pool, Shirley at her side. She'd been reluctant to get back into the water after the incident at Pyramid Lake, but now she felt safe with Shirley shadowing her every move in the water and several other poolside guests watching them. Even Carol, who didn't usually linger by the swimming pool, was there, sitting in a white deck chair, an umbrella shading her as she embroidered an elaborate yellow rose onto a new gray Western shirt. From the moment she'd returned to the Circle E on Saturday afternoon, Mary had noticed that either Carol or Chuck always hovered nearby. The only time Mary didn't feel watched was when she retreated to her room.

Although her hosts' close scrutiny disconcerted her, she tolerated their vigilance, knowing that Ben had told Carol that Mary was still in danger.

"Had enough?" Shirley asked. "You seem to be slowing down a little."

"I think so. I don't have much energy today."

"No wonder, Mary. After all you've been through, there's no need to push it. We'll have plenty of time—about another four weeks, anyway."

"True. It's hard to believe that I've been here at the ranch almost two weeks already."

Mary floated a few feet, then kicked her feet until she reached the edge of the pool. She climbed the steps, pulling off her bathing cap and running her fingers through her hair. It wasn't until she emerged from the pool and paused at the edge that she saw Ben standing next to Carol. He gazed at her as though he were dumbstruck, and Mary felt her face awash with heat. She quickly grabbed her long kimono, pulled it on, and tied it at the waist. Covered now from her shoulders to her feet, Mary greeted the deputy.

"Hi, Ben. I'm surprised to see you here today."

"I had some business at Lake Tahoe to take care of, and I was driving by on the way back to Reno, so I thought I'd stop."

"Cocktails, anyone?" Carol asked. "It's that time." Gesturing toward the patio, she said, "Chuck's setting up the bar now."

The entire group trouped to the patio, and Chuck began taking orders. Most of the guests settled on martinis while Shirley opted for Coke and Mary had a whiskey sour.

"Deputy, what can I get you for?" Chuck asked, joking. "On the house."

"No, thanks, Mr. Ellis. I'm still on duty."

Shirley drifted away to chat with Sally and Bea, leaving Mary alone with Ben.

"Have you thought any more about my suggestion to move to a different place while you're in Reno, Mary?"

"I think I'm OK here. Chuck and Carol have been watching me like hawks. Chuck even installed a new lock on the door of my room and told me to keep it locked all the time. It's a bit nerve-wracking."

"You can't be too careful, Mary, and I'm glad to hear that Chuck and Carol are taking this seriously. Still, I think it would be safer for you to get away from the ranch."

"I appreciate your concern, Ben—really, I do." Mary took a sip of her drink. "I'm still having trouble comprehending that my husband might want to kill me."

"Who else could it be, Mary? From what you've told me and from what I can see for myself, I can't imagine that anyone else would have a motive."

"I can't, either." Mary sighed as she swirled her drink. "I wouldn't have believed John could ever do such a thing if I hadn't seen him drop his mask a couple of times. Ask anyone. They'll tell you that he's the most charming man in the world. Once upon a time, I thought so, too."

"As ambitious as you say he is about his political career, he might have decided that the voters would sympathize with a widower but not with a man whose wife divorced him."

"That's true. With the Catholic constituency of the Congressional district he wants to represent, a divorce will cost him the election. Really, I'm not getting the divorce to be vindictive, but when I found out he married me only to get a leg up in politics and that he wanted children for the same reason, I couldn't stay with him. His cheating, which I hadn't known about, either, until I overheard him talking to his buddy, added to my disgust. Then, when I heard him say that when we had children, he'd send them away to boarding school to keep them out of the way, I felt sick."

Ben nodded. "I understand, Mary. Most people like to keep their kids close."

"I wanted to have children so much, but now it looks as though I may never have any."

"Why not? Surely, you'll get married again."

"You're not Catholic, are you, Ben?"

"No. I guess I'd say I'm a lapsed Presbyterian."

"Then you don't know what it means for a Catholic to get a divorce. The church doesn't look kindly on divorce. A divorced Catholic can't remarry in the church."

"You're saying you can't ever marry again?" Ben's shocked

expression told Mary that she'd been correct that Ben didn't understand the implications of her divorce.

"That's right, unless the church grants me an annulment. An approved annulment is very difficult to get, though. I've already talked to my parish priest back home about it, and he suggested that I remain married and live apart from my husband, even though he admitted that he thought an annulment might be granted in my case."

"I'm sorry, Mary," Ben said, but Mary noticed that he seemed angry. "That just doesn't seem right to me. You have good reasons for divorcing your husband. Anyway, you can remarry legally once your divorce is final. Why do you have to have a church wedding? Just go to a justice of the peace."

"Like I said, Ben. You don't understand."

"You're right. I sure don't. This all sounds crazy to me."

"I am who I am, Ben. And who I am is a Catholic."

Chapter 23

"Sheriff in?" Ben asked Anita as soon as he returned to the office.

"He is, Ben, but he's in a meeting with Al and Fred right now."

"Maybe something's finally breaking in that cattle-rustling case Fred's been working on."

"Could be. I know Al's pulling three deputies off patrol duty tonight to work a stakeout with Fred."

"Say, Anita, I meant to ask you earlier. Have you noticed any stray messages floating around here? This morning Adrian Beaumont claimed he'd left me several messages, but I haven't seen anything from him." Ben frowned. "I wonder if he really did."

"I always leave your messages under Carmine's ashtray, but I don't know about some of the deputies. I'll have a look around and see what I can find."

"Oh, no. Don't bother, Anita," Ben said as he waved her off. "I know you're busy. I can do it myself."

"It's no bother, Ben. After all, if it weren't for you, I couldn't play glamour girl." Anita pointed to the fur stole that she'd draped over the back of her chair.

"You deserve it. We'd do a poor job of keeping this place running without you." Suddenly embarrassed, Ben tried for a lighthearted tone as he said, "I'd be chained to the Underwood if you didn't type my reports for me."

"OK, tell you what. Let's both search." They walked around the bullpen area, scanning desktops, lifting staplers and ashtrays, in an attempt to find the missing messages, but they didn't come up with a single one. Ben wondered again if Adrian Beaumont had lied about leaving him messages, but then again, Beaumont had sounded awfully exasperated that Ben hadn't returned his phone calls.

"Nothing," Ben said. "Time to forget about it. It doesn't really matter now, anyway."

Ben parked himself at Carmine's desk. He felt eager to tell the sheriff that he'd finally come up with the first solid lead in the Beaumont case since he'd discovered that the car wreck that killed Candice Martin was no accident. If the Martin woman had been the killer's target all along, Ben could stop worrying about Phyllis Beaumont's accompanying her husband to Nairobi, where endless opportunities for arranging an "accident" might present themselves out in the wild where Beaumont was directing his latest movie.

The sound of the buzzer on Anita's phone interrupted his thoughts.

"Ben, the sheriff wants to see you now."

Ben patted his pocket to make sure that he had his notebook before he grabbed a pen from the desk and went down the hallway to the sheriff's office. Surprised that Al and Fred were still in the sheriff's office, Ben entered and took the only vacant chair. He felt as though he'd arrived in the middle of a joke that only the others, who were grinning broadly, were privy to.

"What's the matter? Do I have a sign on my back or something?"

The question elicited a loud guffaw from Sheriff Rogers, who stood to shake hands with Ben. "Congratulations on your promotion, detective."

Al and Fred echoed the sheriff's words, each shaking hands with

Ben, in turn, while a dazed Ben accepted their congratulations.

"You want the job, don't you, Ben?" the sheriff asked.

"You bet!"

"Sit down, Ben, and I'll go over some of the details with you." The sheriff turned to Al and Fred. "See you boys in the morning. Good luck on the stakeout, Fred."

After Al and Fred left, Ben settled back in his chair, drew out a Lucky Strike, and lit it. To Ben, the impact of the sheriff's announcement rivaled a Mac truck's running into a wall. He'd joined the department only two years earlier, and most of the deputies had far more seniority than he did.

"I want to thank you for this opportunity," he said formally. The sheriff stared at him. "Oh, hell, I'm happy as a clam to get the job."

The sheriff laughed even louder at Ben's discomfort.

"Seriously, I know there are lots of others who've been with the department longer."

"Can it, Ben. You're the right man for this job. Been watching you working your cases, and I was right when I said that you're a bright guy. Not everybody's cut out to be a detective. It takes both logic and intuition. You got both."

"Carmine?"

"On the mend, but his doctor told him that if he didn't retire, he wouldn't last till the end of the year. Went home yesterday, and his wife made it clear that's where he's staying. Take his open case files over to his house and review them with him in a day or two. He's happy to help you with anything you need, but it'll have to be at his place."

"Yes, sir."

"Go ahead and use his desk. His son said he'd come over to pick up the personal stuff."

"I could take it to him. Save the son a trip."

"OK, sure. Another thing: Carmine was Senior Detective. That's Fred now. He's not your boss, but you'll work cases together once in a while, and when you do, he's the lead. Otherwise, you're on your own. Report directly to me, just like you been doing."

"Will do."

"And Ben, one more thing: there's a good bump in pay. Never hurts to have some extra dough."

"No, sir, it sure doesn't," Ben agreed.

When Ben came back to Carmine's desk, now his own, Anita beamed at him.

"Congratulations, Ben!"

"How did you know?"

"Al just told me to order you some business cards—Detective Ben Cameron, Washoe County Sheriff's Department. That's great!"

"Thanks, Anita."

"You deserve it, Ben."

Chapter 24

Mary slept fitfully, waking often, even though she'd felt exhausted when she'd gone to bed early in the evening. Probably the glass of red wine, along with the two whiskey sours after dinner, caused her restlessness, she thought, as she remembered that she'd also had a whiskey sour when she'd talked to Ben in the afternoon. Suffering from a headache, too, Mary stumbled into the tiny bathroom adjoining her room and looked for the small bottle of aspirin that she remembered placing in the medicine cabinet when she first arrived at the Circle E. She didn't see the bottle, so she rummaged through her make-up case, stowed in her closet, but came up empty there, too. Groggy and dizzy, Mary went back to the bathroom and began pulling everything from the glass shelves of the medicine cabinet. Behind a large jar of Pond's cold cream sat the aspirin bottle. Mary shook out two tablets and swallowed them, without bothering to drink any water. She climbed back into bed, lying on her side and staring at the wall, hoping that sleep would come soon.

Alcohol or fear—either could be causing her distress, she knew, or perhaps a little of both. Despite her confident declaration to Ben a few days earlier that she'd seen heaven and that she wasn't afraid to go there, the time that had passed since her near-drowning had pulled her more and more back into her life, and she no longer wanted to follow the light, not right now, anyway. Someday, her time would come. Now, she prayed that it wouldn't come soon.

To obtain her divorce, Mary knew she'd have to stay in Reno four more weeks—four weeks and one day, to be precise. Four weeks and one day that she'd fear for her life, if she lived that long. Would the fear end when a Reno judge granted her a divorce? Once the divorce decree had been issued, Mary couldn't see any reason that her death would benefit John. Would he call off his hired killer then, or would he want revenge for Mary's ruining his political career?

John wouldn't be able to explain her absence from New York much longer. He'd told everyone that she was vacationing in the West, but that story would wear thin, even before the divorce came through. Once word got out that John was a divorced man, his political future in the Congressional district he wanted to represent would be dead, as dead as he evidently wanted his wife to be. Mary had absolutely no doubt about that. The district's overwhelmingly Catholic constituency wouldn't ever send a divorced man to the House of Representatives. They wanted a married man for their Congressman, a family man, someone with no scandal attached to his name.

How could she have been so naïve, so stupid as to marry John, a man she'd known for only a few weeks before their marriage? She'd let herself be carried away by John's charm. She'd played the perfect patsy, never questioning the man's true motives, never questioning the reason, of all the women he might have picked, he'd chosen Mary Marchetti, an Italian-Irish girl with a Catholic education that didn't go beyond high school. John was a Harvard graduate, the grandson of one of the wealthiest men in America, and the heir to his family's fortune. Any one of the dozens of blue-blooded debutantes who whiled away their college years at Vassar or Radcliffe, just waiting for a proposal, would have been happy to marry John.

Although she hated to admit it, even to herself, John's money had influenced her in ways that she regretted now. Riding around the city in a chauffeured limousine, rather than stuffing herself into a crowded subway car; shopping at Saks and Bergdorf's, rather than Penny's; traveling to Paris and London, rather than Coney Island, Mary had felt like a pampered princess. She still treasured her designer clothing from the haute-couture houses of Dior and Balenciaga—custom-made suits, cocktail dresses, and evening gowns—and she'd taken her clothing with her when she'd departed from the couple's luxurious New York apartment for the last time, although she'd left behind all the jewelry John had given her, placing it neatly on the top of her dresser with a polite note saying that she did not want to keep it. Whenever she felt guilty about keeping her wardrobe, she rationalized the decision because many of the garments had been made exclusively for her or altered to fit her perfectly. She'd refused her New York attorney's advice to allow him to negotiate a better settlement, adamant that she didn't want John's money anymore.

Although she'd never acknowledged it when they were together, not even to herself, Mary realized that her marriage to John Garrison hadn't been like the marriages of her friends, good Catholic girls who'd married guys who loved them and who'd had children already while Mary's husband had pushed her into such a whirlwind of political events and charity board meetings that she'd barely had time to catch her breath long enough to realize that she and her husband seldom saw each other, and when they did, it was usually at a political rally. Even though the financial perks had been exciting, the marriage lacked depth and breadth. In fact, it had never been much of a marriage at all. Mary wished that the church would recognize the situation and grant her an annulment, but she feared it would never happen, and if it didn't, she'd live the rest of her days without a husband or children.

She could understand Ben's shock when she'd explained the situation, but she knew the deputy was most concerned with protecting her from another attack. If he failed to catch her attacker, there'd be no need to worry about obtaining an annulment or anything else.

Mary rolled over and looked at the white ruffled curtain blowing in the wind. She'd opened the window earlier in the evening, but the pleasantly cool breeze that had wafted gently into the room when she'd gone to bed had turned into a gale, and she got out of bed to close the window. A half-moon hung in the dark sky above the grove of cottonwood trees where the Circle E's cottages nestled. The trees swayed as the wind moaned, and she quickly pushed the window down to the sill, closing it with a loud thump that surprised her. She hadn't anticipated that the window would slide so easily.

Mary hoped that the noise hadn't awakened the other guests, especially Faye, who had the room next to Mary's. Someone had heard the sound, though. A man stood between two of the cabins, looking up at the second floor of the ranch house. Mary jumped back from the window, but since she hadn't turned on any lights in her room, she realized that the man probably couldn't see her, anyway. She crept back to the window and looked out, over the lawn to the place where the man had stood a few seconds earlier, but she didn't see him. Mary continued to stare at the cabins until she spotted him again. This time, he was creeping from behind the last cabin in the row.

Mary didn't wait to find out what he'd do next. She flung on the robe that she'd draped over the foot of the bed and flew down the stairs. She made a hairpin turn to her right, at the bottom of the stairway, sprinted down the hallway to the door of the first-floor apartment where Carol and Chuck resided, and pounded on their door.

"Chuck! Chuck!" Mary called until Chuck finally opened it.

"What's wrong, gal?"

"Chuck, there's someone sneaking around outside!"

"What?"

"A prowler. Outside. I just saw him, over by the cabins."

Knotting the sash of her long white robe, Carol appeared behind Chuck. "For heaven's sake, Chuck. Let Mary in." Chuck backed up, allowing Mary to enter the Ellises' living room.

"Someone's lurking around the cabins," Mary told Carol. "I saw him when I got up to close my window."

Chuck, clad in pajamas, lifted his shotgun from its rack above the mantle of the stone fireplace.

"Chuck, you can't walk around outside barefoot," Carol said. "At least put some boots on."

Chuck disappeared into the bedroom and emerged in a minute, wearing jeans and boots.

"You gals stay right here," Chuck said, loading the shotgun. "If I ain't back in fifteen minutes, call the sheriff."

"Be careful!" Carol admonished her husband, as she handed him a flashlight.

"It's him 'as better be careful." Leaving the door to the apartment open, he stamped down the hallway. They could hear the creak of the patio door as Chuck went outside.

"Sit down, Mary." Mary sat in the center of the tan, overstuffed sofa in front of the fireplace. "You're shaking like a leaf." Carol took a knitted, red afghan from the back of the sofa and draped it over Mary. "Are you sure you didn't see one of the guests? Shadows can play tricks on our eyes sometimes."

"I'm positive I saw a man. He was tall, not as tall as Ben—I mean Deputy Cameron—but about Chuck's height."

"Hmmm. Chuck's six feet tall, so that means it couldn't have been Jack or Buster, and there aren't any other men on the place, just the wranglers and Chuck. I don't like this. I don't like this, at all."

"I'm sorry, Carol." Tears welled up in Mary's eyes.

"Oh, no, Mary. It's not your fault, you poor dear." Carol sat down on the sofa, next to Mary, and gently patted her arm. They sat in silence for several minutes until they heard the patio door's creaking again and the tap of Chuck's boots as he came in.

"Chuck?" Carol called softly.

"Yeah, it's me." He came back into the apartment. "He ain't out there now," Chuck said, as he returned the shotgun to its rack above the mantle. "But I found this behind the cabins." Chuck held up a man's red-and-black Western kerchief and handed it to Carol. "It sure ain't mine, and our boys always wear blue ones."

"That's right," Carol said. "I embroider our Circle E logo on all the wranglers' neck scarves, too. Maybe we should call the deputy."

"It's after midnight. Ain't much he can do now. We'll wait to call him in the morning, if Mary don't mind."

"Mary, you'll stay with us for the rest of the night," Carol insisted.

"Oh, I wouldn't want to be a bother."

"It's no bother, Mary. We have a guest room, and it's all made up. Our apartment here used to be the original ranch house before we built on to accommodate guests."

"All right. I guess I will, then. It gave me the creeps seeing that man standing outside, looking up at me."

Chapter 25

Despite his elation about his promotion to detective, Ben had one more item on his agenda before he'd allow himself to celebrate. He flipped through his pocket notebook until he found the number the Cal Neva's showroom manager had given him for the Les Brady Band's booking agent in Hollywood. He needed to track down the band to find Billy Littleton, Candice Martin's former boyfriend, now the chief suspect in her murder.

Ben pulled his pack of Luckies from his shirt pocket and set it on top of Carmine's desk. He wondered how long it would take him before he started to think of the desk as his own, rather than Carmine's. The heavy ceramic ashtray on the desktop brimmed with cold ashes, and Ben was about to dump them into the small trash can next to the desk when he saw bits of torn paper in the bottom of the receptacle. Retrieving the pieces of paper, he reassembled them.

Adrian Beaumont hadn't lied about calling Ben. The shreds of paper, now resembling a jigsaw puzzle, told the tale. Someone had deliberately shredded the messages and hadn't bothered to conceal what he'd done. Only one person would stoop to such pettiness: Overmeyer. Ben could almost feel his blood pressure rising as he thought about the obnoxious deputy.

"Ben," Al called, as he came into the bullpen. Ben swept the ripped messages back into the trash can and dumped the ashes on top of them. No need to involve Al in his ridiculous feud with Overmeyer. He'd settle it in his own time, in his own way. Al clapped Ben on the shoulder. "I'd like to take you and the boys out for drinks after work tomorrow to celebrate your promotion. OK with you?"

"Sure thing. Thanks, Al."

"Good. I'd do it tonight, but it's my grandson's third birthday. The wife and I got him a trike. Hope he likes it."

"He will, Al. Boys always like anything with wheels."

"Guess that's right. Even the big boys. Now don't think you have to solve all of those cases tonight. We got no shortage of 'em, you know."

"That's for sure," Ben agreed. After Al left, Ben looked in both deep bottom drawers of the desk, where Carmine kept his open case files and felt momentarily panicked by the number of them. Adding the cases Ben was already working, he knew that the only way to get a handle on the volume of work was to methodically review each case and then to prioritize them. If he remained with the Washoe County Sheriff's Department the rest of his working life, which he fully intended to do, he'd face a never-ending battle against the bad guys. That was what crime solving was all about, and Ben hoped he'd measure up to the challenge.

Today's break in the Beaumont case had encouraged that hope, and now he needed to pursue the lead. He called the long-distance operator and gave her the number of the Hollywood booking agent. Ben waited while the phone rang several times, but, just as he was replacing the receiver, he heard an answer. Unfortunately, an answering service operator picked up the call. She would leave a message for the agent, she said, but she didn't know when he'd check in. Sighing, Ben hung up. Getting in touch with the agent might take a little longer than he'd anticipated.

After calling Carmine's house and receiving a go-ahead to talk with the former detective the next afternoon, Ben boxed the files and stowed them inside his pickup. Then he headed to his apartment to call his parents and share the good news of his promotion to detective. He never considered using the phone at the sheriff's department to call home. Any long-distance calls made from the office had to be carefully logged. They were expensive, and there had to be a good reason for making any call out of the Reno area.

Splurging on a call to his parents, Ben talked with them for several minutes beyond the usual three-minute caution that he customarily asked for from the operator. They were as elated as Ben at their son's promotion to detective, and Ben promised them that he'd visit as soon as possible so that they could celebrate together.

After lugging the boxes filled with Carmine's files upstairs to his apartment, he spent the rest of the evening reviewing them. He quickly noticed that Carmine placed only factual reports and statements in the files, never any speculation about any of the many crimes he investigated. Carmine's system made a lot of sense. Keeping hunches to himself until they panned out had served the chief detective well during his career. Once he connected the dots, an arrest followed, and Carmine had accumulated an impressive arrest record.

If Ben could do the same, he'd have a fine career, one that surpassed what he'd ever imagined for himself. Living through the Great Depression had made an indelible mark on Ben's psyche, and he'd been so obsessed with finding a good, steady, secure job that he'd given little thought to expanding possibilities beyond that.

After a couple of hours browsing through the files, he returned them to the boxes. He felt ravenous and more than a little restless, so he decided to make a food run. When Ben pulled into the crowded lot of the A & W, he snagged a spot, gave his order to a gangly teenager on roller skates, and listened to the jukebox blaring "Sincerely" by the Maguire Sisters from large speakers mounted on the outside of the building. He smoked until his order arrived and the strains of "Unchained Melody" filled the evening air. Stubbing out his cigarette in the truck's ashtray, Ben devoured two cheeseburgers, onion rings, and French fries, washing the greasy mélange down with ice-cold root beer from a large frosted glass mug. He turned his lights on to signal the carhop that he was done. Feeling generous, Ben left a dollar tip for the teenager on the tray, and when she came to detach the tray from his window, her eyes widened when she saw the bill. Ben almost regretted leaving it when the girl seemed about ready to cry, but she recovered herself, stuffed the dollar into her pocket, thanked him, and skated away smiling.

Chapter 26

"Mary, are you awake?" Carol tapped on the guestroom door and cracked it open slightly when Mary answered.

"Just getting out of bed now." Wrapping her robe around her, Mary came to the door.

"Oh, good. I'm going to call the deputy, Mary. It's a little after eight right now."

"OK, I'm headed back upstairs. I'll be down for breakfast in about half an hour."

"Did you lock your room last night before you came downstairs?"

"No. I was so scared that I didn't even think about it."

"I'll have Chuck go up there with you and check it, then. Wait just a second."

After Chuck appeared, carrying a mug of coffee, Mary followed him to her room at the top of the stairs. She knew that she hadn't shut her door when she'd rushed downstairs in the middle of the night, but she didn't remember leaving it wide open.

Wide open it was, though.

"I'll have a look-see." Chuck handed Mary his coffee mug. "Better stay out here in the hall, while I check your room." Through the open door, Mary watched as Chuck surveyed the room, peeked into the closet and the bathroom, and got down on his knees to peer under the bed. "So far, so good." He propped his elbows on the mattress to push himself back up. "Damn!"

Mary rushed in, sloshing the coffee on the oval rag rug beside the bed before she set the mug down on the top of the dresser. "What is it, Chuck? What's wrong?"

"Dang knee's paining me something awful."

"Let me help you get up."

"I got it, Mary." With a grunt, Chuck pushed off the bed and struggled to his feet. "Don't pay me no never mind. It's just the arthritis in these old bones."

"Thank you for checking my room. I'm sorry to be so much trouble."

"It ain't you that's the troublemaker, Mary. Keep this door locked." After Chuck stepped out into the hallway, Mary turned the deadbolt. Glancing around the room, she saw that nothing appeared to have been disturbed, and she doubted that anybody had been in her vacant room during the night. Still, she'd welcomed having Chuck check the room for her. After seeing the mysterious man outside, she felt thoroughly spooked.

Hurriedly, Mary bathed, dressed in her Western garb, and applied her make-up. She went downstairs to the dining room, eager to be surrounded by other people, although her safety-in-numbers idea hadn't applied when she'd been pushed into the street in Reno or almost drowned at Pyramid Lake. Although she'd had no idea that she might be in danger then, she certainly knew it now. Joining Shirley, Faye, and Carol in the dining room, she poured herself a cup of coffee.

"You really should eat something, Mary," Carol said. "You need to keep up your strength."

Mary smiled. Carol's solicitousness made Mary think of her mother. Carol had no children, but Mary guessed that she enjoyed mothering her guests.

"This Mexican egg dish tastes yummy," Shirley said, "if you like spicy chili peppers."

"I think I'll just stick to coffee for now." The thought of eating spicy food when her stomach already felt queasy didn't appeal to Mary. "Maybe some toast."

For the first time, they heard the ranch's new doorbell ring. Chuck had installed it, along with a new deadbolt. Now guests had to ring for entry to the front door, although previously the front entry had never been locked, not even at night.

Trailing Chuck, Ben came into the dining room.

"Deputy, won't you join us for breakfast?" Carol asked.

"All right. Don't mind if I do. Everything looks mighty good." Ben helped himself from the ample buffet set out on the sideboard, heaping a plate high with fried potatoes, ham, and sweet rolls before setting it on the table. Then he filled a mug with coffee, added some cream, and set it beside his plate.

"I understand you folks saw a prowler last night."

"What?" Shirley dropped her fork, and it fell, clattering, onto her plate.

"Mary saw a man lurking outside by the cabins," Carol explained. "It was after midnight. We thought we should report the incident to the deputy."

"By the way, ma'am, it's detective now."

"Promotion?" Chuck asked.

"Yes, sir." Ben grinned. Mary noticed that he'd let being called deputy pass once, but not the second time.

"Ben, that's great!" The others chimed in to second Mary's congratulations, which Ben seemed happy to acknowledge.

Mary watched as Ben quickly cleared most of his plate before he pulled his notebook from his pocket.

"Tell me exactly what you saw, Mary." As Mary described the

man she had seen and his movements, Ben took notes. Chuck showed Ben the kerchief he'd found lying on the ground next to the last cabin in the row, the one occupied by Shirley. Ben turned to Shirley. "Did you hear any noise outside last night?"

"No, not a thing, but I'm a sound sleeper. My parents used to tell me that a herd of elephants could be stampeding through my room, and I'd never wake up."

"How about you, ma'am?" Ben asked Faye.

"No, I didn't hear a thing."

"Mr. Ellis, I'd like to look around outside. Could you show me where you found the neck scarf?"

"Yup." Chuck motioned for Ben to follow him, and they went out through the French doors that led to the patio. In a few minutes, they returned. Ben entered the open French doors first with Chuck a few steps behind him.

"Mrs. Ellis, I'd like to have a word with you and Mr. Ellis. Mary, you, too."

"We're leaving," Shirley said.

"No, no. Stay put. We'll go back to our apartment. Breakfast won't be over for an hour, and I don't want to tie up the dining room." Leaving Shirley and Faye, Carol led the others to the apartment she and Chuck shared at the back of the ranch house. The group seated themselves in the living room.

"Did you find anything new out there this morning?" Carol asked.

"No, the ground's fairly hard, as you know, since we haven't had any rain lately, so there are no footprints. The neck scarf that Mr. Ellis found last night is about it, and that doesn't really tell us much. There must be hundreds of cowboys in the area who wear a kerchief just like that one. I'll check with the other guests. Maybe someone saw or heard something that would help me track down the man.

One thing—he's not the man who came to Mary's hospital room with a syringe the other night."

"How do you know?" Mary asked.

"You said the man you saw last night was about Mr. Ellis's height."

"Yes, I'm sure about that because he was standing right next to the lilac bush, and I'd say it's about six feet high."

Chuck nodded. "Yup, same height as me."

"OK. The intruder at the hospital definitely wasn't that tall. I'd estimate that he was five-six or so, no taller, so it couldn't have been the same man. Even so, you need to be especially cautious, Mary. I wish you'd consider moving."

Carol and Chuck looked at each other. "We're keeping a close eye on her," Carol interjected before Mary could respond.

"I'll think about it, Ben, but nothing happened here last night, not really. I'll admit I felt frightened last night, but in the light of day, I'm not sure that I had anything to worry about. The man never came near the house. He was by the cabins when I saw him."

"But you said he was looking up at you."

"He was, but now that I think about it, when I closed my window, it hit the sill kind of hard and made a noise. Maybe that's why he looked up at me."

"Could be. In any case, I'll nose around and talk to the other guests. Is everybody still on the place this morning, Mrs. Ellis?"

"Everybody except Sally, Bea, and the new lady—the one who's staying in the cabin where Phyllis, I mean *Candice*, stayed. They all went into town early to get their hair done. They probably won't be back till this afternoon."

"I'll talk to whoever's around right now, but I'll have to catch up to those other ladies later. I'll be tied up for the rest of the day today."

"I'd better get down to the corral now. It's time for my riding lesson," Mary said, as she rose and left the apartment with Ben. Carol called out that she'd come down to the corral to watch her in a few minutes.

"Looks like the Ellises are taking your safety seriously. I just hope it's enough. Is money the only reason you're insisting on staying here at the ranch? I could talk to Mr. and Mrs. Ellis and ask them to give you a refund. It certainly wouldn't be unreasonable under the circumstances, and they seem like fair people to me. I'm sure they'd understand."

"Please don't do that, Ben. I'm not a child. If it comes to that, I'll talk to them myself, but I did pay for six weeks in advance with the understanding that the payment wasn't refundable, and it also includes Carol testifying as my witness in court. I don't want to have to start all over at square one with the six-week waiting period."

Chapter 27

Mary had made a point that she was no longer a child. Ben could see that Mary was a woman, not a child, plain as day. The way she filled out her plaid Western blouse and her jeans left no doubt on that score. Mary looked adorable in her Western clothing, just like a cowgirl, a very pretty one. She'd brushed her new bangs over the gash in her forehead, and if Ben hadn't known better, he would never have noticed the telltale sign of her injury. Briefly, he wondered whether his growing attraction to Mary was interfering with his judgment about her case.

Although frustrated at Mary's reluctance to move to a safer location, Ben hadn't pressed the issue. Her attacker surely knew that she was staying at the Circle E, and he saw no reason to tempt fate. Despite Mary's bravado, he believed that she was frightened, although evidently not frightened enough to take action that could save her life. He'd noticed that she hadn't mentioned being prepared for heaven again, and he felt thankful, at least, for that. The more seriously she took the threat on her life, the better. With his added responsibilities as a detective, Ben couldn't hang around all the time to protect Mary. He planned to spend most of the afternoon with Carmine, reviewing open case files, and after work, he'd join Al and the deputies for drinks to celebrate his promotion. He'd have to depend on the Ellises and Mary's promise to stay at the ranch to keep her safe. So far, the attempts on her life had happened away from the ranch, although her sighting of the mysterious man was worrisome.

Back at the office, Ben found an envelope on his desk, addressed to "Sheriff, Attn: Deputy Ben Cameron, Reno, Nev." Despite the lack of a full address, the letter had reached its destination. There was no return address. Ben ripped the end of the envelope and shook its contents out onto the desktop. Folded inside a sheet of stationery from the Mapes, Ben found a check, the amount more than adequate for its purpose, signed by Adrian Beaumont. Eager to rid himself of the responsibility of the check, Ben let Al know that it had arrived and arranged for Anita to deposit it into the Sheriff's Benevolent Fund. He placed a long-distance call to Candice Martin's brother in Southern California, but there was no answer. His luck was no better with a second call he made to the Les Brady Band's booking agent in Hollywood. Again, the answering service took a message, but the operator there couldn't provide Ben with any other phone number for the elusive man. Just like his old Army days, Ben thought: hurry up and wait.

While Ben waited, he looked over the files that he hadn't read the previous evening. He'd lugged the boxes of open case files back into the office because he hadn't wanted to leave them sitting in his truck. Just the other day, someone had smashed the window of Big Swede's Chevy sedan, parked right outside the sheriff's office. He'd left a package on the front seat—a package that had evidently tempted a passerby. Despite the broken window, Big Swede had laughed when he'd told the tale. In the package had been a couple of dead rattlesnakes left on his neighbor's front porch. Big Swede had promised the irate homeowner that he'd take care of the evidence in what he called "The Case of the Snakes on the Stoop."

Although the thief had gotten his just deserts in that case, Ben wasn't about to take any chances with his case files. In his own mind, he'd already made the transition from calling them Carmine's files to calling them his files, and he took a proprietary interest in preserving them.

After a couple of hours, it was time to load them up in his truck again. Carmine lived in a pleasant residential area about a mile southwest of the office. It took Ben only a few minutes to drive to his house. Seeing no driveway, he parked in front of the house where a young man in shorts and a short-sleeved shirt, shirttails flapping, was pushing a rotary mower across the front lawn. He stopped when he saw Ben's truck and walked over to greet Ben.

"Detective Cameron?" Ben nodded. "Come on in. Pop's expecting you."

"OK. Let me just grab these boxes." Ben hefted three large boxes onto the sidewalk, stacking them one on top of another. They felt heavier every time he moved them.

"I'll bring 'em. You go ahead. Pop's waiting for you in the front room." Ben knocked a couple of times on the front screen door and called Carmine's name.

"Come in, Ben." Ben blinked as he entered the dark room. As his eyes adjusted to the dimness, he could see Carmine sitting on the sofa. A crucifix hung on the wall behind him, and family photographs, all in light wood frames, covered the other walls. The living room was crowded with spare-line Danish modern furniture, made with blond wood and turquoise-colored, knife-edge cushions. Tuned to Reno's sole television station, KZTV, a large console set dominated the small room. Ben recognized the show that played—*The Brighter Day*—a soap opera that his mother watched every day.

"Here you go," the young man said, depositing the boxes of files on the floor next to the front door.

"Ben, my son Joey."

Ben shook hands with Joey. "Thanks for your help."

"Don't mention it." Joey turned to his father. "Say, Pop, you wanna sit outside while you and the detective talk? I'll take the files out there for you."

"Sure, Joey." Joey held his father's arm as Carmine struggled to get up from the sofa. "Hold onto me, Pop," he said, as he led the older man through the kitchen and out the back door. Shaded by a huge lilac bush, a glider with a green and brown, striped canvas cover sat in the corner of the backyard. There were a picnic table and a couple of nearby lawn chairs, a white Adirondack chair and a metal-framed chair that matched the glider. Joey guided his father to the glider and held onto him as he sat down. Ben, who'd never been able to get comfortable in an Adirondack chair, opted for the metal-framed chair.

"I'll bring out the boxes."

As they waited for Joey to return, Ben pulled out his pack of cigarettes and offered one to Carmine.

"No, thanks, Ben. I got something better here." Carmine reached into his pocket and withdrew two cigars along with a lighter. He held a cigar out to Ben. "You want one? The finest hand-rolled Cubans— they were a birthday present from Joey." Ben nodded and Carmine snipped the ends off both cigars.

Ben accepted the cigar and sniffed it appreciatively. He leaned forward while Carmine lighted Ben's cigar and then his own. Inhaling deeply, Ben took a drag on the cigar, paused, and then exhaled.

Joey came out and deposited the boxes of files on the picnic table next to Ben. "Good thing Mama's at Rosa's house this afternoon. If she saw you smoking, she'd have a fit."

"I know it. Don't tell her, OK, Joey?"

"I won't, Pop. Yell if you need anything. I'm going to finish mowing in the front and then trim the hedge."

"OK, Joey." After Joey returned to his yard work, Carmine turned to Ben. "Man couldn't ask for a better son. He'll be a rock for the family when I'm gone."

"But you're feeling better, aren't you?"

"Better, but not good. I don't have long, Ben. I can feel it here." Carmine thumped on his chest. "And my wife Sofia, she knows it, too, but she doesn't want to admit it." Carmine's appearance—his pallor, labored breathing, weight loss, and slow, unsteady movement—all confirmed what the veteran detective had just told Ben, who felt tempted to argue the fact or speak some words of comfort, but restrained himself.

"I'm sorry."

"We all got to go sometime. I've had a good life—five great kids, ten wonderful grandkids, the best wife any man could ever have and a decent career to boot. Sure, I wish I could have more time, but that's in God's hands. Twenty-five years ago, I was a young guy like you, just starting out. The time goes faster than you can imagine, Ben, but you're not here to listen to an old geezer like me tell you his troubles. Let's get down to business."

Ben lifted several file folders from one of the boxes Joey had placed next to him on the picnic table and opened the first one. After he recapped the case, he asked for Carmine's impressions and suspicions. In his own indecipherable, except to Ben, special shorthand, Ben jotted down what Carmine could add to the facts already in the file in his pocket notebook. He slid the file beneath the others, and they continued with the process until they'd discussed each case in the stack of files. Then Ben returned those files to the box and grabbed another handful of them.

The open cases included vandalism, burglaries, armed robberies, auto theft, embezzlement, assault, attempted murder, bigamy, rape, and one homicide. With only two detectives in the Sheriff's Department, specialization wasn't possible, and detectives also investigated any death that wasn't natural, ruling out murder as a possible cause of death.

Carmine didn't need much prompting to launch into his ideas about the disposition on each open case, some of which he doubted would ever be solved because of the lack of evidence. Ben noticed that, despite his infirmity, Carmine had an excellent memory.

Ben and Carmine had just finished going over all, but one, of the files in the first box. When Ben picked up the last file folder and read the name on it, Carmine rubbed his forehead and grimaced. Ben looked at the older man in alarm.

"Want to stop now?"

Carmine sighed. "No, it's OK. I was never able to make a case on that one. The coroner wanted to rule it a suicide. I know it was murder, but he didn't believe there was evidence of homicide. Finally, I convinced him to at least rule it an accidental death, for the peace of mind of the family."

"How's that?"

"A ruling of suicide would have been devastating. Mrs. Desmond, the lady who died, was Catholic and so was her family, all except for her husband. A Catholic who commits suicide can't have a Christian burial in consecrated ground, but if the death is accidental. . ."

"But in this case?"

"I have absolutely no doubt that Mrs. Desmond was murdered. Like I said, though, I could never prove it."

"What happened?"

"Mrs. Desmond was staying at the Verdi Guest Ranch. This was about two years ago, could have been before you joined the department, Ben."

Ben nodded. He didn't remember the case.

"Anyway, the ranch is one of the nicer, small guest ranches in the county. Two sisters run the place. They have quite a stable, and they cater to people who like horseback riding. Guests can bring their own horses, and that's what Mrs. Desmond did. The sisters let her store her horse trailer and truck in one of their outbuildings. Long story short—they found her in the cab of her truck, dead of carbon monoxide poisoning. The door of the building was shut, and the truck was still running."

"I assume that the door wasn't locked."

"That's right. The circumstances seemed to point to suicide. It looked as though Mrs. Desmond could have gotten out of her truck if she'd wanted to and left the building, but she didn't. The first deputy to arrive on the scene figured she was despondent over her upcoming divorce and decided to end her own life. Initially, that's what I thought, too, but after I interviewed the sisters and nosed around, I came to a different conclusion. Since the lady was a devout Catholic, I found it hard to believe that she'd risk eternal damnation—Catholics consider suicide a mortal sin, you know—by killing herself. In fact, she didn't really want to go through with the divorce, according to what she told the sisters. Although she was willing to leave her husband, she wanted to separate, rather than divorce."

"I take it her husband pushed for the divorce."

"Right. It was all his idea, and he's a very rich, very powerful man who wanted an heir. The Desmonds had been married for seven years and had no children. Desmond had an affair with his secretary, and when he found out she was expecting, he told his wife he wanted a divorce so that he could marry the next Mrs. Desmond."

"He sounds like a real prince."

"A prince and a murderer, if I don't miss my guess. He's the only person I found who had any reason to want to get rid of Mrs. Desmond. She'd called him a few days before her death to tell him that she wasn't going to go through with the divorce. From what Mrs. Desmond told the sisters, he was livid. He said that no child of his was going to be illegitimate."

"You think he killed her himself?"

"No, he was too smart for that. He had to have help, and he also made sure that he had an ironclad alibi."

Although Ben didn't like what he was hearing, delving into Mrs. Desmond's case would have to wait until another time. A quick glance at his Timex told Ben that he should be leaving now so that he wouldn't keep Al and the deputies waiting for him at Buck's Saloon.

Chapter 28

Although the day after Mary's sighting of the mysterious man near the Circle E's cabins passed uneventfully enough, when the other guests began to return to their rooms and cabins for the night, Mary felt hesitant to retire to her own room. Should she feel afraid that the man would return? She knew that Chuck would be patrolling the area around the ranch house until the wee hours of the morning, and that knowledge helped, although it didn't quite alleviate Mary's concern.

In any case, she didn't want to spend another night in Chuck and Carol's guestroom, so she locked her door behind her, and before she went to bed, she pushed the dresser in front of the door to block it. If anyone tried to open the door, she'd at least hear the noise. She doubted that someone would try to get into her second-story window. That would require a ladder, and Chuck would surely notice someone placing a ladder on the side of the ranch house, but, just in case, Mary closed and locked the window. Then she placed one of her suitcases open on its side under the window, a glass ashtray on its top. Like the dresser, if it were moved, it would make enough noise to serve as a warning. If the man tried to enter her room from either direction, she could at least scream to alert the household.

Once her barriers were in place, Mary slipped into bed and

silently said her prayers. Preparing herself for a sleepless night, she lay on her back and closed her eyes. She thought that she could at least rest quietly, but she surprised herself by drifting off. She didn't waken until well after dawn. When she opened her eyes and glanced around her room, she saw that nothing had been disturbed during the night. Her precautions evidently hadn't been necessary, after all. Perhaps she had overreacted, she thought, as she climbed out of bed.

Mary took her time getting ready for the day. She added some drops of scented oil to her bath water, filled the old-fashioned claw-footed tub almost to the brim, and soaked until her skin began to wrinkle. She put on a pink sundress decorated with tiny appliqued rosebuds on the bodice and stepped into her light tan, high-heeled sandals. She carefully applied makeup, first covering the bruises on her legs. Next, she put liquid base makeup on her face, gently patting it around the purplish wound on her forehead. A dusting of powder on top of the base makeup almost concealed the area. Mary enhanced her eyes with deft touches of dark brown mascara, eyeliner, and eyebrow pencil, smoothed creamy pink blush on the apples of her cheeks, and glazed her lips with pink lipstick.

Ben had said that he'd be back to question Sally and Bea, since they'd already left the ranch to go into Reno before he'd arrived yesterday, in response to Carol's report of a prowler. Mary wanted to look pretty, not like a woman who'd been beaten up, when she saw him the next time. She felt sure that his interest in her case had as much to do with his interest in her as it did the case. The way he looked at her left no doubt in Mary's mind that Ben felt attracted to her, and she realized that she enjoyed the tall detective's admiration. Not that anything could come of it. The more she thought about the possibility of obtaining an annulment, the more unlikely it seemed that the Church would grant her one. Sighing, Mary left her room to go downstairs to breakfast, but not before she double-checked that she'd locked her door.

When Mary entered the dining room, she realized that she was too late for breakfast, although not too late for coffee, which was always available in a large urn on the sideboard during the day. She helped herself to a cup and carried it outside to the deserted patio. She looked across the back lawn to the swimming pool. While a couple of the guests paddled lazily in the cool water, others lay on long deck chairs, sunning themselves.

Hearing voices, Mary turned and saw Carol and Ben coming through the French doors.

"Why don't you wait here, detective? I'll go find Sally and Bea. They may still be in their cabins. I know that they didn't get back here until almost midnight last night, and I was beginning to worry." Mary knew that Carol, like a mother hen, never went to bed until all her guests were home for the night. She remembered Carol's lecture the first day she had arrived at the Circle E and the emphatic way Carol had told Mary that it was crucial that Carol see her guests every day so that she could swear to their six-week residency as a witness in divorce court.

"OK. Thanks, Mrs. Ellis." When Carol headed for the cabins, Ben turned to Mary and smiled, his grin spreading as he noticed the dress she wore. "You look beautiful, Mary." As soon as he said it, his face turned red in embarrassment.

"Thank you, Ben." Mary felt every bit as awkward as the lanky detective seemed to feel, but, at the same time, she was pleased that he had noticed the care she'd taken with her appearance in anticipation of this very moment. Now that it had come, she found herself tongue-tied. She didn't have a crutch to cover her shyness as had Ben, who had pulled out his pack of Lucky Strikes and begun fiddling with a book of matches to ease his discomfiture.

"Cigarette?" he offered, extending his hand toward Mary.

"No, thanks, Ben. I don't smoke."

"Oh, right. I should have remembered." His face turned redder at this lapse as he put a flame to the tip of his Lucky Strike and inhaled. "No disturbances last night, I take it?"

"No. Nothing's happened since I saw the man."

"Well, if it isn't the long, lean deputy," Sally burst out, striding onto the patio, trailed by Carol and Bea. "How've you been, honey?"

Ben choked and began waving his cigarette smoke away with his hand. Taken aback, Mary glared at Sally, then thought better of it. Although Sally was a notorious flirt, Mary hadn't forgotten that Sally had rushed to help to save her life on the beach at Pyramid Lake.

"Uh, fine. You?"

"Fine and dandy, deputy."

"By the way, it's detective now."

"Ooh, someone's on his way up in the world." Sally giggled. "Are you here to do some detecting?"

"That's right."

"Why don't we all go into the dining room and have some coffee while the detective talks with you?" Carol suggested, and they followed her through the French doors. They helped themselves to coffee, and Ben waited until the women had sat down before he took a seat at the head of the table, Mary on his left side and an empty chair on his right. As soon as Ben sat down, Sally jumped up, claiming that she had forgotten to put sugar in her coffee. Catching Bea's eye, Sally smirked as she sat down next to Ben when she returned to the table. Lowering his eyes, Ben sighed and stared at his coffee cup.

"What's this all about, detective?" Bea asked.

"If you two ladies hadn't been gone until almost midnight last night, you'd know what happened," Carol said, sounding mildly irritated.

Bea raised an eyebrow, surprised by Carol's tone, but Mary knew that the Circle E's owner had been shorted on sleep the past two nights and attributed her prickliness to tiredness.

"I think that's our prerogative, isn't it, Carol?"

"Of course," she replied, conciliatory now, the perfect hostess. "I didn't mean to imply that it isn't."

"Let's get down to business, ladies." Ben said, scooting his chair a few inches to the left. "This won't take long. Now, the night before last, Mary saw a man near the cabins sometime after midnight. The prowler dropped a red neckerchief on the ground out there. I wonder whether either of you ladies noticed any strangers lurking around the place. Did you hear any noise or see anyone that night?"

Bea looked at Sally and snickered. "Not me. I didn't hear a thing."

Ben turned to Sally. "What about you?"

"Um, that was no prowler."

"How do you know?"

"He's one of the wranglers from the Bar Z Ranch. Just paying me a friendly little visit."

"I'll bet," Bea said.

Mary noticed that Carol didn't look a bit amused. The Circle E wranglers had strict orders not to fraternize with the guests, although the rule didn't preclude their accompanying them into town to gamble. Far too much potential for trouble, Carol always said, and house rules forbade female guests from entertaining men in their rooms, too.

"Sally, could I have a word with you, please?" Carol asked, although her request sounded more like a command.

"Uh, oh," Bea said. "Somebody's in the dog house."

"Oh, shut up, Bea!" Sally said, as she meekly followed Carol out of the dining room.

Chapter 29

Driving back to the office, Ben couldn't get Mary out of his mind. He knew that if they'd had a few more minutes alone, he wouldn't have resisted the urge to take her in his arms and kiss her. He allowed himself the little luxury of imagining a romance with her, even though he knew that he should be concentrating on protecting her and bringing her attacker to justice. Still, the lovely picture of Mary in her pretty pink sundress lingered. He found himself so distracted that he came close to rear-ending a Studebaker stopped at a red light on Virginia Street.

The near collision snapped Ben out of his reverie, bringing him back to thinking about his to-do list for the day. He intended to spend the afternoon with Carmine again, going over the rest of the open case files; that is, if nothing else came up in the meantime. He still hadn't heard back from the Les Brady Band's agent, and he was beginning to wonder whether the man had dropped off the face of the earth. Counting the call Ben had made to him early in the morning, again with the answering service picking up the call, Ben had tried to contact the agent five times. If he didn't hear back from him today, he'd have to try another way of finding out the band's Western tour schedule.

"Oh, here he is now," Anita said as she flagged Ben down the minute he walked through the front door of the Sheriff's Department. "Ben, phone call for you on line three. I'll put it on hold."

Ben nodded his thanks and sprinted to his desk. Picking up the phone, he almost identified himself as Deputy Cameron, but caught himself in time. When he heard a woman asking him to hold for the booking agent, he breathed a sigh of relief. A minute later, he knew just where to find Candice Martin's ex-boyfriend. Billy Littleton. The man Phyllis Beaumont had called a "two-bit clarinet player" was staying at a downtown hotel in Sacramento, where the band would be playing its second session of a two-day gig at a ballroom on the outskirts of Sacramento.

Certain that an in-person interview with the clarinet player would be preferable to a phone call, Ben sought out the sheriff and told him that he had located Littleton and intended to go to Sacramento to question him right away.

"Good lead, Ben. Hope it pans out."

"Yes, sir."

"You'll be out of your jurisdiction, so we'll need to go through channels if you think he's our guy."

"Yes, sir. I thought I'd try to catch him at his hotel. The agent told me the band's first show's at eight this evening. That should give me plenty of time as long as he's around. I'm hoping he'll still be at the hotel when I get there. I'm going to try to go at it sideways, nothing blunt or accusatory. Just try to draw him out and get a feel for what he knows."

"OK. That might work—probably work better than bringing the Sacramento police into it and using one of their interrogation rooms at the station."

"Do I have to let the SPD know I'm in town to question a suspect?"

"There you're on tricky ground, but probably not in this case.

Why don't you call me after you've talked to the guy, and we'll take it from there."

"Will do."

Telling Anita that he'd be out of town for the rest of the day, Ben left the office. He'd reached the edge of town before he realized that he wouldn't get too far unless he gassed up. He stopped at a service station to fill his tank. While the attendant pumped gas, checked the pickup's oil, and washed the windshield, Ben went to the pay phone inside the station and called Carmine to postpone their appointment. He paid the attendant and headed out Fourth Street, which became U.S. Highway 40, going through the Sierra Nevada Mountains, over Donner Pass, and descending to Sacramento on the other side of the mountain range. Driving the scenic route, with its twists and turns, could make faint-of-heart drivers nervous, but Ben was accustomed to mountain driving, and he felt no such qualms. In a few hours, he pulled up outside the hotel housing the members of the Les Brady Band and parked nearby.

"Here to see Mr. Littleton," Ben said, quickly flashing his badge at the hotel desk clerk, a young man wearing thick eyeglasses with tortoise-shell frames. Dressed in his only suit, a hand-me-down charcoal pinstripe from his father, rather than the standard deputy's uniform that he'd worn for the past two years, Ben didn't draw the stares he would have, had he worn his uniform.

Although Ben had expected the clerk to question his authority, especially since he wasn't a California lawman, the bespectacled man didn't bat an eye as he readily gave Ben Littleton's room number and offered to call Littleton to let him know that Ben was on the way up. Ben declined the offer, bypassed the elevator, and took the steps, two at a time, to the third floor. He found Littleton's room, number 320, at the end of the hallway and knocked on the door.

"Yeah, yeah. Just a minute." Shirt open, Littleton opened the door. His hair looked damp. "Oh, I thought it was room service." He sounded disappointed.

"Detective Cameron from Washoe County," Ben said, holding up his badge. He deliberately omitted any mention of Nevada, figuring that Littleton probably had no idea what county he was in at the moment, especially since the band had been on the road for several weeks. "I'm following up on an accident, and I wondered if I could ask you a few questions."

"Sure," Littleton said, buttoning his shirt. "Come on in and have a seat." He gestured toward the only chair in the room while he sat on the edge of the bed. "Don't think I can help you much, though. I was asleep when the bus went off the road the other night. I don't really know what happened."

"I'm afraid there's been some confusion, Mr. Littleton. I'm here about another accident."

"Oh?" Littleton frowned.

"Two weeks ago near Lake Tahoe, a car went off the side of Mount Rose, and the driver was killed."

"I don't know anything about it. We were only in Tahoe the one night."

"Mr. Littleton, the driver of that car was Candice Martin."

"Candy? Candy's dead? Are you sure there's no mistake?"

"No, sir. No mistake. We have a positive identification."

"My God!" Littleton's face crumpled. He doubled over as racking sobs convulsed his body. Ben stared at the clarinet player. This certainly wasn't the reaction he'd expected. Evidently, Littleton still cared for his ex-girlfriend. Ben had seen enough people who'd been given the bad news of a loved one's demise that he didn't doubt the genuineness of Littleton's reaction. Ben shifted uncomfortably in his chair and waited until Littleton pulled himself together, wiping his eyes with a large white handkerchief that he pulled from his pocket.

"I'm sorry, Mr. Littleton. I was told that Candice was your former girlfriend. I didn't realize that you two were still close."

"Close? Yeah, you could say that." Littleton paused. "Candy was my wife."

"What?" Now it was Ben's turn to be shocked. If Candice and Billy Littleton were married, he wondered why nobody in Candice's family knew.

"That's right. We got married in Las Vegas a few days before the band's tour began."

"Her family didn't mention that she was married. I take it they didn't know."

"You take it right. They don't like me, especially that brother of hers. He thinks all musicians are bums. We weren't going to tell Candy's family that we got married until after the tour was over. Then we would have had enough money to put a down payment on a house. The band's been signed for a two-year run in Los Angeles as soon as this tour's over, and I won't be on the road. We had plans, detective. But now—I don't know what I'm going to do. I can't believe she's gone." Littleton burst into noisy sobs again, and since he didn't seem to hear the persistent knocking at his door, Ben got up and pulled the door open.

"Room service, sir. Sign here." Ben obliged, signing his own name and then noting "for Mr. Littleton" on the slip of paper that the waiter presented to him. "Where would you like me to put your tray?"

"Uh, I'll take it. Hold on a minute." Ben grabbed the tray and placed it on the only table in Littleton's hotel room before returning to the door. He reached into his pocket, pulled out some change, and deposited it in the waiter's outstretched hand. The waiter nodded his thanks. If he'd noticed the sobs emanating from the room, he gave no indication of it. Ben figured he'd probably trained himself not to intrude on the hotel guests. Ben took the coffee cup from the tray, went to the sink in the tiny bathroom that adjoined Littleton's room, and filled it with cool water. Littleton's sobs had subsided by the time Ben returned and handed him the water. Littleton accepted the cup and took a long gulp of water before setting it on the bedside stand.

"I still can't believe Candy's gone. My God! Did she suffer, do you think?"

Ben hesitated. He knew that Candice had been behind the wheel of a car that was hurtling down Mount Rose with no brakes, and she must have been absolutely terrified, especially in the few seconds after the Cadillac left the road and plunged down the mountainside. When the car crashed into the Ponderosa pine, Candice's death had been instantaneous, according to what the coroner had told Ben, so he repeated the coroner's words to Littleton. Hoping to prevent Littleton from asking for more details, Ben changed the direction of the conversation.

"Mr. Littleton, didn't you think it was strange that you hadn't heard from your wife in the last two weeks?"

"No. That's what we'd arranged. Right before our tour started, Candy was offered an acting gig in Reno. She told me that it would last for six weeks, and she'd make quite a bit of money, but it was all hush-hush, and she wasn't supposed to discuss it with anyone. Well, I thought it was fishy, but she insisted on going through with it. She said we could use the money, and I couldn't argue with her there, so I went along. We arranged to meet just once during the time—at the Cal Neva the one night the band played there. If I'd known that would be the last night I'd ever see her. . ."

"So no letters, no phone calls?"

"No, that was our plan. We'd go back to Los Angeles after her job and my tour were over, and we'd start a new life together. Say, do you know what her acting job was? She never would tell me. I tried to get it out of her when we met at Lake Tahoe, but no dice."

"I'm afraid I do." Ben proceeded to fill Littleton in on the reason Candice had gone to Reno for a six-week stay. He didn't omit the fact that she had been murdered because he knew that the coroner would be making his report public at the end of the day. After Cal Harris had reminded Ben of his promised scoop, Ben had leaked the news to the persistent reporter, and soon everybody would know that the accident had been no accident, anyway. Although he hated to do it, he asked Littleton if he knew of anyone who might want to harm his wife. As he paced the floor, hitting his left hand with his right fist repeatedly, an angry Littleton swore that nobody had any reason to kill Candice, and Ben believed him.

Ben had been sure that he was about to get his man, the man who'd murdered Candice Martin, but Littleton's revelations had thrown his theory—that Littleton had rigged the Caddy's brakes so that he could do away with his ex-girlfriend—into a tailspin. Now, he had to start the accident investigation all over.

He didn't relish his role as the bearer of bad tidings, either. Hoping to mollify the grieving man somewhat, Ben told him that he might want to get in touch with Candice's brother regarding her funeral and that all the funeral expenses for Candice would be paid for by the Washoe County Sheriff's Benevolent Fund. He explained that her family in Southern California had begun making the arrangements for her body to be transported back there for burial. Although the arrangements were made possible by the donation from the Beaumonts, Ben didn't mention Phyllis Beaumont's name again. When he'd told Littleton that Phyllis had hired Candice to impersonate her, Littleton had called Phyllis some choice names. Evidently, he'd never thought much of her. Ben speculated that Candice must have known how her husband felt about Phyllis, and that may have been one reason she'd refused to tell him the details of her acting job in Reno.

Leaving the miserable man to his grief, Ben retreated from his room, quietly closing the door behind him. As he started to walk toward the stairway, he could hear the muffled sounds of crying coming from Littleton's room. He almost felt a little guilty about having suspected Littleton, but he knew that was ridiculous. As an investigator, his duty lay in pursuing all the leads, no matter where they took him. The first thing he intended to do when he returned to Reno was go over all his notes on the Beaumont case to make sure he hadn't missed anything along the way. But first, he planned a more enjoyable break from his job.

In the lobby, he approached the desk clerk. "Pay phone?" he asked.

The young man with the thick eyeglasses gestured to his left. "Right around the corner, sir."

Ben nodded his thanks, rounded the corner, and stepped into the first empty telephone booth. He dialed the operator and, asking her for a three-minute reminder, dutifully deposited his coins.

"Hello." Ben's mother sounded out of breath as she answered the phone. Most days she spent a couple of hours in the afternoon baking desserts for the family. Ben could picture her wiping her flour-covered hands on her cotton print apron before she picked up the receiver.

"Hi, Mom."

"Benny!" Ben's mother was the only person in the world he allowed to call him Benny. He would have cheerfully clobbered anyone else who called him by the childish name. "Are you OK?"

"Sure, I'm fine. Why wouldn't I be?"

"You only call during the daytime on the weekends."

"Nothing to worry about, Mom. I'm calling from Sacramento. I had to come over on business, and I thought I'd drop in and spend the night."

"Wonderful! We can celebrate your promotion sooner than I thought. I have a beef roast with your name on it."

"With mashed potatoes and brown gravy?"

"Just the way you like it. Lemon meringue pie for dessert, too."

"That sounds great. I should be there within the hour."

"Wait till your father hears you're coming today! We're both so proud of you, Benny, getting such a big promotion. I didn't even know that you wanted to be a detective, son."

"Neither did I, Mom. Neither did I."

Chapter 30

"Mary, let's go into town tomorrow. We could shop or maybe play some blackjack. I'm getting tired of doing nothing except swimming and taking riding lessons." They sat on the edge of the swimming pool, splashing their feet in the water. The sun hung low in the sky, and all the other guests had gone into Reno for the evening, some to see a show in the Sky Room at the Mapes and others to gamble. Cocktails in hand, Carol and Chuck sat on the back patio, watching them.

"You go, Shirley. I think I should stay at the ranch."

"Tell me what's going on, Mary. Why is Carol always hanging around? And if she isn't, Chuck is. And why did the deputy—er, detective—take Sally's rendezvous so seriously?"

"I . . . I'm not supposed to say anything."

"Says who? Mr. Cute-Gary-Cooper-Lookalike? He can't order you around, Mary. Now are you going to tell me or what?" Shirley had a persuasive way about her. Mary remembered the day she'd first met Shirley and how easily she'd confided in her then. Now she wanted to tell Shirley what had really happened at Pyramid Lake and later that night when Ben had tried to catch her attacker, but she hesitated. He'd been adamant that she shouldn't tell anyone. Only Carol and Chuck knew the danger Mary faced, and they knew it only because Ben wanted them to watch out for her.

A fleeting thought came to Mary, one so ugly that she could hardly believe it. What if Shirley had been the one who'd pushed her in front of the cab? What if Shirley had been the one who'd tried to drown her at Pyramid Lake? On both occasions, she'd been with Shirley. That day on the sidewalk, in the midst of the crowd, they'd lost sight of each other. What if Shirley had deliberately hung back, only to position herself so that she could give Mary a surreptitious shove? And at Pyramid Lake, where had Shirley been when someone pulled her under the water? Like a fish, Shirley could swim underwater with ease. During the swimming lessons she'd given Mary, Shirley had demonstrated that she could hold her breath for an incredibly long time.

Almost as quickly as Mary suspected her friend, she dismissed the idea that Shirley could have tried to harm her. Hadn't Shirley helped her after she'd fallen in front of the taxi? Hadn't Shirley tried to save her after she'd nearly drowned in the lake? And what possible reason could Shirley have to harm her, anyway? Ben thought Mary's husband had hired a killer to attack her. But Shirley? Ridiculous! The wife of a famous movie star, Shirley was a rich woman who'd been battered herself. No, it was impossible.

"Mary? Mary? Haven't you heard a word I've said? You're a million miles away tonight."

Guilty that she'd ever entertained such thoughts, even for a moment, Mary turned to her friend. "Yes, I guess I am. I'm going to tell you everything, Shirley, but you have to promise you won't breathe a word of it."

"Cross my heart and hope to die," Shirley said, gesturing.

"All right." Mary didn't omit any details as she explained the danger she faced and the reasons Ben thought her husband had hired a killer to make sure that his wife never obtained a divorce. Wide-eyed, Shirley listened to Mary's story.

"My God, Mary! No wonder you were so upset when you saw Sally's wrangler outside the other night. You thought he was here to attack you."

"Embarrassing, but true. Sally's such a flirt; I should have realized what was going on."

"I would have reacted the same way you did, Mary, and I don't blame you for being scared, but you need to take care of yourself, and you've got to get out of here."

"But, Shirley, nothing's happened to me at the ranch, so I think I'm safe here. When I saw the man the other night, I admit I was really scared, but look how that turned out. I should have guessed Sally could be entertaining."

"There's more to Sally than meets the eye. She's the one who took over when I was trying to revive you with that old resuscitation technique I learned in lifeguard training way back in high school. I didn't realize that the recommendations had changed, but she did, and she jumped right in to save you."

"Yes. I'm very thankful to both of you. I wonder how she knew that."

"She told me that she'd seen a demonstration at a charity board meeting she attended. It's a miracle she remembered what to do, but thank goodness, it worked. Anyway, Mary, I still think you should move. Better safe than sorry."

"But I paid for the entire six weeks in advance, with a stipulation of no refund, and I'm running out of money. I can't afford to move."

"You can't afford *not* to move. Surely, Carol and Chuck would make an exception in your case if they understood the situation."

"They do understand it. Ben briefed Carol before I left the hospital, and I know she told Chuck. They've been watching me like a hawk since I got out of the hospital."

Shirley frowned. "I still don't understand why you can't get your money back."

"Well, I'm going to let you in on another secret. Carol actually brought up the subject herself and said that she'd like to give me a refund so that I could move and stay someplace else incognito, but she and Chuck are practically bankrupt. They don't have the money."

"What? I don't understand. They never scrimp on anything around here."

"That's part of the problem. Carol told me that Chuck wanted to lay off the staff during the slow winter months and make some other cuts, but she wouldn't do it. Even though they have all the guests they can handle right now, their business has declined quite a bit over the past few years."

"That's odd. I thought everybody came to Reno for a divorce."

"More in the thirties and forties, according to Carol. Business boomed back then. She says some of the states have changed their divorce laws, and it's affecting the ranch."

"I never would have guessed."

"Me neither. I think it nearly killed Carol to tell me about their business problems. She's a proud woman."

"You can't let that stop you, Mary. What if I lend you the money to move? You can pay me back later.'"

"That's very generous of you, Shirley, but I think I'll stay put for now. Like I said before, all the trouble's happened someplace else."

"I hope you know what you're doing, Mary. If you change your mind, my offer's still good."

Chapter 31

"Good morning, Ben."

"Morning, Anita. Say, do you know if Virgil's scheduled to work today?"

"Let me check." Anita consulted her copy of the daily duty roster. "Yes. He should be reporting any minute for routine patrol duty."

"Oh, good. I'll check with Al. Maybe he can spare him for a couple of hours." Ben found Al sitting in his office, his feet atop his desk. As soon as Ben entered, he swung his legs down and put his feet on the floor.

"Only a few months left till retirement, Ben. I'm practicing trying to relax. It's not as easy as you'd think."

Ben laughed. "You told me you'll be busy with all your projects around your house when you retire, remember?"

"Yeah. It makes me tired just thinking about it. How'd it go in Sacramento?"

Ben filled Al in on the new developments in the Beaumont case. Since he planned to revisit the evidence now that he'd ruled out Billy Littleton as a suspect and Candice Martin Littleton as the intended victim, he intended to take another look at the Cadillac, still stashed in the impound lot at Joe's Junkyard. Since he needed a mechanic to help him, Ben asked Al to assign Virgil to assist him when he reported for his shift. After checking the duty roster, Al agreed to reassign the rookie deputy for the morning.

Back at his desk, Ben had just started to flip through the dog-eared pages of his pocket notebook when several deputies came in, reporting for their day shifts. They'd read Cal Harris's story in the *Reno Evening Gazette*, and they flocked to Ben to get the scoop on the Beaumont murder case. Besides Ben, only Virgil and the brass had known that the Beaumont accident case had become a homicide investigation. Ben wished he could have held back the story longer because now the murderer would be alerted that the sheriff's department was onto him, but he'd made a promise to the reporter to give him a scoop in return for his help in planting the item about Mary, and he had to keep his word. In any case, the coroner couldn't have stalled much longer before making his ruling public.

Pulling Virgil aside, Ben told him that he'd been reassigned for the morning and to see him right after roll call. Within a few minutes, Virgil was back, and they headed out to Joe's Junkyard in Virgil's patrol car. This time, Joe's employees paid no attention to the men as they drove through the junkyard to the impound lot and unlocked its gate. Ben had brought everything they needed to lift fingerprints from the car, although he was kicking himself for not having done it sooner. The car appeared to be undisturbed, and Ben asked Virgil to point out the areas that the person who had tampered with the brakes would have likely touched. Unfortunately, Virgil had touched some of the same areas himself, and his prints would be there, too, but Ben hoped to find the killer's as well. For over an hour, they worked, mostly under the car, locating and lifting numerous fingerprints. Ben hoped that they wouldn't all turn out to be Virgil's.

"I think that's it," Ben said finally. They stood up, brushed off their clothing, and returned to the car. "Thanks for your help, Virgil. I wouldn't have known where to look myself."

Virgil nodded. "Being a mechanic comes in handy sometimes, especially since I can repair my own car, but I like this job better. Believe it or not, my old boss Mac called me a few days ago and begged me to come back to work for him. What guts! The guy still owes me for my last week of work. He claimed he won a big jackpot, and he promised to pay me my back wages and give me a raise if I came back, but I told him no dice."

"You said he had a gambling problem, right?"

"A big gambling problem. He may have won a jackpot, but he's going to give it right back to some casino and then some. You know, I really hope all those fingerprints we just got aren't mine."

"So do I, but don't blame yourself. I should have thought about fingerprints when we came out here last time, but I really wasn't expecting you'd find that the brakes had been tampered with. I thought that we'd probably confirm that a mechanical problem caused the accident."

"Live and learn, I guess. Do you have any idea who rigged the car?"

"No. I sure don't. I have a pretty good idea of who ordered it done, but he's not even in the country right now, and when he returns, it won't be to Reno."

"Beaumont?"

"Yup. I don't think I'm ever going to be able to prove it, though. The Beaumonts have reconciled, and Phyllis Beaumont never believed that her husband arranged to set up the accident, so she wouldn't cooperate with an investigation targeting him, anyway."

"I hear Beaumont paid the funeral expenses for the woman who died in the crash."

"He did. I'd say it's the least he could do, under the circumstances." Virgil pulled the patrol car over to the curb in front of the sheriff's office to drop Ben off. "Thanks for your help, Virgil."

"Any time. Good luck with the fingerprints."

Back in the office, Ben looked for Jeff Jergens, the deputy who did fingerprint comparisons for the department. He also showed the other deputies how to lift fingerprints at crime scenes, but most of them paid little attention to the technology, and they were more likely than not to leave their own fingerprints all over a crime scene. Now that Ben investigated crimes, he was beginning to understand how useful fingerprints could be as solid, physical evidence of a crime, and he vowed to take more care in preserving them in future investigations. He found Jergens pouring a cup of coffee in the break room, and Jergens promised to process the prints, eliminating Virgil's and isolating any others.

Next on his agenda was another trip to Carmine's to go over the rest of the open case files. He called the former detective and after being assured that "there's no time like the present," he ignored his growling stomach and hopped into his pickup, arriving a few minutes later. It had been hours since he'd consumed the crisp bacon and scrambled eggs his mother had prepared for him early in the morning before he drove back to Reno from Placerville. When Carmine greeted Ben at the door, his rumbling stomach spoke before he could.

"Sorry about that," Ben mumbled, embarrassed.

"Come on in, Ben. I had Joey set up the files on the kitchen table." Carmine led Ben to a cozy alcove with a booth large enough to seat three people on each of the cushioned bench seats. The file boxes sat at the end, next to a window curtained with white ruffled voile, and file folders were laid out neatly in rows. Carmine produced a large platter of oatmeal cookies and placed it in front of Ben. "Coffee?" Ben nodded, and Carmine carefully poured them both a cup from a large dripolator coffee pot. "Cream? Sugar?"

"Oh, don't bother." Ben desperately wanted some cream, but he also didn't think that Carmine should be exerting himself at all, even if only to pour some cream into a pitcher.

"I'll get both."

"Shouldn't you be sitting down?"

"Don't worry, Ben. I feel better today, but I'm not gonna overdo it." He gestured toward the cookies. "Help yourself."

Ben took him at his word. Before Carmine returned with a pitcher of cream and a bowl of sugar, Ben had already eaten four cookies. Filled with plump raisins and bits of walnut, they were soft and chewy.

"These are really good. Did your wife make them?"

Carmine nodded as he munched a cookie. "She took the rest of them to her club meeting this morning. She probably won't be back for a while, so we'll have to fend for ourselves until Joey comes home."

"Is he at work?"

"No, he just went to the hardware store for some hinges. He's fixing the cabinet in the bathroom. Joey's a science teacher at the high school, so he's off for the summer, but he's working nights, helping some professor at the university on a research project."

"A college graduate?" Ben's surprise came through in his question. He didn't know many people who had college degrees. He'd never considered getting any education beyond high school himself.

"Yeah. The first in our family. He's a bright boy, my Joey." Carmine took another cookie and pushed the plate closer to Ben. "Finish those, or Sofia'll think you didn't like them."

"We couldn't have that now, could we?" Ben asked, his eyes twinkling, as he helped himself to several more cookies, cleaning the plate. He took out his notebook, and they were soon immersed in a discussion of the open cases that Ben had inherited from Carmine. When they'd finished, Ben filled Carmine in on the details of the Beaumont case and Mary's case.

"The other day, when you told me about the woman at the Verdi Guest Ranch who died of carbon monoxide poisoning, it kind of rang a bell. That makes three cases involving women who came to Washoe County for a divorce, and now two of them are dead and one's been attacked. It seems like too much of a coincidence to me."

"You may be right, Ben. And now that you mention it, I know of a couple of other cases that might fit the same profile—both supposedly accidents. Both people were here to establish residency so that they could get a divorce."

"So five women may have been targeted by a murderer? It seems far-fetched, but, on the other hand, maybe not."

"Actually, one of the accident victims was a man—the victim of a hit-and-run accident. He was walking along the side of the road near the ranch where he was staying, and he was hit by a black pickup truck, according to witnesses. The driver didn't stop or even slow down, for that matter. It's still an open case. Fred's handling it, but I'm sure it's on the back burner at this point since it happened nearly three years ago."

"Do you remember anything about the man's background?"

"As I recall, he was from New York, and his wife was the one with all the money. It seems to me he was thirty or thirty-five, and she was about twenty years older. She owns a cosmetic company, Ritzy Lady. Fred said that she didn't seem too upset by her husband's death when he talked to her on the phone. She paid for his burial here in Reno, but she didn't come out herself."

"She could have arranged for his 'accident.' Maybe she didn't want to share the wealth when they divorced."

"It's possible. Check with Fred. He might be able to tell you if he found out anything about the settlement the husband was supposed to get after the judge granted their divorce."

"I'll do that. Do you remember the man's name?"

"Let me think. Brady. No. That wasn't it. Bradley. Bradley Carlton." Ben jotted down the name in his notebook, along with all the details Carmine remembered. "Now let me tell you about the other one, too. It was last August." Ben poised his pen and began scribbling as Carmine launched into a description of a prospective divorcée who had drowned close to Sand Harbor Beach at Lake Tahoe. A socialite from Belle Aire, Elizabeth Huffington, staying at the Tahoe Pines Ranch, was swimming in the Lake Tahoe waters with several other guests from the same ranch. By the time they missed her, it was too late. When swimmers pulled her from the cold waters, they tried to revive her, to no avail.

Ben flipped through his notebook, comparing the five cases. "August, you say? I guess I was on vacation at the time. I remember hearing something about it when I got back, but I didn't have any reason to be suspicious then. What are the odds of four ranch guests, all here to get a divorce, dying in Washoe County, all within the last three years?"

"Probably about a billion to one. Really we have five targets, including the Marchetti woman. You're onto something here, Ben. Except for Mrs. Desmond's staged suicide, everything's been made to look like an accident."

"There must be some connection besides the fact that they all were here for a divorce. I'm assuming that their spouses had motives, but they didn't want to get their own hands dirty. Maybe they all hired a local hit man."

"That's possible, but he must be a freelancer. The mob guys around here stick with their own."

"If that's what happened, I wonder how they made the connection. Two of the victims come from New York. The other three were from Southern California. The spouses are all prominent people, but I doubt that they're connected that way. I have a feeling there's a missing link somewhere."

"Let's go back to what they all have in common—a prospective divorce, but they didn't all stay at the same guest ranch, so the ranch itself isn't a common factor, although two of them stayed at the Circle E recently."

"They must all have had lawyers. Maybe a local lawyer set up his clients."

"That doesn't seem likely, but I'll grant you that the whole situation seems strange."

"Maybe we're making too much of a leap here. Maybe it's a crazy mass murderer who preys on divorce ranch guests."

"Another possibility, I suppose, but why make the deaths appear to be accidental?"

"I don't know. What I have is a lot of questions and no answers."

Chapter 32

"Mary, hurry up!" Shirley could see Mary's open door from the living room downstairs. "We're going to be late for our riding lessons."

Mary rushed out of her room. Peering over the railing at the top of the staircase, she waved at her friend below. "Be right there. I have to put on my boots."

"I'll wait in the dining room, but hurry, Mary. I want to get down to the stable before Faye makes off with Daisy."

Mary knew that Daisy was the only horse that Shirley felt comfortable riding. Although her athletic friend had no equal in the water, horseback riding didn't come easy for her. Shirley was no Dale Evans, but her enthusiasm for riding lessons had rubbed off on Mary. Arching her right foot, Mary pulled on her leather, pointed-toe boot with less difficulty than she'd had the day before. Practice made it easier, she realized, as she repeated the maneuver with her left foot. Mary ducked into her bathroom long enough to swipe on some pink lipstick before pulling her door closed and making sure that she locked it.

Without bothering to hold onto the wooden bannister, Mary began to descend the stairs. Suddenly, she tripped. She imagined pitching forward through space with nothing to anchor her, screaming with shock before she landed hard on the bare wooden plank floor at the bottom of the stairs, and moaning with pain before she drifted into unconsciousness. Luckily, reality trumped imagination, and she was able to grab the bannister firmly to prevent herself from falling too far, although her feet landed a few steps below where they'd been when she tripped. Her boots thudded against the wooden steps, and Shirley, who had stepped into the dining room for a moment to take a sip of coffee, heard the noise and came running back into the living room, followed by Carol and several other guests. Mary gripped the bannister tightly, her body twisted sideways.

"Mary, are you all right?" Shirley asked.

"Yes, but that last step was a lulu," she said, trying to make a joke. Clinging to the bannister, she slowly made her way down the rest of the stairs.

"What happened?" Carol asked as the women crowded around Mary.

"Just clumsy, I guess," Mary said, not wanting to alarm Carol. "No harm done." Mary pretended not to hear Sally whispering to Bea that she'd never seen a woman more accident-prone than Mary. She probably would have thought so herself if she hadn't come to believe that her "accidents" had all been deliberately arranged.

When the little knot of women dispersed, Shirley asked, "Do you want to skip the riding lesson today?" Mary could tell that Shirley was still in a hurry to beat Faye to the stables.

"Of course not. You go on ahead, and I'll meet you there in a couple of minutes. I just want some coffee, but I'll make it snappy."

"OK." With a little wave, Shirley rushed off.

As soon as her friend left, Mary took Carol aside, linking arms, and guided her outside to the deserted patio, away from the guests, who'd returned to the dining room.

Glancing back to make sure that Carol had closed the patio door,

Mary spoke in a low voice. "I'm going down to the corral for my riding lesson now, but please call Ben and ask him to come out here. I didn't want to say anything in front of the others, but I didn't just trip on nothing. There was something on those stairs."

"Oh, Mary, no!"

"I'm not kidding, Carol. I didn't see what it was, but there was something on the steps. I felt it."

#

When Ben arrived, he asked Mary to show him where she'd landed on the stairs after she'd tripped, and he immediately examined the staircase. He found scuff marks from her boots where the heels had scraped across the step when she'd saved herself by gripping the bannister.

"Did you see anything on the step or hear anything fall when you tripped?" Ben asked.

"No, nothing, but I felt something. I know I touched something with my boot."

"Carol, how about you?"

"I was in the dining room when it happened, so, no, I didn't notice anything. When I came back in after Mary asked me to call you, I looked around, but I didn't see anything then, either. I can't imagine why anything would be on the steps unless maybe someone dropped it by accident. The housekeepers know better than to set anything on the steps."

Ben came down and went around to the side of the staircase. He looked at the wood-turned spindles that supported the bannister, but the dim light in the paneled room made it difficult to see.

"Got a flashlight, Carol?"

"Sure. I'll fetch it." She quickly returned, carrying a long black flashlight and handed it to Ben. Mary recognized it as the same one she'd given Chuck the night she'd seen the mysterious stranger outside.

Ben clicked it on and aimed the beam up and down, along one of the spindles on the right side of the staircase; then he swung the flashlight around, illuminating the left spindle on the same step. He rubbed a spot on the spindle with his index finger and peered at it before turning off the flashlight.

"Can we talk in private?" he asked.

"Let's go back to my apartment. I wish Chuck were here this morning, but he drove a couple of the guests into Reno." Ben and Mary trailed Carol down the hallway next to the staircase to the owners' apartment at the back of the house. She closed the door firmly and indicated that they should sit down. Mary perched on the edge of a wooden rocking chair while Ben settled on the sofa, and Carol sat in an armchair next to Mary.

"Mary's right, Carol. Something was on those stairs, and Mary's lucky she didn't fall all the way to the bottom. She could easily have broken her neck. I saw marks on the spindles, faint, but unmistakable. A wire, or possibly fishing line, was strung across the stairway and tied onto the spindles. Now, ladies, I was afraid something like this might happen. Someone right here at the ranch rigged up this trap, and until I know who that someone is, Mary's going to have to stay elsewhere."

"But what about testifying as her witness? I can only testify to the days she actually stayed here."

"Nobody's asking you to lie, Carol. We'll consult Mary's lawyer about how to proceed. If she has to start over to establish her Nevada residency, so be it. Mary's life's in danger, and we can't keep pretending that she's safe here."

Although Mary heard the conversation, she felt strangely removed from it, almost as though Ben and Carol were talking about someone else. The push in front of the cab; the pull on her leg, forcing her underwater; the mysterious man in disguise, coming to attack her at the hospital; and the trap on the staircase all seemed incredible and unreal, as though she were having the worst nightmare of her life. How could her husband even consider the idea of hiring someone to kill her? She shuddered, knowing that she, once a valuable asset to him, had now become a liability, and John Garrison never hesitated to rid himself of liabilities.

"You're right, detective. I never should have resisted Mary's moving." Carol rose and went to the ornately carved, antique roll-top desk that sat in the corner of her living room. She opened a ledger filled with Circle E business checks, scribbled on one, ripped it from the ledger, and handed it to Mary. "Mary, here's a refund for the rest of your time."

"Thank you, Carol. I wish I didn't have to leave."

"I wish you didn't, either, and I'm sorry I stalled about giving you this, but I had to make sure the funds were available. Yesterday, Chuck sold Rosie and Tulip at the horse auction in Carson City— they're too high-spirited for most of the guests to ride, anyway—so you don't have to worry about your check bouncing. Chuck's right— I've been far too extravagant with expenses. The divorce business has started to wane, and we're really going to have to tighten our belts if we want to hold on for a few more years. That's probably the least of our worries now, what with some maniac running around here, trying to attack our guests. I wonder who it could be."

"I was afraid someone here at the ranch might be involved," Ben said, "and the stairway incident definitely confirms my suspicion. I'll need to get some information from you about both the employees and the guests, but that'll have to wait until Mary's moved."

"I guess I should go pack."

"I'll come with you to keep watch, Mary. I'm not letting you out of my sight until we get you settled someplace safe."

Chapter 33

As good as his word, Ben whisked Mary away from the Circle E. The wranglers had taken several of the inexperienced riders, Shirley among them, on an easy ride, sticking to a wide, flat trail that circled the ranch's property, and Chuck had driven the other guests into Reno for a day of shopping and gambling, so Mary couldn't bid her new friends goodbye. The less said, the better, in Ben's opinion. He warned Mary against contacting anyone she'd met because he wanted to prevent the would-be killer from finding her. After a brief consultation with Mary's lawyer, Bill Cooper, who assured Mary that he'd be able to use two witnesses to her residency, rather than the usual one witness, and receiving the attorney's pledge that he wouldn't discuss Mary or her case with anyone without her approval, Ben took Mary to the bank, where she cashed the check Carol had given her and purchased several travelers' checks. Avoiding the sheriff's office, Ben stopped at a pay phone and made a few calls. Then he took Mary to her new Nevada residence, where her hostesses were given only her first name. If anybody were tracking Mary Marchetti, Mary Garrison, or Mrs. John Garrison, they'd be out of luck.

Ben had just finished bringing the sheriff and Al up to date on Mary's case when he received a call from one of the jailers, telling him that the burglar he'd arrested at the flea market was begging to talk to him. The jailer said that he could bring Adam Walker to the small conference room at the jail, where lawyers met with their clients, if Ben wanted to hear what Walker had to say. Although Ben hated the jail and avoided it whenever possible, Walker's request piqued his curiosity, so Ben agreed to see Walker in the conference room right away. Ben arrived first. The only furniture in the room was a small wooden table with a chair on each side of it. If an attorney brought an associate along for a conference with a prisoner, a jailer would provide another chair. Otherwise, extra chairs were never permitted because a prisoner might decide to grab one and wreak havoc before a jailer could rush in to intervene.

Ben took the seat facing the door, and he barely recognized Walker when the jailer brought him in. He wore the baggy gray uniform that the Washoe County Jail provided all its prisoners, and his head had been shorn nearly bald. Without his tangle of greasy hair, the tattooed Walker looked even younger than he had at the flea market. Ben noticed that the handcuffed man had lost some of his swagger, too. He looked more like a whipped pup than the enterprising huckster who had tried to sell Ben a stolen rifle at the flea market. Walker dipped his head as the jailer instructed him to sit in the chair opposite Ben and to stay put. Locking the door, the guard positioned himself outside it.

"What's this about, Walker? You know we've got you dead to rights. Every single item you had with you at the flea market had been reported as stolen property, and a couple of the owners identified you in the line-up yesterday as the man they saw running from their house, leaving a trail of their silverware behind. So don't even try to tell me you didn't steal that stuff. Your story about selling it for your grandfather is nothing but a fairy tale."

"But I *was* sellin' it for my grandfather. He needs the money bad."

Ben groaned. Walker wasn't the brightest burglar he'd encountered. "That may be, but stealing isn't the way to earn money. Didn't you ever think about getting a job?"

Walker hung his head. "Don't know how to do much," he mumbled.

"Well, maybe you'll get some training in prison. Start over and go straight when you get out, and we won't ever have to arrest you again."

"I'm gonna get a long sentence, huh?"

"That's up to the judge. Why did you want to talk to me, anyway? I don't have anything to do with all that."

"Some of the other guys told me that if I knew somethin', you know, somethin' important about another crime, I could make a deal with the D.A. and maybe get a lighter sentence, but he won't talk to me. I thought maybe you could, you know, put in a good word for me."

"I can't guarantee anything, you understand. It's up to the district attorney whether or not he makes a deal, and from what you've just told me, he's not inclined to do that, probably because he has a real solid case against you."

"But what if I could tell you who killed that lady up on Mount Rose? My cellmate's sister brought us the paper yesterday, and I read all about how that lady died because someone messed with her car."

Restraining his eagerness, Ben took a deep breath. He didn't want Walker to know how excited he was at the suggestion that the prisoner might be able to provide him a lead on the Beaumont case. "If you know anything about that, I'd strongly advise you to tell me."

"If it pans out, will you talk to the D.A.?"

"Let's quit beating around the bush. Do you know who did it?"

"I might."

"Walker, I'm ready to leave right now if you won't talk. If your information helps us find the killer, yes, you bet I'll go to bat for you with the district attorney. That's the best I can do. I already told you he's the only one who can cut a deal for a lighter sentence."

"OK," Walker sighed. "I'm at the Silverado Bar about a week ago, and this guy I never seen before's all liquored up. It's gettin' late—no one there except him and me. The barkeep says 'last round,' and the guy takes a swing at him, misses him by a mile, so I says 'hey, buddy, let's get out of this dive.'"

"Were you drunk, Walker?"

"No, I swear. I only had a couple beers."

"OK, go on."

"So we go out to his truck. He can hardly stand up. I stuff him into his truck, and he says he'll give me five bucks to drive him home, so I say OK. He keeps mumblin' about brakes, but I don't think anythin' of it until we get to his place, and, out of the blue, he says don't tell anyone but he rigged up a car so's the brakes would fail and it ran right off the side of a mountain. Then he starts bawlin'. I tell him I want the five bucks he promised me, and when he hands it over, I get the hell out of there."

"What's this man's name?"

"Dunno."

"You're going to have to do better than that."

"Uh," Walker squinted. "He never told me his name, but it was on his shirt, you know, like a gas station attendant." Walker pointed to the shirt pocket of his prison uniform. "Right about here—Mac."

"Can you tell me where his place is?"

"Sure. Left him sittin' in the parkin' lot of his garage—over on East Fourth Street, right next to the Five Star Motel."

"All right, Walker, you may be onto something here. I'm going to check into your story. In the meantime, don't discuss it with anyone. One more thing: can you describe his truck?"

"Just an old black pickup. Nothin' special."

#

Virgil was coming off duty for the day when Ben flagged him down.

"The sheriff approved some overtime for you this evening if you're game."

"Great! Give me a minute to call Cindy and let her know I'll be late."

Ben nodded. He could barely contain his excitement. They could be arresting Candice Martin Littleton's killer if Walker's information panned out. Ben planned to bring Mac in for questioning, and he hoped Virgil's familiar presence would prevent Mac from clamming up. He'd been drunk when he talked to Walker, but Ben feared that Mac wasn't likely to be so free with a confession when confronted by two lawmen, even if one of them was his former employee, an employee he'd obviously valued since he'd asked Virgil to return to work for him at his garage.

"Has your former boss ever had any trouble with the law?" Ben asked on the drive to Mac's Motors, after he'd filled Virgil in on the latest developments.

"Far as I know, a couple of DUIs."

"Does he strike you as the kind of person who would rig a car's brakes to fail?"

"Maybe, if he felt desperate enough, yeah."

"Let's park the squad car where he can't see it, then. He might get spooked." Virgil angled the car into a narrow space on the side of the Five Star Motel, and they hoofed it around the front of the building, approaching Mac's Motors from the west. Leaning under the hood of a battered Pontiac sedan, Mac hovered above its engine, examining a hose. The mechanic turned around when he heard them and, squinting, shaded his eyes with his grease-covered arm. Ben noticed that "Mac" was embroidered on the shirt's pocket, just as Walker had described.

"Virgil? You decide to take me up on my offer?"

"No, we're here on another matter."

Ben, dressed in his suit, pulled out his wallet and displayed his badge. "Detective Ben Cameron, Sheriff's Department. Like to ask you a few questions."

Mac's eyes darted back and forth between Virgil and Ben. "Sure. What's all this about?"

"Downtown," Ben said, ignoring his question.

"Up to my elbows in grease. Mind if I clean up first?"

"Go ahead." While Mac stepped into his office, Ben lit a Lucky. He took a couple of drags on it before it occurred to him that Mac might not come back. "Virgil, is there another way out of that office?"

"Nope. One tiny window way up high, not big enough for a man to get through." A come-the-dawn look passed over Virgil's face. "But he keeps a shotgun in the corner!"

Ben dropped his cigarette and drew his gun from his shoulder holster. Virgil reached for his own gun, as Ben signaled to him, and they positioned themselves on either side of the door. By seconds, a metallic click preceded the appearance of a gun barrel in the doorway, rapidly followed by a shotgun blast. If Mac had intended to aim to hit them, he'd miscalculated by a mile, as the shot shattered the window of a tan Studebaker in for repair and punctured its door.

"You fool!" Virgil shouted.

Ben grabbed the shotgun's barrel and, pulling Mac outside, wrenched it from his grip. Virgil pounced on his former boss, knocking him to the ground. Mac landed hard on the gravel. Before he could move, Ben yanked his arms behind his back, handcuffing him and pulling him to his feet. Mac's face and forearms oozed blood from scraped skin, and a red stream trickled from his nose, spotting his grease-stained work shirt. Virgil picked up the shotgun and pulled Mac's office door closed. Sandwiching their prisoner between them, Ben and Virgil hauled him to the patrol car and settled him in the back seat.

"Virgil, sorry I took a pot shot at you," Mac whined, as Virgil started the car. "I didn't mean no harm."

"I'm not buying that for a minute. Why'd you shoot that twelve gauge?"

Mac shrugged.

"You went off the rails somewhere along the line, and now you're going to have to pay the piper."

"Don't know what you mean."

"So I suppose you don't know anything about the accident up on Mount Rose a couple of weeks ago?" Ben interjected.

"Don't know nothing about that lady's brakes."

Ben and Virgil looked at each other. "I didn't say anything about brakes," Ben continued. "Neither did the newspaper article about the accident. It mentioned that the car had been tampered with. Period."

Chapter 34

Like Carol and Chuck Ellis, the Granger sisters acted as hospitable hosts. Mary felt comfortable at their ranch as well as relieved to escape the danger lurking at the Circle E. Warning Mary not to contact anyone at the Circle E during the rest of her stay in Nevada, not even her friend Shirley, Ben had whisked her away from the ranch. She knew the detective believed that one of the Circle E's guests was a hired killer, disguised as a prospective divorcée, and she feared that Shirley topped Ben's suspect list. With a pang of guilt, Mary thought of her own momentary doubt about Shirley. Although Shirley had been on the scene of three attacks, she couldn't be the person who had sneaked into the hospital in search of Mary because Ben said that person was a man. Although that fact didn't completely eliminate Shirley as a suspect because she could have an accomplice, Mary couldn't think of any reason that Dale Snow's wife would involve herself in such a scheme. Besides, she liked the ebullient Shirley who had welcomed her to the world of the Nevada divorce ranch and who had made her feel at home in a strange land.

"Breakfast!" Maggie Granger, one of the sisters who owned the Verdi Guest Ranch, called. Mary joined Maggie and her sister Beth at their kitchen table. Although the sisters had closed their guest ranch operation in anticipation of converting their business exclusively to horse boarding, they had agreed to house Mary when Carmine, at Ben's request, had explained her dangerous situation to them. With no staff to help them in the interim, the sisters busied themselves with caring for their own horses, maintaining their property, and cooking their own meals.

"I made eggs Benedict, Mary," Maggie, a stocky woman in her fifties, said. "I hope you like it. "Homemade cinnamon rolls, too."

"Everything looks delicious," Mary said, sipping her coffee. "Did you do the cooking when you ran your guest ranch?"

"Mercy, no. I'm not good at managing crowd-sized portions. We had a wonderful cook, but she wanted to retire, so closing the guest operation didn't put her out."

"We hated to lay off our staff, but they've all landed on their feet, thank goodness," Beth, a round middle-aged woman with cropped gray hair, added. "I really think changing to a horse operation will work out well. It's always been all about the horses for us. We learned to ride when we were toddlers, didn't we, Maggie?"

Maggie nodded. "Mary, you said you'd taken a few riding lessons at the Circle E. I hope you'll continue here."

"I'd like to." Although Mary felt grateful for a safe place to stay, she'd wondered how she'd occupy her time since there were no other guests staying at the ranch. She'd also noticed that the sisters had drained their swimming pool.

"Let's get you on Patches after breakfast, Mary," Beth said. "She's a nice gentle horse for a beginner."

"We'll give you some carrots to feed her," Maggie added, "and she'll befriend you for life."

"Have another cinnamon roll, Mary," Beth urged. "It won't hurt. You're so thin, Patches won't even know that she has a rider."

Much to Mary's delight, Patches, a chestnut and white pinto with a docile temperament, took to her right away, consuming a bunch of carrots, leafy stems and all, and standing patiently while Mary struggled to saddle her after Beth demonstrated the proper technique. Mary had never saddled a horse—at the Circle E, the wranglers had always saddled the horses for the guests—and it took her a while to get the hang of it, but Patches never budged until Mary mounted and urged her to a walk. Patches' slow, steady gait made riding her easy, and Mary spent a pleasant morning while she circled around the corral. Beth gave her some pointers about correct posture and demonstrated trotting, although Mary didn't feel ready to attempt a faster pace yet.

After a lunch of hamburgers and potato salad with the Granger sisters, Mary spent the afternoon writing letters to her family and friends. In a cheerful tone, she recounted anecdotes about some of the guests at the Circle E, deliberately omitting any mention of the danger she faced. She knew that her parents, especially, worried about her, and she didn't want to add to their distress. She didn't mention her move from the Circle E to the Verdi Guest Ranch, north of Reno. Ben had arranged for Chuck to drop off any mail that might come for Mary at the Sheriff's Department. Mary knew that Ben made it a priority to make sure that nobody discovered where she was staying now. Only Ben, Carmine, and the Granger sisters were aware of her current whereabouts, and none of them would reveal her secret.

By evening, Mary felt at loose ends. The sisters dined early, and the evening stretched on without much to do except watch television shows that Reno's only channel broadcast, but since reruns dominated the summer schedule, Mary soon tired of watching. Maggie suggested that Mary might find a book to read in the ranch's library, and Mary dutifully followed her into a large room in the back of the house that doubled as both library and office. The book collection took Mary's breath away. Built-in shelves, packed with books, lined all four walls of the room. Avid readers, the Granger sisters had accumulated thousands of nonfiction books on a wide range of subjects, in addition to classic volumes of Shakespeare and other famous writers, as well as bestselling novels and hundreds of Westerns and mysteries. Although Mary had never read a Zane Grey or a Louis L'Amour novel, she selected one of each along with a book about horses, attracted by the cover photo of a pinto.

"Look, Maggie, doesn't that horse remind you of Patches?"

"It does. In fact, it *is* Patches."

"Patches is a cover girl?"

"She sure is. The publisher who puts out those books about horses was a guest here at the ranch a few years ago. She asked to use Patches and some of our other horses on her book covers, and we liked the idea. Our horses have modeled for professional photographers more times than I can count. I have some albums of stills that they gave us if you'd like to see them."

"How wonderful! I'd love to see them."

Maggie pulled three large albums bound in hand-tooled leather from the corner shelf in back of her desk. They returned to the living room just as Beth switched off the television, and the three women sat side-by-side on the sofa with Mary in the middle, an album on her lap, as they paged through it, showing Mary the photographs of their horses and some other scenes around the ranch. As far as Mary was concerned, Patches was the main enticement. Mary liked her easy-going manner, and she found the little horse's chestnut and white markings striking. As she turned the page from a particularly handsome image of Patches, she paused at a group photograph that looked less polished than the other pictures.

"Did the publisher's photographer take this picture?"

"You found me out, Mary," Maggie said. "No, I took it myself with my Kodak. Of course, the quality's not as good as the professional's, but I like to keep some group pictures of our guests, so I took one about every six weeks or so. We called these ladies the 'ditzy dozen.' They were always pulling pranks on each other and doing zany things."

"Maybe one too many," Beth said.

"Oh, Beth, you don't really think so, do you?"

"I've often wondered."

Confused, Mary looked from one pensive sister to the other, but the two women offered no explanation, and Beth turned to the next page of the photo album, a large black-and-white picture of the same group of women clustered around Patches. Looking closely at the photo, Mary caught her breath as she spied a familiar face.

"She looks like a lady I know," she said pointing to the woman's image.

"You mean Helen?" Maggie said. "Helen Lester's her name. She was here about two years ago, but she didn't stay long enough to establish residency. I remember that she decided to reconcile with her husband."

"Helen Lester? That's not the name she's using now."

"Maybe she changed her mind again, and either remarried or took back her maiden name."

"I don't think so. I think she changed her name for an entirely different reason."

Chapter 35

Since Mac refused to talk after tripping himself up when he inadvertently admitted knowledge about the tampering of the wrecked Cadillac's brakes, Ben and Virgil delivered him to the jail. After Ben filled out an incident report, he went home, satisfied that they had caught Candice Martin Littleton's killer, but he wondered whether he had enough evidence for the district attorney to make a case against Mac for the murder. So far, Mac had racked up charges of resisting arrest and assault, maybe even attempted murder, which would keep him locked up for a while. Tomorrow, Jeff Jergens, the deputy in charge of fingerprint matching, could compare the fingerprints the jailer had taken when Mac was booked with the ones Ben and Virgil had gathered from the underbelly of the wrecked Caddy. Ben eagerly awaited his findings. If Jergens matched them, the fingerprint evidence would bolster the D.A.'s murder case.

The following morning, Jergens' ear-splitting whoop of excitement fulfilled Ben's hopes and brought the sheriff striding into the squad room to see what all the yelling was about. When he learned that Jergens had identified solid matches to Mac on four prints from the Cadillac, he shook hands with Jergens. Ben and Virgil, who'd waited impatiently while Jergens examined the evidence, did the same.

With physical evidence backing the confessions Mac had made about the crime, the case looked solid to Ben, but to prevent the mechanic from claiming that he'd worked on the car when the owner had brought it into his shop for repair, Ben called Chuck Ellis to inquire about when Candice, posing as Phyllis Beaumont, had driven the car during her short stay at the ranch. According to Chuck, Candice hadn't driven the car at all once she arrived at the ranch, except for her ill-fated trip to Lake Tahoe, but she had asked Chuck to take the car into town for a routine oil change. Luckily, he'd taken it to the Cadillac dealership, rather than to Mac's Motors. After hearing this bit of news, Ben felt confident that Mac's attorney wouldn't find any loopholes in the case against the wayward mechanic, and he grinned, slapping his hand on the top of his desk. His first case solved—a huge accomplishment. Even in his triumph, however, the nagging thought that he had captured only the low man on the totem pole rankled. Although he hadn't given up on making a case against the instigator of the crime—Adrian Beaumont, undoubtedly—he realized the difficulty in succeeding. With Beaumont out of the country, Ben couldn't question him. Unless Mac rolled over, making the connection between the mechanic and the movie director might be impossible. Finding out whether Mac had received a great deal of money as a payoff from Beaumont might prove impossible, too, given that Mac gambled, often winning and losing large sums, but he intended to look into Mac's financial affairs, anyway. In his short time as an investigator, he'd been surprised more than once. Something just might turn up unexpectedly.

After the sheriff and deputies returned to their duties, only Ben and Anita remained in the squad room. Although the fingerprint matching worked in Mac's case, Mary's attacker had left no fingerprints on either the syringe or the stethoscope left at the hospital. Until she'd been deliberately tripped at the Circle E, Ben had assumed that the attacker in disguise as a physician had been a man. Now he felt certain it was a woman—someone Mary knew at the Circle E. Since only three men—Chuck and the two wranglers—lived on the place, and none of them had been in the vicinity of any of Mary's accidents, Ben decided the perpetrator must be one of the guests who had gone on the outing to Pyramid Lake with Mary.

Ben felt irritated at himself for not seeing it sooner, and he realized that he often jumped to conclusions. Sometimes they were right; sometimes they were wrong. He told himself that if he didn't break that habit and fast, he could end up a second-rate detective. On the other hand, his job required some level of intuitive thinking, but intuition proved useless unless backed by evidence.

The constant clattering of typewriter keys ceased, and Anita smoothly rolled the last page of the report she had just finished from her Underwood, a machine of the same vintage as the one sitting on Ben's desk.

"I don't know how you can type so fast on that old machine," Ben commented. "It seems to me it's about time to replace some of our equipment."

"I wouldn't mind having a new typewriter. This one's keys stick sometimes, but I guess I've gotten used to it, so it doesn't slow me down too much."

"Say, Anita, I know this is going to seem like a strange question, but humor me. Do you ever read any movie magazines?"

"With two little kids and a full-time job? I don't have much time for either movies or movie magazines anymore. Why do you ask?"

"Just thought maybe I could take a shortcut to identifying someone. I need to find a picture of Dale Snow's wife."

"Oh, I love him. Even though it's been a good long time since I've seen a movie, I know who he is! If anyone's seen a picture of his wife, it would be my neighbor LuAnn. She can tell you anything and everything about all the Hollywood stars, and she never throws her movie magazines away. Want me to give her a call?"

"I'd sure appreciate it. If she could come up with a picture of Snow's wife, it would be a big help."

Ben turned back to study Mary's case file while Anita dialed her neighbor, but before he even opened the file, the sheriff called him into his office to discuss the presentation of their case against Mac to the district attorney. After reviewing all the evidence again, the sheriff called the district attorney's office and made an appointment for them to bring the case to him. Although Ben and the sheriff agreed that they had enough evidence to support a first-degree murder charge against Ronald "Mac" McCormick, the district attorney determined the actual charges. The appointment made, Ben returned to the squad room to find a plump redhead with a freckled face talking to Anita.

"Ben, look what my neighbor brought." Anita held up a dog-eared copy of *Stars and Styles*. "This is my neighbor LuAnn Howard."

"Is this what you're looking for, detective?" LuAnn asked after they had exchanged polite pleasantries. She turned to a photo spread titled "At Home with the Snowdens," featuring a full-page photo of Dale Snow leaning against a mantle on which his two best-actor Oscars were prominently displayed. "The story starts here, but on the next page, you can see both Dale and his wife."

She flipped the page to a photo of Shirley Snowden posing with her husband beside their swimming pool. The picture left Ben in no doubt that Mary's friend Shirley, the woman he'd pegged as the most likely suspect in Mary's attacks, really was the wife of the famous film star. Considering her status, he decided that he'd have to look closer at the other guests. Shirley was who she said she was, and Ben could think of no reason for her to involve herself in the heinous attacks on Mary.

"That's exactly what I was looking for, Mrs. Howard," Ben said. "I appreciate you going to the trouble of coming all the way down here to show it to me. Let me take you two ladies to lunch at the Mapes. It's the least I can do."

Anita lost no time in grabbing her hat and handbag. "That sounds better than the cheese sandwich I brought."

"I just love the restaurants at the Mapes." LuAnn beamed. "They have such scrumptious desserts!"

Ben ushered Anita and LuAnn to the Mapes, and during lunch he tried to keep up with their conversation, but their girl talk sometimes eluded him. He couldn't help but think that it would have been more pleasant if he and Anita had lunched alone. It was too bad that Anita didn't have a man to share her life and be a father to her boys. Daydreaming, he imagined himself in that role, but he snapped out of his reverie when the time came to order dessert. As he ate his whipped-cream-topped cheesecake, he had to admit that LuAnn Howard was right: desserts at the Mapes were delicious.

Back at the office, fortified by a large lunch, Ben yawned. Eating a big meal often made him want to take a nap, but he poured a cup of coffee to keep himself awake. After staring at his reports in Mary's file while he drained his coffee mug, Ben decided to take another look at the only physical evidence he had—the brown paper bag and its contents that the head custodian had discovered at Reno Regional Hospital.

Even though they hadn't found any fingerprints on either the syringe or the stethoscope, Ben figured maybe the bag or its contents might yield a clue to the identity of the attacker. Removing the bag from the evidence locker, he took it to his desk and carefully inspected each item, but he found nothing new until he came to the stretchy cap that nestled inside the toupee. Inside the skull cap, clinging to the stretchy fabric, Ben discovered several hairs. With painstaking precision, he used tweezers to pluck them, one by one, from the cap, placing them on a piece of typing paper. Some of the hairs were black, others white, and they each measured about four inches, certainly longer than most men wore their hair. Like Ben, many men sported flattops, and a lot of others wore crew cuts, but none of the men Ben knew had long hair. This finding supported Ben's new theory that the perpetrator was a woman, not a man. The color of the hairs didn't point to the woman he had once suspected. Shirley Snowden's hair was brown, not a mixture of black and white.

"Ben, telephone for you," Anita said.

Still staring at the hairs he'd extracted from the skull cap, Ben picked up the phone.

"Ben, it's Mary. I called a couple of times earlier, but you were out both times. I guess I should have left a message." The timber of Mary's voice caught Ben's attention. She sounded breathless and excited. "Could you come out to the ranch? I found something that you should see. I think it could be important."

"I'm on my way."

Chapter 36

Brushing aside the sheer white curtain at the window next to the front door of the Granger sisters' ranch, Mary watched for Ben. She frowned when a black Oldsmobile turned into their lane and parked right outside the front door. Mary expected Ben to drive either his red pickup truck or a sheriff's department patrol car. Resolving that she wouldn't answer the door, she backed away from the window so that the driver couldn't see her, but she was still able to see outside. The driver emerged from the Olds, and as soon as Mary saw that the caller was Ben, after all, she flung the door open.

"Mary, you look startled. Is everything all right?"

"Yes, everything's fine. I just expected to see your truck or a patrol car."

Ben glanced over his shoulder. "Let's go inside."

"Of course," Mary agreed, backing up so that Ben could enter the ranch house.

"I borrowed one of the deputies' cars because I didn't want to take a chance that someone might follow me. Everybody at the Circle E knows I drive a red pickup or an official car."

"Do you really think someone's following you?"

"No, but where your safety's concerned, I don't want to take any chances. We moved you out here so that nobody knows where you're staying, except me and Carmine, and I intend to keep it that way. You're using the Circle E as your return address for all your correspondence, right?"

"Yes, just like you suggested, and I haven't called anyone except you."

"I'm really sorry that you have to go through all this, Mary, but we can't take any more chances. You'll stay here in seclusion until your day in court."

"I'm reconciled to doing that, Ben. The Granger sisters have been very sweet to me, opening their home even though they're not in the guest ranch business anymore."

"Carmine said they're good folks. He got to know them when he was investigating a case."

"Maggie and Beth are out tending to the horses right now. Come on into the kitchen, Ben," Mary said, leading Ben to the back of the house, "and I'll show you why I called. Let's sit here at the table." Mary picked up a photo album that lay on the kitchen table and opened it to the picture of Patches, surrounded by the group of women that Maggie had called the "ditzy dozen."

"This picture was taken of some of the guests here two years ago. Recognize anyone?"

Ben pulled the album closer and looked at the photo. "I sure do."

"You don't seem surprised."

"Well, I wasn't expecting it, but, on the other hand, I'm not shocked. Things are falling into place. In fact, seeing Bea's picture there confirms what I was beginning to suspect."

"Maggie said her name was Helen Lester, not Bea Carstairs."

"I doubt that either is her real name."

"Why do you suppose she was here? The Granger sisters told me that she left because she was reconciling with her husband."

"I suspect she left because she had finished her job. Causing accidents seems to be her specialty, and there was one here a couple of years ago. Just think about it, Mary. Bea knew that you and Shirley were going into Reno the day you were pushed into the street. She could have easily hidden in the crowd, and you wouldn't have noticed her. She may even have used a disguise like she did at the hospital. At Pyramid Lake, she visited the beach with you and the rest of the ladies. She could have been the person who pulled you under the water, and at the Circle E, she had ample opportunity to rig a wire across the stairs to trip you and time to take it down, too."

Queasy at the thought of Bea as a hired killer, Mary listened to Ben's reasoning. It was difficult to believe that Bea, who'd seemed so harmless, could have plotted and carried out the attacks on her. Ben reached over and put his hand on Mary's.

"Mary, I'm afraid that the only hard evidence I have are the hairs I found in the skull cap that she wore under her toupee when she disguised herself to come after you at the hospital. I really doubt that's enough to convince the district attorney to charge Bea. Rest assured, I'll try, though. I'm going to bring Bea in for questioning. In fact, just to make sure she's on the premises when I show up, I'll call Carol right now to find out where Bea is, if the Grangers don't mind me using their phone."

Mary accompanied Ben to the stables where Beth Granger gave him the go-ahead to use their phone. He promised that the department would pay for any long-distance charges he incurred since he didn't know whether a call to Reno from Verdi would fall in the local category or not. Mary waited outside the door as Ben, wasting no time, placed the call from the extension phone in the office at the stables. Although she couldn't hear what he said during the short conversation, she did hear the oath Ben uttered after hanging up the phone.

"She's vanished, Mary. Bea took a powder right after we left the ranch yesterday. According to Carol, she cleared out without a word to anyone, including the Ellises. You can best bet all the information she gave the Ellises when she booked her stay is phony. She left in a taxi. I should be able to find out where the cab driver dropped her, but I'll bet the bus depot or the train station. She could be anywhere by now, and she'll be using a different name to boot."

"Do you think she'll try to come after me again?" Mary shivered as she wrapped her arms around herself. "After I died and came back, I thought that I could accept whatever happened. But now, well, I guess I'm really back on earth because I'm scared, Ben. I'm really scared." She leaned against Ben as he circled her with his arm.

"We're going to do something about that right now, Mary," Ben said decisively. "I think I have a plan that just might work. Sometimes the best defense is a good offense." As they walked back to the ranch house, Ben explained what he intended to do.

An hour later, Mary, wearing her jeans, Western boots, and Stetson hat, pulled low over her eyes, slipped out of the car Ben drove and hastily entered the back door of a tavern on West Fourth Street, accompanied by Ben, who had parked in the deserted area behind the building. They moved down a hallway and entered a door marked "Private," where a thin man dressed in a tan summer suit awaited them. Ben shook his hand and introduced Mary to the reporter.

The cramped, windowless room, obviously the bar's office, was sparsely furnished with a small desk and a couple of chairs. Cal Harris motioned for Mary and Ben to sit down while he took the chair behind the desk.

"Don't worry about anyone spotting you, Miss Marchetti. The owner of this place is a friend of mine. He's in front, behind the bar, and when I came in, there wasn't a customer in the place. Nobody knows you're here, and I'm sure the detective can get you back to wherever you're staying without anyone knowing."

Mary nodded. Ben had been watching to see if they'd been followed when they left Verdi, but there hadn't been a car in sight when he pulled out of the Granger sisters' lane.

"Here's what I've come up with." Harris set a typewritten note on the desk so that Mary and Ben could read it. "Of course, you understand I'll have to double-check with the sources named to confirm what I'm reporting, so you better give the Ellises and Cooper a heads-up that I'll be calling them. I wrote this article based on what you told me, Ben."

Candidate Garrison's Wife Reno-Vated

Mrs. John Garrison, wife of New York Congressional candidate John Garrison, is in Reno to establish the six weeks' residency required by Nevada law in order to seek a divorce from her husband of two years. The former Mary Marchetti, who arrived in Reno by train two-and-a-half weeks ago, is thought to be staying at the exclusive Circle E Guest Ranch, south of the Biggest Little City. Ranch owners William "Chuck" Ellis and his wife Carol Ellis would neither confirm nor deny that Mrs. Garrison is staying at the Circle E.

According to Bill Cooper, Mrs. Garrison's Reno attorney, Mrs. Garrison will seek a divorce, citing grounds of "extreme cruelty." Frank Valspar, who represents Mr. Garrison, said that his client would deny any and all claims made by his wife, the plaintiff, but that a property settlement has already been reached, negotiated by the couple's respective lawyers in New York.

John Garrison is running for U.S. Representative from the 30th District in New York, an area heavily populated by voters of Italian and Irish descent. Garrison's wife's dual Italian-Irish heritage and her work on behalf of numerous charitable causes in the district were widely believed to be defining factors in Garrison's Congressional race. When asked what effect the Garrisons' divorce would have on his bid for Congress, Garrison's spokesman refused to comment. The district's seat in the House of Representatives is traditionally one of the most influential in Congress. The seat has never been held by a divorced man.

Mary quickly scanned the article. "Do you really think this will work, Ben? John's going to be absolutely furious when word gets out that I'm divorcing him."

"If I didn't think it would work, I wouldn't suggest it. Until now, your husband's had the upper hand. This is going to turn the tables. He hired Bea to arrange an accident so that he could gain sympathy as a widower. He figured you'd be long gone before your case ever came up, and he could keep your intention to divorce him from the public. Once this article runs in a New York paper, the whole world will know, and there's no point, other than sheer revenge, of his continuing to try to harm you. From what you've told me about him, your husband sounds like a pragmatist. After he reads this, I'll bet he figures out a way to build his political career as a divorced man. Be prepared for some nastiness in the press because he'll probably blame you for the divorce and impugn your character."

"Better my character than my life. People who know me know the truth. It doesn't matter what anybody else thinks."

"All right," Harris said. "Here's how it works. This article will run in tomorrow's *Nevada State Journal*. Frankly, it's not of much interest locally, so it'll probably be buried in the back. I'll let the wire service know that it's a national story, and the New York newspapers will pick it up from the wire service. Of course, I'll tip some of the New York editors that the story's going to be on the wire. They'll take it from there. You can best bet, they'll write their own follow-up stories about the effect your divorce will have on the election."

"I wish it hadn't come to this," Mary said, "but thank you for your help, Mr. Harris."

"Just repaying a favor from the detective here. This morning, he gave me an exclusive about the arrest of the mechanic who rigged the brakes on the Beaumont car to fail."

"Ben, you didn't tell me."

"It happened just last night. The man owns a garage called Mac's Motors."

"A mechanic? So nobody at the Circle E was involved?"

"Somebody who knew Candice was planning to go to the Cal Neva had to have tipped Mac off, and that person was most likely staying at the Circle E. At first, I thought Mrs. Smythe, the woman who left abruptly not too long after you arrived, may have been involved, but I checked her out, and she's clean. I have my suspicions about who did it."

Mary guessed that Ben referred to Bea but that he didn't want to give the reporter any names.

"Sounds like another story to me," Harris said, his wolfish eyes gleaming.

"Only a hunch. If I can develop a solid case, you'll be the first to know, Cal. One more thing—could you hold off on contacting Garrison for a couple of hours? There's something I need to take care of first."

Chapter 37

"Urgent call for Mr. John Garrison from the Washoe County Sheriff's Department in Nevada," Ben declared. "It's about his wife."

"One moment, sir," replied a man with a clipped British accent. Ben assumed that he must be Garrison's butler.

"This is John Garrison." The distant voice sounded tinny on the telephone, but Ben noticed an expectant tone, too.

"Mr. Garrison, this is Detective Ben Cameron from the Washoe County Sheriff's Department in Reno. I'm calling about your wife."

"Yes?" The anticipatory tone grew stronger. Ben detected a note of poorly concealed excitement in the candidate's voice.

"Your wife's suffered a series of accidents since arriving in Reno."

"She's not . . .?"

"Dead? No, Mr. Garrison, your wife is perfectly fine." Garrison emitted a barely audible sigh. Ben could imagine his disappointment.

"We're doing everything possible to protect your wife and to ensure that she doesn't have any more accidents during her stay in Nevada."

Quickly recovering his political savvy, Garrison said, "I appreciate the sheriff's department's help."

"Glad to oblige."

"I'm a big supporter of law and order, you know."

"I'm sure you are, Mr. Garrison," Ben said mildly. "It's not the wild West out here anymore. We've modernized our methods of crime fighting. The long arm of the law can reach all the way from Nevada to New York, if necessary." Ben added, "But I'm sure it won't be necessary in this case."

"I don't know what you mean, detective," Garrison, wary now, said.

"I think you do. Good-night, Mr. Garrison." Ben hung up without waiting for Garrison to reply.

During the entire conversation, Ben held his anger with Garrison in check. Although he'd have preferred to lash out at the man, he believed that his controlled warning would serve its purpose better than an angry tirade. If Mary's situation hadn't been so dangerous, Ben would have been almost amused by the candidate's response to Ben's call. Garrison had no idea that his world was about to come crashing down. Of course, he'd receive an alert when Harris called him to try to get a comment on the divorce article. He might even attempt to suppress the story, but Harris had assured Ben that editors wouldn't be intimidated by the likes of Garrison, not when they had a story that could affect a New York Congressional election.

After Ben had taken Mary back to the Grangers, he'd made a point of extracting her promise, as well as the Grangers', that she'd remain in seclusion and refrain from calling anyone, except Ben or the sheriff's department, during her remaining weeks in Nevada, even though he believed that Garrison would back off after the story about his divorce ran. Ben doubted that he'd replace Bea with a different hired gun, but common sense dictated caution.

He thought of Mary and how beautiful she'd looked when he'd left. She'd reached up—a far reach for her to a man who stood a foot and a half taller than she did—and guided his face to hers, grazing his lips gently with her own.

"Thank you, Ben," she'd said softly. "I'll never forget what you did for me." Sweet, poignant, final. Although Ben knew that he'd see Mary again, he also knew that she'd decided against any romantic relationship between them.

"Cameron? Cameron? Are you deaf, man?"

Ben started, nearly upending the ashtray, where his burning cigarette, now mostly ash, rested. He looked up to see Overmeyer moving a chair beside Ben's desk.

"Talk to you a minute?" Overmeyer asked in a low voice, his eyes darting around the squad room. "Confidentially?"

"Uh, sure." Ben sat back in his chair, but Overmeyer pulled his own chair closer and leaned over the desk toward Ben, motioning the detective closer. Inclining his head slightly, Ben made his only concession to Overmeyer's gesture.

"I know we haven't always seen eye-to-eye," Overmeyer said, in what Ben considered a huge understatement, "but it wouldn't be fair for my brother to suffer because of it."

"OK." Ben hadn't switched gears yet. He had no idea what Overmeyer wanted.

"Glad you agree. Since you got tapped first and Virgil second, it's my brother's turn now. He's been passed over twice for no good reason, and he don't even want to apply for the deputy's job again— your old job." Ben knew that Overmeyer thought his brother should have been hired two years ago, rather than Ben. "I talked him into it, though. He can't get hired if he don't apply."

"That's true," Ben agreed.

"So you'll put in a good word for him?"

"The sheriff does all the hiring. I don't have a thing to do with it."

"You can put in a good word for my brother Tim. Rogers likes you. He'll listen to what you have to say."

"Well, I don't know about that."

"He promoted you, didn't he? Ahead of lots of guys who been here longer. Yeah, you're the golden boy." Ben noticed that even when Overmeyer was wheedling him for a favor, he couldn't help getting in a little dig.

"But I don't know your brother."

"Tim's a good guy," Overmeyer assured Ben. "Be a crackerjack deputy—better 'n me." That declaration didn't exactly constitute a ringing endorsement, considering what Ben knew about Overmeyer's abilities. Still, he couldn't fault a man for trying to help his own brother.

"I'm sure the sheriff will choose the best man for the job."

"Right. Appreciate your help, detective." Overmeyer stood, extending his hand. Ben shook it, just as the sheriff burst into the squad room.

"Ready to roll, Ben? Appointment with the D.A.'s in ten minutes."

"Yes, sir." Ben grabbed the Beaumont/Martin case file, earning a knowing smile from Overmeyer as, whistling, he departed.

Half an hour of District Attorney Korel's grilling him on the details of the Beaumont/Martin case was plenty for Ben. True to his word, Ben credited Walker with providing the tip that led to Mac's arrest, and he successfully lobbied Korel to make a plea agreement with the hapless burglar. In Mac's case, the D.A. settled on charges of resisting arrest, assault, and first-degree murder, but he wanted Ben to look into Mac's financial dealings to find evidence to back up the murder-for-hire theory that the district attorney planned to present at Mac's trial.

When he returned to the office, Ben watched for Virgil to return from his day-shift patrol as the deputies assigned to night duty drifted in to report. As soon as Virgil showed up to clock out, Ben took him aside and told him what the district attorney had said about Mac's case.

"Do you know where Mac banked?" Ben asked. "I think you mentioned that his checks didn't always clear, so I assume he has a checking account."

"Yeah, he does. Overdrawn most of the time. It's at the Washoe Heritage State Bank."

"I guess I'd better check his bank records to see whether he deposited any large sums."

"That would go against the grain. Money burns a hole in his pocket. He never could stay out of the casinos."

"Do you happen to know where Mac gambled, Virgil?"

"Seems to me he did most of his gambling at Fabio's Club."

"Isn't Fabio connected?"

"That's the rumor. I doubt that he'd tell you anything. There's something else that I should have thought of earlier, though. When he was feeling flush, Mac used to drive up to the Cal Neva at Tahoe. Maybe he ran a tab there."

"Worth checking. It wouldn't hurt if we could find a witness who saw him there on the night he rigged the brakes, even if the D.A. thinks the fingerprints give him enough solid physical evidence to charge Mac. If I could just find the money trail that leads back to Beaumont. . ."

"You're sure Beaumont put him up to it?"

"Pretty sure, but someone else must have brokered the deal. I doubt that Beaumont and Mac ever met."

"Tomorrow I'm scheduled to patrol the Tahoe area. You want me to stop in at the Cal Neva and nose around?"

"I'd appreciate that. Guess I should get over to the jail now—have to keep a promise."

#

"Ben," the excitement in Virgil's voice came through loud and clear as soon as Ben picked up the phone. "We got him dead to rights."

"What?" Ben asked, snapping his radio off.

"I'm calling from the Cal Neva, and guess who lost a bundle here at blackjack the night of the accident?"

Ben grinned. "Mac."

"That's right. I talked to a dealer who saw him here, and he's willing to testify. It gets better than that. After Mac lost what little cash he had with him, he insisted that he had a big line of credit with the casino. The dealer didn't believe him, but it turned out to be true. He ran through the entire five thousand in a couple of hours."

Ben emitted a low whistle. "Good work, Virgil! With an eyewitness who can put him there and the fingerprint match, the D.A. shouldn't have a bit of trouble making his case."

"Nope. I knew Mac was a gambler, and he may not have been the best boss in the world, but I sure never would have pegged him as a killer. Just goes to show what some people will do when they're desperate, I guess."

"Did you happen to find out how Mac came to have a line of credit there?"

"Yeah, I did, from the casino's cashier. Seems that, about a week before the accident, a woman called to make arrangements for a wire transfer to the casino's account to be credited to Mac."

"A woman, huh?" Ben scratched his chin. "Any idea who she was?"

"No, but the cashier said the call definitely came through from the Los Angeles area. She remembers the operator saying that when the call was connected. She remembered it because it's unusual for gamblers to arrange credit ahead of time, especially for such a large amount."

"Virgil, I think you've just picked up the first clue we've had to Beaumont's middle man. Or, in this case, I guess I should say middle woman."

Chapter 38

For the first time in her life, Mary skipped Sunday Mass. Although she'd prayed, as she did every morning, she missed the familiar comfort of the formal service. If she followed Ben's advice to remain in seclusion until her day in court, she'd miss Mass more than once. Mary looked at the calendar hanging on the Grangers' kitchen wall and counted the days until she'd appear at the Washoe County Courthouse to petition the judge for a divorce. Twenty-three. Twenty-three more days of hiding. Twenty-three more days of being a married woman.

She wondered at Ben's confidence that exposing her divorce plans to public scrutiny would cause her husband to back off, but she hoped he was right. It felt good to take action, rather than wait in fear of another accident. If she'd had any lingering doubts about her decision to divorce John, they ended the moment she realized that her husband wanted her dead, rather than divorced.

Sighing with regret, Mary knew she'd done the right thing in discouraging Ben's obvious interest in her. She couldn't claim that she didn't find him attractive, but, clearly, a future with the tall detective was impossible for many reasons. It wouldn't be fair to pretend otherwise, because Mary realized that she, unlike Sally, couldn't be comfortable with a mere flirtation or a casual affair. In that way, Mary thought that she and Ben shared common attitudes, and if they continued to play at romance, one or both of them would be hurt.

When Maggie called her to the phone to take a call from Ben, Mary jumped, as though her thoughts of him had precipitated the call.

"Mary, I'm leaving for Los Angeles in a few minutes, but I wanted to let you know that I'll call into the office when I know where I'm staying. If you need to contact me, you can get the number from Anita, our receptionist, or the sheriff."

"Los Angeles?" Mary fought a sense of panic, feeling as if she were about to be deserted by the one man who'd tried to protect her. Despite their over-before-it-really-began romance, she'd known that Ben would be nearby to help her if she needed him. Now he'd be hundreds of miles away.

"An unanticipated trip. Yesterday, one of the deputies uncovered some information about the Beaumont/Martin case. I don't know yet how it ties into your case, but I believe there's a connection. If Bea tipped off Mac so that he could rig the brakes on the Beaumonts' car and if she also arranged your accidents, those two are linked somehow. Since Mac isn't talking, and Bea's flown the coop, I'm following the lead where it takes me, and, right now, it's taking me to Los Angeles."

Attempting to suppress her anxiety, Mary took a deep breath. She struggled to speak calmly as she said, "I'll pray for your success and your safe return, Ben."

"Mary, please do me a favor. Think very carefully about your husband's associates and who he may have come into contact with, and let me know if you can think of any connection to Los Angeles."

"Hmmm. John's lived in New York or New England his entire life. He's traveled to Europe, but never to the West Coast, so, offhand, I can't think of contacts he might have in Los Angeles, but if I remember any, I'll call you."

"OK, Mary. I'd better hit the road now. It's a long drive to L.A."

Chapter 39

After a restless night spent trying to sleep on a lumpy mattress in a cheap-but-clean motel in Pasadena, Ben walked to the restaurant next door and ordered the breakfast special—ham and eggs with fried potatoes and toast on the side. The waitress planted a pot of coffee on his table, leaving him to pour it himself. He inhaled the steam as he filled his cup. He lit a cigarette, alternately puffing on the Lucky and sipping coffee doctored with a generous dollop of cream while he waited for his breakfast to be served and contemplated his first move. In California, far from his lawful jurisdiction, Ben lacked official status, but he planned to notify the Pasadena and Los Angeles police of his investigation, as a courtesy, and request their help, if it came to that.

When the waitress deposited his breakfast in front of him, Ben stubbed out his cigarette and dug in. The food, mediocre but plentiful, satisfied his appetite, and the coffee tasted good. He finished the special and ordered a huge cinnamon roll to top off the ham and eggs. After emptying the pot, he finished his fourth cup of coffee, well-fortified for the day ahead.

Since Beaumont's home and his lawyer's office were both in Pasadena, Ben decided to stop by the Pasadena Police Department first. Burt Connelly, the detective he spoke with, showed some interest as Ben began to explain the Beaumont/Martin case, but a call to the scene of an armed robbery in progress interrupted their conversation. The detective took off with Ben in his wake, and he was left standing in the police department's parking lot with a brief directive to "keep me posted."

Ben climbed back into his truck and unfolded the city map of Pasadena, located the Beaumonts' address, and plotted his route to their house. He'd been expecting a mansion, but the house was a fifty-year-old craftsman set on a large lot, well back from the street. The narrow driveway, lined with neatly clipped hedges, led to a small detached garage, and hedges framed the sidewalk leading to the front door. A short Mexican man wearing a wide-brimmed hat manicured the bushes with long shears. Ben tried to talk to him, but he indicated the front door and kept repeating "señora," until Ben understood that he should talk to the woman in the house. A quick rap on the door brought a buxom woman wearing a white apron to the door.

"I spoke to a lady on the phone," Ben began, but the woman interrupted him.

"You from Fred's?" Ben had no idea what she was talking about. "The market, you come from the market?"

Ben shook his head, but the woman kept her own head down and didn't notice.

"We pay. You know we pay, but I got no cash today. You go."

"I'm sorry, ma'am. I think there's been some mistake. I'm not from the market."

"You go," she repeated and shut the door. Ben shrugged. As he passed the gardener on the sidewalk, the man tipped his hat politely and returned to his pruning. Undeterred, Ben hopped back into his truck. He hadn't thought he'd learn much at the Beaumonts' house, but it had been worth a shot. He checked his map again, noted the route, and headed for Beaumont's lawyer's office in downtown

Pasadena. Ben found the five-story office building easily enough, and he drove around until he found a metered parking spot a couple of blocks away. After feeding the meter several pennies, he hoofed it to the imposing structure.

Checking the building directory next to the elevator in the marble lobby, he found the offices of Benson & Alder on the third floor and decided to take the stairs, rather than waiting for the elevator. Climbing the steps, two at a time, he reached the third floor, where the elevator operator patiently held the door open for an elderly couple walking at an excruciatingly slow pace. Ben found the law office at the end of the hallway.

Based on the outside of the building and its marble lobby, he'd expected something grander, but the secretary's tiny windowless office contained only her desk and three chairs for waiting clients. An elaborately framed photograph of the secretary, dressed in a bridesmaid's gown, and her lookalike, wearing a wedding gown, sat on the desktop beside two books, *Miss Pringle's Guide to Elocution* and *How to Prepare for an Audition*. Noting the books, Ben supposed the young woman was an aspiring actress, forced to make a living as a secretary while she waited for her big break.

Dressed conservatively in a buff-colored linen summer suit, the secretary looked up from her typing and peered over her cat's-eye-shaped, blue-frame glasses when Ben entered. Even with her bleached blond hair coiled in a bun, when she took off her glasses, Ben could see that she was a beauty. "Good morning, sir. What time is your appointment?" The secretary spoke slowly and carefully, effecting a British accent but not doing it very well. Ben thought he detected a trace of another accent, although he couldn't place it.

"I don't have an appointment, Miss Rinaldi," he said, glancing at her name plate on the front of her desk, "but I'd like to see Mr. Alder on a matter of some urgency."

"I'll see if Mr. Alder can work you into his schedule. May I tell him what this is regarding?"

"I'd rather discuss that with Mr. Alder."

"All right." She exited through a door behind her desk. Reappearing a few minutes later, she sat down, turned to her appointment book, and poising a pen above it said, "He can see you at two o'clock this afternoon. Will that be convenient for you?"

"That's fine."

"Name?"

"Ben Cameron." As she entered his name in the appointment book, he beat a hasty retreat before she could ask him any more questions. He didn't want to alert the lawyer that he wasn't a client.

As he walked back to his truck, he decided setting appointments probably made more sense than just showing up, interrupting work days, so when he spotted a phone booth in a corner drugstore, he called Excelsior Studio and asked for Beaumont's secretary. She agreed to see him in an hour.

Scrambling to find his way to Hollywood amid the maze of freeways, he pulled up at the gate to Excelsior Studio with five minutes to spare. A uniformed guard greeted him.

"Ben Cameron to see Miss Anderson."

"Yes, sir. She's expecting you. Building C, to your right." The guard lifted the pickup's windshield wiper and positioned a long strip of cardboard under it. "This here's your pass. Don't remove it until you leave the studio or your pickup will be towed. Go ahead now."

After the guard pressed a button, the gate swung open and Ben pulled through, turned right, and parked next to the door to Building C, which looked like an airplane hangar, but housed the studio's administrative offices.

Miss Anderson's office, unlike the cramped secretary's office at Benson & Alder, presented a luxurious appearance. Plush beige carpet covered the floor, overstuffed sofas and chairs sat in coordinated groups around the huge room, large paintings in elaborate gilt frames decorated the walls, and, set back in a discreet corner, a desk perched on delicate curved legs sat, empty except for a white-and-gold French telephone. A plump white-haired woman in a lavender dress, glasses dangling on a chain around her neck, emerged from a side door as Ben entered.

"Miss Anderson?" Ben asked, unable to keep a note of surprise from his voice. Based solely on her soft voice on the phone when he'd called looking for Adrian Beaumont right after the car crash three weeks earlier, Ben had pictured her as a much younger woman.

Smiling, she nodded. "Have a seat, detective." She motioned toward a sofa while she sat in the chair opposite.

"This is your office?"

"The outer office, yes. As you can see, I don't do much work here. It's more of a reception room really. I have my typewriter and office equipment in the back."

"Quite a layout."

"Only the best for Mr. Beaumont. He's an important man around here. I suppose you're wondering why he has an old lady as his secretary."

"Oh, no, ma'am!" Ben protested, although that's exactly what he had been thinking.

"Don't kid a kidder, young man. I'll tell you how I got this job. It was all Mrs. Beaumont's doing. She's not about to let her husband subject himself to temptation right in his own office. She says it's bad enough that he's around cute young things when he's directing a movie. That's one reason she likes to have a part in all his movies, but it doesn't always work out that way. Of course, the other reason is that she fancies herself a great actress. Mr. Beaumont's a little more realistic about his wife's acting ability."

"Sounds like that could cause some conflict. Have you ever observed any violence between them?"

The elderly secretary eyed Ben suspiciously. "You're thinking that Mr. Beaumont had something to do with that car crash, aren't you?"

"It's my job to look into all the possibilities."

"Mr. Beaumont loves his wife, detective. He'd never do anything to harm her."

"The first time I talked to you following the accident, you said that you didn't know that Phyllis Beaumont was out of town. Had you heard that she wanted a divorce?"

"No." She frowned. "Phyllis is such a flighty little thing," she murmured. "In any case, they're back together."

"Yes, I know." Since Miss Anderson's knowledge of her boss's private life seemed limited, Ben decided to take a different tack. "Have you ever called the Cal Neva?"

"I've never even heard of the Cal Neva. What is it?"

Ben sighed. "It's a casino at Lake Tahoe."

"Why on earth would I call a casino?"

"So the answer is 'no'"?

"Of course."

"All right. I remember that you told me you wrote Christmas cards for the Beaumonts. Do you handle any other personal chores for them?"

"Oh, yes. I run some errands, hire caterers for their parties, and so on."

"How about their bills? Do you handle the Beaumonts' checkbook?"

"As a matter of fact, I do. Mr. Beaumont has their household bills sent here, I write the checks to pay them, and after he signs them, I try to make sure they're mailed on time."

"You said you 'try' to pay on time. Is there some reason that you can't always do that?"

Miss Anderson hesitated. "Well, I hate to say this, but there's not always enough money in the Beaumonts' joint account to cover the routine bills. I've asked Mr. Thorpe over and over again to make deposits, but he's not very prompt about it."

"And who is Mr. Thorpe?"

"Walter Thorpe, Mr. Beaumont's business manager. Mr. Beaumont's a very rich man, but he's also a very busy man. He's more interested in making movies than he is in investments. Mr. Thorpe takes care of Mr. Beaumont's finances."

"So if Mr. Beaumont needed to pay a large bill—say, five thousand dollars—would you write the check or would Mr. Thorpe take care of it?"

"Mr. Thorpe would be responsible for taking care of a bill of that size. I just write the checks for routine household expenses, and the studio takes care of all Mr. Beaumont's business expenses."

"Does Mr. Beaumont make many big-ticket purchases; for example, jewelry, art, vacation trips, that sort of thing?"

"Why, yes. He often buys Phyllis jewelry at Blake's, and he's purchased several pieces of antique furniture at Cavanaugh's."

"These stores—are they in Los Angeles?"

"Beverly Hills."

Ben stood. "Thank you, Miss Anderson. I appreciate you taking the time to see me today on such short notice."

"You're looking in the wrong direction if you think Mr. Beaumont arranged for that accident. He wouldn't hurt a fly."

Funny, hadn't Phyllis Beaumont told Ben exactly the same thing? But Ben knew better. He'd seen the director punch Phyllis's paramour, Bill Mead, in her hotel room at the Mapes. Still, all he'd learned so far was that Beaumont had an incompetent business manager, although he supposed it possible that, at Beaumont's request, Thorpe had arranged the Cal Neva credit on Mac's behalf.

Virgil said a woman had called, but she could have worked for Thorpe. Having ruled out Miss Anderson as the woman who made the call, Ben could think of only one other possibility: the secretary at Benson & Alder. At the direction of her boss, she could have called the Cal Neva to set up Mac's payoff.

Puzzling over the problem, Ben battled his way through heavy traffic, arriving back in Pasadena in time to grab the blue-plate special at the corner drugstore where he'd used the pay phone earlier. Since the hot roast beef sandwich and mashed potatoes slathered in gravy didn't quite fill him up, he ordered a slice of peach pie topped with vanilla ice cream, consuming the dessert in a few quick bites. Although he felt tempted to order another piece of pie, he refrained, after checking his Timex. If he wanted to appear on time for his appointment with Beaumont's lawyer, he needed to get going.

Ben found the reception area vacant when he arrived at Benson & Alder right on the dot for his two o'clock appointment. An old man poked his head around the corner of the door that led into the inner sanctum. "Mr. Cameron?"

Ben nodded.

"Come on back."

Ben followed him to a well-appointed office.

"Let me get all the pertinent information first." The old man picked up a pencil and a yellow legal pad. "Full name?"

"Sir, I'm not here as a client."

"Oh? You're listed in my client appointment book."

"Possibly your secretary misunderstood. I'm a detective with the Washoe County Sheriff's Department." Ben opened his wallet and displayed his badge.

"Washoe County? That's in Nevada, isn't it?"

"Yes, sir. I'm based in Reno. I'm in town investigating a homicide. A young woman posing as Phyllis Beaumont was murdered, but Mrs. Beaumont was the target."

"Good Lord! That's unbelievable!"

"According to Carol Ellis at the Circle E in Reno, your office made the arrangements for Phyllis Beaumont to stay there. Is that correct?"

"My secretary keeps track of all that. Most of my clients are wealthy gents, and they pay for their wives' stay in Nevada, if they want a quick divorce. We settle the financial matters here, before the ladies leave town."

"Mr. Beaumont told me that he was willing to give his wife anything she wanted. Is that true?"

"Most foolish. I cautioned him. But then, he may not have had it to give."

"What do you mean?"

"I'm telling tales out of school, but his retainer check bounced. My secretary had a devil of a time chasing down his business manager to pay Mr. Beaumont's bill. Most unusual."

"I see. Did you ever get the impression that Adrian Beaumont is a violent man?"

"No, but I don't know him well. I met with him just once in person. He actually cried when he told me his wife wanted a divorce. Most distressing."

He'd feared that the lawyer would refuse to answer his questions, especially considering that Ben had no jurisdiction in California. After sizing up the lawyer, Ben doubted that he'd participated in the scheme to kill Phyllis Beaumont. He'd answered Ben's questions in a straightforward manner, even though he had no obligation to do so. Ben had hoped to talk to the secretary, but he'd have to come back later to do that since she still hadn't returned to her post when he left the law offices of Benson & Alder.

Stopping at the drugstore pay phone, he called Blake's Jewelry in

Beverly Hills and asked for the accounting department. The mention of Adrian Beaumont's name brought forth a diatribe about "that weasel" Walter Thorpe, accompanied by a torrent of expletives from the store's accountant that shocked even the seasoned army veteran. He didn't bother to call the antique store.

Since the incompetent Thorpe evidently handled every aspect of Beaumont's finances, Ben decided to visit him next. He'd just reached for the phone to call Miss Anderson to find out where Thorpe's office was located when he decided to check the phone directory that hung from a chain in the booth. He placed the directory on the little shelf under the phone and checked the yellow pages under the financial advisors category. No Thorpe. But he hit pay dirt in the white pages. Walter Thorpe lived in Pasadena. Ben jotted down Thorpe's address and phone number.

Ben whistled in shock when he saw Thorpe's mansion, an edifice far grander than Beaumont's craftsman. The inhospitable property was surrounded by wrought iron, a fence and two locked gates, one blocking the sidewalk that led to the front door and the other guarding the cement driveway that ended in a large garage.

Looking around, Ben found a small call box next to the front gate. He pushed the button, but nobody responded. He decided he'd stand a better chance of catching Thorpe at home in the evening, so he left after giving the button another futile stab. If a money trail from Beaumont to Mac existed, Ben reckoned, Thorpe had served as a conduit.

Returning to his motel room, Ben shucked off his shoes and hung his suit jacket on a lone wooden hanger. A sign under the telephone announced FREE LOCAL CALLS. He'd given up on pay phones since he'd exhausted his supply of pocket change. He called Walter Thorpe's home number, but nobody answered. He resolved to try the call every half hour until evening, when he planned to go back to

Thorpe's house if he hadn't reached him by then. In the meantime, he dialed the Pasadena Police Department and asked for Detective Connelly.

"Getting anywhere on your murder investigation?" Connelly asked.

"Not too far, but I wonder if you've heard of Walter Thorpe. He lives here in Pasadena, and he works as a business manager for Adrian Beaumont."

"Thorpe? Yeah. Hold on." Ben could hear shouting in the background. "Meet me at the station at eight tomorrow morning. Gotta roll on another call." Connelly hung up, leaving Ben wondering what the Pasadena detective knew about Thorpe.

From the beginning, the Beaumont case's unexpected twists had presented a challenge to Ben. What part had Thorpe played, if any? And was the Beaumont case really connected to the other deaths of divorce-seeking dude ranch guests in Washoe County?

Trying to see connections between the cases, Ben pulled out his notebook and constructed a chart, listing the names of the victims in the left margin and factors that could connect them at the top: place of residence, where they stayed in Reno, their lawyers' names, their spouses' lawyers' names, how they died, possible motives.

Clearly, a rich spouse had motive in each case, and every death had been made to look like an accident or, in Mrs. Desmond's case, a suicide. As for the rest, two victims came from New York and three from Southern California.

Now that he'd written the facts on the chart, he could see that both Mary's husband and the other New York victim's prominent wife had retained the same law firm. In California, the victims' husbands—Beaumont, Desmond, and Huffington—were represented by Benson & Alder: two by Benson, and Beaumont by Alder. Only two victims—Candice, playing her role as Phyllis

Beaumont, and Mary—had stayed at the Circle E; the others had stayed at other guest ranches.

Ben drew a line between the New York law firm, Henson, Jones, Filbert, and Jenner and the Pasadena firm of Benson & Alder. What or who linked them? Ben looked at his Timex—six o'clock. That made it nine o'clock in New York, too late to call a law office. Ben made a note, picked up the phone, and asked the motel desk clerk to give him a wake-up call at six the next morning. Much as he hated to add an expensive long-distance call to his motel bill, the call could reveal a valuable clue if his hunch paid off.

Ben put his shoes back on and shrugged into his suit jacket for a drive-by of Thorpe's mansion. If he could catch the business manager at home, he wanted to be dressed properly. Ringing the bell at Thorpe's gate yielded no better results than it had earlier. Ben strolled down the street and around the corner, where he could see a dim light in the back of the house. If Thorpe was home, he evidently preferred to remain incommunicado. Ben hoped Connelly would shed some light on the elusive business manager when he met with him in the morning.

In the meantime, Ben's growling stomach demanded food. He drove around until he spotted a brightly lit steakhouse, its parking lot full of cars. He snagged a space for his pickup and joined the crowd, consuming a sixteen-ounce T-bone with all the trimmings before his hunger waned.

Returning to his motel room, he slept soundly, despite the lumpy mattress, until a buzzing noise emanating from his telephone woke him. As soon as he realized that the noise was his morning wake-up call, he rolled out of bed. He rang the long-distance operator and placed a call to Henson, Jones, Filbert, and Jenner in New York, specifying a direct connection so that whoever answered the phone at the law offices wouldn't realize that the call came from out of town.

"Henson, Jones, Filbert, and Jenner. How may I direct your call?"

"May I speak to Miss Rinaldi, please?"

"You mean Mrs. Tollson?"

"I didn't realize Miss Rinaldi had married."

"Oh, yes."

"In that case, I guess I'm a day late and a dollar short," Ben said, playing the fool. "I dated Miss Rinaldi a few years back, but I've been in the army, and I haven't seen her for a while. So some lucky devil snagged her already, huh?"

"Oh, my, I'm afraid you're more than a day late," the operator said, dropping her officious tone. "She got married two weeks ago. Such a lovely ceremony."

"Maybe I should call her sister instead. She isn't married yet, is she?"

"Oh, no. She was the maid of honor at Vivian's wedding. But you're out of luck if you plan on seeing her."

"Why's that?"

"She doesn't live in New York anymore. She flew in from L.A. just for the wedding."

Bingo! Ben's hunch had paid off big time. The law offices on the East and West Coasts were connected not by a relationship between lawyers, but between secretaries. Sure now that the woman who had called in Mac's credit to the Cal Neva was Alder's secretary, Ben wanted to rush over to the law office to question her as soon as she arrived, but he'd agreed to meet Connelly at eight. That gave him two hours to shower, shave, and find a better place to breakfast than the dive next door.

Connelly met Ben at the station door.

"You want to know about Thorpe? I'm on my way to wrap up the case we've been building against him. Come on, and I'll fill you in."

Ben hopped in the passenger seat of Connelly's car. "Where are we headed?" he asked.

"CPA's office. He consults for the department on financial crimes. I had a few complaints about Thorpe from his clients, and it sounded as though he's been robbing Peter to pay Paul, using some kind of a Ponzi scheme, so I asked our accountant to look into it. We got lucky and Thorpe's bank turned over all his records without a warrant. Doesn't always happen, but, like I say, we got lucky. What's your interest in Thorpe? How's he connected to your murder investigation?"

"I'm not sure, but I'm beginning to think he may be involved as a middleman. He handles all Beaumont's finances. I don't see how Beaumont could have paid off his hired killer without going through Thorpe. I tried to track him down yesterday, but I never made contact."

"Here we are," Connelly said, parking in front of a small bungalow, now converted to an office. "Let's see what our accountant has to say."

They entered the building where a wiry man with thinning hair and rimless glasses peered at them over stacks of ledgers. After an hour of explaining the details of Thorpe's scheme to swindle his clients, the accountant paused.

"The bottom line, gentlemen, is that Thorpe's perpetrated a gigantic fraud on his clients. Instead of investing his clients' funds, he's been financing his extravagant lifestyle with their money."

"You'll be able to testify at trial?"

"Oh, yes. The trail's crystal clear if you know what to look for, and Thorpe's been very careless of late. One of his clients demanded his money back, and Thorpe had to drain all the others' accounts to satisfy the guy. He's skating on very thin ice right now."

"What would happen if another client had to divide his assets, say because of a divorce?" Ben asked. "Would Thorpe be able to come up with enough money?"

"No."

"What are you thinking, Ben?" Connelly asked.

"I'm thinking that Thorpe arranged the murder himself. It cost him several thousand, but that's nothing compared to what he'd have to cough up if he had to disperse the large settlement Adrian Beaumont agreed to give Phyllis." Ben looked at the accountant. "Am I right that Beaumont's worth millions?"

"Yes, at least, he was wealthy before Thorpe spent most of his money."

"So if Mrs. Beaumont died, let's say in an unfortunate auto accident, Thorpe wouldn't have to come up with the settlement money, and Beaumont would be none the wiser."

Chapter 40

Bill Cooper rose and faced the judge. "I'd like to request a private hearing and sealed records in the matter before the court."

"Mr. Valspar, any objection?"

"No, sir."

As the court reporter dutifully recorded the proceedings in Courtroom 210 at the Washoe County Courthouse, Mary glanced to the left. Her husband's attorney sat at a table opposite hers. In the front row, seated behind Mary and her lawyer, were the three witnesses her attorney would call to establish her Nevada residency—Maggie Granger, Carol Ellis, and Ben, who would testify to the reason she needed two witnesses, an unusual circumstance, but one Cooper had assured her wouldn't prevent the judge's granting her a divorce.

As soon as her request for a divorce on the grounds of extreme cruelty was placed before the court, her husband's lawyer rose to say that the respondent denied all such allegations.

"So noted," the judge said. "Will you be presenting evidence?"

"No, sir."

"What's that all about?" Mary whispered to Cooper.

"Just routine, my dear. He's not going to question anyone." Cooper patted Mary's hand. "It'll all be over in a few minutes."

Carefully, Cooper led Maggie, Carol, and Ben through their testimony to establish Mary's six-week residency in Nevada. As Cooper had predicted, her husband's attorney did not object. Then it came time for Mary to testify. After she swore to tell the truth and settled herself in the witness box, she clutched the smooth wooden rail in front of her with trembling hands. Her knuckles turned white from the force of her grasp as she listened intently to the first question posed by her attorney.

"State your name for the record, please."

"Mary Garrison."

"Where do you currently reside?"

Mary gave the address of the Grangers' ranch house in Verdi before her lawyer led her through a few more questions about her residency in Nevada.

"When you came to Reno, did you plan to live in Nevada indefinitely?"

Mary removed her hands from the railing and folded them primly, out of sight, in her lap. Like a child about to tell a whopper, she crossed her fingers.

"Yes, sir."

"Is it still your intention to live in Nevada?"

Mary squeezed her fingers more tightly and answered in the affirmative.

"Do you desire to resume the use of your maiden name, Mary Marchetti, if your divorce is granted?"

"Yes, sir."

"Thank you." He turned to the other attorney. "Your witness."

"No questions."

"You may step down," the judge said, and Mary returned to her seat beside Cooper.

"I hereby grant the plaintiff's petition for divorce and the resumption of her maiden name." With a tap of his gavel, the judge declared, "Case closed."

Everybody in the courtroom stood while the judge made his exit, and then Cooper turned to Mary and shook her trembling hand. Cooper patted her arm. "It's over, my dear. You're a free woman now."

Mary nodded, a tear trickling down her face. She hadn't expected to feel quite so overwhelmed, not that she regretted ending the marriage, but she'd gone through hell to accomplish her six-week solution, and she didn't know if she'd ever get her life back in order, but, at least, she'd taken the first step. With Maggie and Carol flanking her and Ben trailing behind the three women, Mary walked down the courthouse steps into the bright sunshine. She felt a tingle of hope, as though the warm sun on her face reflected a new life.

Carol wished Mary luck, gave her a quick hug, and strode off to meet Chuck around the corner at the Riverside Hotel and Casino.

Until her court appearance, Mary hadn't seen Ben since the day they'd met with Cal Harris to circulate the story of Mary's intention to divorce her husband. Except for the meeting with Harris, Mary hadn't left the Grangers' ranch since she moved there. Besides avoiding further "accidents," Mary had had to worry about the possibility of having her reputation besmirched. While Ben had been conducting his investigation in Los Angeles, he'd called her to let her know that a New York private detective, retained by John Garrison, had arrived in Reno to dig up some dirt on her. If Garrison could find evidence of Mary's cavorting with another man before the divorce, the ambitious politician could try to turn the tables and gain sympathy from his district's voters, casting himself as the innocent spouse of a cheating wife.

The private eye had tried to locate Mary at the Circle E, but Chuck had shown him his shotgun and the door. With no information forthcoming from the Circle E owner, the frustrated detective had tried to ferret some nuggets of information from the sheriff's department, but he'd had no better luck with the sheriff or any of the deputies, and Ben had refused to talk to the man. After two weeks in Reno, the detective still hadn't been able to locate Mary, let alone gather evidence of an affair. Mary had been relieved to hear that the private detective had left town when Ben had called to tell her the sheriff had spotted the P.I. at the bus station, boarding an eastbound Greyhound.

Keenly aware that she hadn't invited Ben to visit her, even after her husband's henchman had hightailed it back to New York, Mary looked past Maggie and saw that Ben was smiling at her. She'd worried that he felt angry with her, although their phone conversations had been cordial. Cordial, but impersonal. Ben had slipped into the courtroom at the last minute, and Mary hadn't spoken with him before the brief trial began.

"We should be getting on to the station, Mary," Maggie said. "I hope you don't mind if I don't wait with you until the train comes, but our contractor's supposed to meet Beth and me at the ranch in half an hour to go over the plans for our new stable."

"So you're going back to New York right away, Mary?" Ben asked. She nodded.

"That's cutting it close. When's the train due?"

"Right about now, I'm afraid. I figured I could leave either today or tomorrow, depending on how long we were in court, so I came prepared. I left my bags in Maggie's car."

"I can take Mary to the station, Maggie," Ben volunteered. "My pickup's right around the corner in front of the sheriff's office. Lead on, and I'll grab her bags."

A pang shot through Mary. She'd be alone with Ben one last time. She thought about objecting, telling Ben that she'd go with Maggie, as planned, but she didn't want to delay the woman who'd opened her home to her, even though Maggie and her sister Beth no longer operated a dude ranch. Instead, she went along with Maggie and Ben, watching as they transferred her bags, and gave Maggie a good-bye hug.

Ben opened the passenger door of his pickup, and Mary climbed in carefully, trying to keep her skirt from hiking up over her knees. She remembered struggling to get into his truck the day he'd accompanied her to Mass and they'd breakfasted together. She also remembered how safe she felt when she was with him.

"All set?"

"All set," she answered as Ben pulled away from the curb. "You know, Ben, I didn't expect to feel so nervous in court. I was shaking the whole time."

"You did fine, Mary."

"I don't know how to thank you for everything you've done for me. If it hadn't been for you. . ."

"No thanks necessary." He grinned. "We Western lawmen take our jobs seriously, and we're always happy to oblige a lady," he drawled.

Mary laughed. Leave it to Ben to lighten the mood. As they neared the train depot, they heard the long, low whistle of a train rolling into town.

"Not a minute to spare," Ben said, as he zipped into a parking spot, helped Mary out of the truck, and hefted her bags. "Why the train again, Mary? I thought you wanted to fly back to New York."

"I did. It's a long haul on the train, but I upgraded to a Pullman berth this time. It costs more than coach, but it's cheaper than flying."

Standing on the platform, they watched the *City of San Francisco* glide into the station. The engine flew past them, and gradually the train slowed and stopped. They headed for the Pullman cars.

"Looks like this is it," Ben said, setting Mary's bags down on the concrete platform. He looked down at her. "You're sure you wouldn't like to keep your promise to stay in Nevada?"

"I had my fingers crossed when I said that."

"Uh, huh, figures," he said good-naturedly. He pulled Mary close, bent down, and kissed her forehead. "Good-bye, Mary."

"Good-bye, Ben."

Ben handed Mary's bags to the porter as she ascended the steps to the train car. She turned and waved before stepping aboard.

Inside her compartment, Mary pressed her face to the window and looked out, searching for the tall lawman. A head taller than the rest of the bystanders, he was easy to spot. As the train rumbled out of the station, she saw Ben one last time. He caught sight of her, too, and waved.

She'd arrived on the train in June, a married woman. Now, in July, she was leaving on the train, a divorced woman. After six weeks in Nevada, she was going home.

Chapter 41

On a cool December evening, Ben drove up the Mount Rose Highway again. He'd driven the route several times since he first investigated the accident that had taken Candice Martin Littleton's life, but he never passed the spot where the Beaumonts' Cadillac had hurtled off the side of the mountain without thinking about it. This evening, though, his thoughts quickly returned to his passenger. Ben was taking Anita to the Christmas Tree for a steak dinner. Not long after he passed the accident site, the twinkling lights of the restaurant came into view, and Ben turned left, off the highway, into the eatery's parking lot. He walked around the pickup, opened the door for Anita, and helped her out. She held his arm, balancing on her high heels, as they walked across the bumpy parking lot.

The hostess was seating another couple when they entered.

"Have I told you how beautiful you look?"

"Only about a dozen times, but, don't worry; I'm not tired of hearing it," Anita joked. The soft curls of her strawberry blond hair framed her face, and she'd enhanced her eyelashes with mascara, a cosmetic she never wore to work. Her simple black sheath dress showed off her fine figure to advantage, and the silver fur stole she wore added a touch of glamour to her ensemble. Ben couldn't take his eyes off the lovely woman he'd been dating for the past five months.

The hostess returned and seated them, and although the restaurant was crowded and noisy, they didn't notice.

"Would you like some wine?" Ben asked.

"That would be nice, but I'm no connoisseur. I've heard that red wine goes with steak, but I have no idea which kind to order."

"Me, either," Ben confessed. "Let's ask the waiter to recommend one."

The wine poured, Ben and Anita sipped it while they waited for their steak dinners to arrive.

"The kids loved those catcher's mitts you gave them, Ben."

"Good. They'll be playing in real baseball games before you know it."

"I suppose so. Even though they're four and five, I sometimes still think of them as babies, but they're growing up fast."

"You're a great mother, you know."

"Thanks, Ben. I just wish I could have stayed home with them instead of having to work, but, thank goodness, my mother's able to take care of them when I'm at the office. I've been lucky that way."

Anita tore off a piece of roll, neatly buttered it, and popped it into her mouth. "Do you ever hear from Mary?" she asked in a casual manner, but Ben knew her question was far from casual. He figured Anita suspected that Ben had had a crush on Mary, and she was probing to find out if he still harbored feelings for her.

"She sent me a newspaper article, along with a brief note a couple of weeks ago." Seeing the look of disappointment on Anita's face, he hastened to add, "It's the only time I've heard from her. We're not corresponding." Anita looked relieved, and Ben continued. "I think she sent it because she wanted me to know that her husband left New York after dropping out of his race for Congress. According to the article, his poll numbers plummeted after the news broke that his wife was divorcing him. Mary's note said she heard he was returning to New Hampshire, where he grew up, to try to establish a political career there. It's too bad that we weren't able to make a case against him. Since Rinaldi's sister skipped to Rio, and we still haven't been able to locate Bea—probably not her real name, anyway—the NYPD didn't get too far with the New York end of our conspiracy case."

Distracted from her concern about Ben's possible feelings for Mary, Anita said. "Well, at least, you're going gangbusters on your end of the case. I hear Mac's going to accept a plea deal."

"He might have gotten a death sentence if he hadn't. I think that's what made him finally come around. I figured out the parts the Rinaldi woman and Thorpe played, but until Mac squealed I didn't know how Thorpe had connected with him. It all goes back to Mac's gambling addiction. Turns out Mac owed Fabio's Club a bundle, and Rinaldi's brother manages the club. They worked out a deal to pay off his gambling debts with a little extra, to boot, in the form of a big credit at the Cal Neva. I'm almost sure it wasn't the first time Mac took on a contract. He may have been responsible for a hit-and-run, but he claims to know nothing about that accident. The D.A. is still going back and forth with his California counterpart about whether to extradite Thorpe to Nevada or have him stand trial in California first. One thing's for sure: there's no shortage of charges—murder, embezzlement, fraud, conspiracy."

"How are you coming on those other two cases—the supposed suicide out at the Verdi Guest Ranch and the drowning at Lake Tahoe?"

"We're going at it by following the money trail. It worked to nail Thorpe. Maybe it'll work to incriminate the other guys. Rinaldi claims her only part was calling in Mac's credit to the Cal Neva. I know better, though. She and that sister of hers were running a murder-for-hire business right under their employers' noses, and the attorneys had no idea what was going on. The two secretaries were both in good positions to know when a rich client might find it appealing to do away with an inconvenient spouse. Add their brother, with his street connections, who could arrange the hits in Washoe County when the spouses showed up to establish their six-week residency, and you have the world's worst family business."

"Unbelievable! What a first case!"

"You can say that again. Carmine's downright flabbergasted by the conspiracy angle."

"How is Carmine, anyway? He never visits the sheriff."

"Holding up pretty well, I think. More good days than bad lately."

"I always did like Carmine, but I can't say that I miss his cigars."

"Oh? He's shared a few of his primo Cubans with me, and I think they're swell." Ben grinned.

"Ben Cameron, don't you dare smoke one of those horrible, nasty, smelly things around me!"

"No, ma'am! I wouldn't dream of it."

"I'll take your word for that. Carl was smoking one of his awful cheap cigars yesterday, and it smelled up the entire squad room. I had to get the fan out to circulate the air. By the way, I noticed you two buried the hatchet. There were a couple of times when I thought you might come to blows right there in the office."

"So did I. Funny thing, though. Overmeyer thinks I talked the sheriff into giving his brother my old deputy slot, but I never said a word to the sheriff. I even told Overmeyer I hadn't spoken to the sheriff on his brother's behalf, but he doesn't believe me. Actually, his brother is shaping up to be a good deputy. Too bad I can't say the same thing about Overmeyer, but, at least, he's loyal. I will say that much for him."

The waiter appeared and set their plates in front of them. Ben's

T-bone steak covered most of his plate, while Anita's petite fillet mignon occupied a small spot on hers. Ben looked at Anita's entrée, tiny compared to his T-bone, and shrugged before attacking his giant-size steak with gusto. Meanwhile, Anita sliced a sliver of her fillet, speared it with her fork, and savored the small morsel. They took their time eating, lingering over apple pie and coffee.

"Have I told you how beautiful you look?"

"Only about a dozen times."

Rising, Ben circled the table and held Anita's chair for her. He picked up the silver fur from the back of her chair where Anita had draped it earlier, and they strolled, hand-in-hand, to the restaurant's door. Holding up the stole for Anita to slip into, Ben caught a glimpse of its new lining. Its former cream-colored lining with Phyllis Beaumont's initials monogrammed on it had been replaced with a new silver-gray silk charmeuse lining with *Anita* embroidered in script letters.

"Your first name," Ben observed. "How come no initials?"

"I might not always have the same initials."

"You mean, they'd change if you get married?"

"That's right."

"Hmm, we'll just have to see what we can do about changing those initials, won't we?"

Eyes shining, Anita looked up at Ben and smiled. "Yes, we will."

ABOUT THE AUTHOR

An instructor at five colleges over the years, Paula Darnell has a Bachelor of Arts degree in English from the University of Iowa and a Master of Arts degree in English with a Writing Emphasis from the University of Nevada, Reno. Having lived in Reno for sixteen years, she was inspired by the local history and found the 1950s, when Reno was considered the Divorce Capital of the World, to be an interesting era in which to set a mystery. *The Six-Week Solution* is the result. Paula is also the author of the DIY Diva cozy mystery series. She now resides in Las Vegas with her husband Gary and their Pyrador Rocky.

www.ingramcontent.com/pod-product-compliance
Lightning Source LLC
Chambersburg PA
CBHW050817190726
48286CB00007B/1900